Partners in Crime

by

Rolando Hinojosa

A Rafe Buenrostro Mystery

Arte Público Press
Houston
1985

This volume is made possible through support from the National Endowment for the Arts, a federal agency, and the Texas Commission on the Arts.

Arte Público Press
University of Houston
University Park
Houston, Texas 77004

Library of Congress No. 84-072298
ISBN 0-934770-37-9

Printed in the United States of America

And a man's foes shall be they of his own household.

St. Matthew 10:36

Virgil: Crimine ab uno/disce omnes.

Aeneid, ii. 65

Latet anguis in herba.

Eclogue, iii. 93

THE KLAIL CITY DEATH TRIP SERIES

Estampas del valle y otras obras

Klail City y sus alrededores

Korean Love Songs

Claros varones de Belken

Mi querido Rafa

Rites and Witnesses

Dear Rafe

The Valley

**Wherein a stupid murder
almost ruins two days of saltwater fishing.**

1

A note, folded and scotch-taped to the telephone dial; he could hardly miss it, and it contained no surprise, either: "Oakland 3, Reds 1. I now owe you $20." It was signed *C*.

The *C* stood for Culley Donovan, his partner and chief of detectives for the Belken County Homicide Squad.

Rafe Buenrostro smiled, opened a side drawer on his desk, and slid that IOU along with the others signed by Donovan during that October 1972 World Series.

It had been a cool October in Oakland and Cincinnati, but it was a hot one in The Valley, in Klail City, Belken County, Texas. It was also a dry October, and the hot weather would continue as it usually did until Christmas or until the first norther came rumbling down from the Panhandle. But, until *that* happened: no rain. Besides, the hurricane season had been declared officially over by the U.S. Weather Service office in Jonesville-on-the-Rio. And that was that.

Rafe Buenrostro looked at his watch; the glass was scratched somewhat, but he could read the time plainly enough: 1:10 p.m. Now, if he could log in two uninterrupted hours of typing, he'd have his preliminary report ready for the District Attorney's office, and he could then begin his weekend fishing with a clean slate.

It had been a stupid murder, he thought. And here he was, six hours after it happened, putting it down on paper; and not through a particularly enterprising piece of detective work, for that matter. Fell on his lap, as it were.

An idiotic murder, he thought. And then, not for the first time in the last eleven years, "Most of them are."

He shook his head again, and he began laying his notes in some semblance of order next to the typewriter. He was about to type the report when Culley Donovan came in.

"Pitching'll do it every time, Buster Brown."

Buenrostro looked up, grinned at him, and went back to his notes.

"Damndest relief pitching I've ever seen," said Donovan. He drew two ten-dollar notes from his wallet and put them in the coffee drawer, alongside the IOUs.

"I hope you and Dorson enjoy the coffee; that's hard-earned money in there."

Rafe Buenrostro laughed this time as he centered the form sheet.

Donovan: "You know, you don't know the first thing about baseball, and here you've got me twenty bucks in the hole."

And then: "Is that the Billings thing?"

Nod.

"Tell you what, I'll handle the telephone calls while you get that report in; you got your gear ready, Rafe? You packed and everything?"

"Sure am; as soon as I get this out of the way, I expect to be doing some saltwater fishing out on the Gulf. How's that sound?"

Culley Donovan nodded and said, "I'll tell you how it sounds, it sounds a whole hell of a lot better than Sam Dorson's cackle when he sees the twenty bucks."

Sam Dorson was another member of the Belken County Homicide Squad. Of what Harvey Bollinger, the District Attorney, was pleased to call *his* Homicide Squad.

The trouble with that *his* of Bollinger's was that Sheriff Wallace "Big Foot" Parkinson disagreed—in public—with the District Attorney. This particular bone of contention had been going on for years, as long as Rafe Buenrostro could remember. He was now thirty-seven years old, and he had been on the force for eleven years.

For accounting and inventory purposes, the Belken County Homicide Squad consisted of five men, five desks, four waste paper baskets, three typewriters, three telephones, one clothes rack, and Sam Dorson's long bench. Dorson had pushed it into the office one morning without any explanation, and there it remained in front of his desk.

There were also eighteen filing cabinets in the long room and other office supplies all of which, then, were paid for out of Bollinger's and Parkinson's budgets.

An opinion had been sought from the state's Attorney General, and that splendid officer concluded on the side of what his Opinion Committee called *obvious logic*, a strange phrase in the law, by the way. The Opinion Committee further determined that the Homicide Squad (five men, five desks, etc.) was responsible to the two county entities by virtue (another strange word in the law) of a shared budget responsibility.

And that, too, was that.

Joe Molden and Peter Hauer rounded out the five-man unit; both had transferred from Grand Theft-Larceny to the Homicide Squad in April of that year.

Hauer was called Young Mr. Hauer by Sam Dorson, for reasons best known to Dorson, and if there was resentment on the part of Hauer, he didn't show it. At least not in public.

Joe Molden, also in his early thirties, believed he had a strike against him from the very start: he was Sheriff Parkinson's nephew, and despite assurances by Donovan of impartiality and fairness, Molden usually felt insecure and unwanted.

Buenrostro and Dorson thought Molden had no reason to feel that way, but there it was.

The Squad managed to solve the relatively few county cases handled in the course of every fiscal year; the secret to much of this was plain, plodding work. And, county murders were fewer and not as frequent when compared to the murders committed within the jurisdiction of each of the Valley's small towns and cities. The second ingredient that led to the solving of cases was dedication to detail, to the job at hand, and to the amassing of hard facts which would then be translated into evidence. Nothing fancy about it.

The Squad had most recently worked on a murder on one

of the nearby farms. It was a case of incest, murder, and suicide. All five members of Homicide had agreed that the case "had been a bitch," but as usual in this type of case, the newspapers were not told of the incest.

The reporters, who had not been allowed in the room, who had not seen the room—a usual procedure of Donovan's—wrote several pages on the blood-filled room, the bodies, of an unknown intruder, of strange writings on the walls (there were none), and on the ghastly scene of the double murder. That last part was correct.

It had been a double murder, and it had been a sad one, too: a seventeen-year-old had shot his fourteen-year-old sister and himself on a bright Easter Sunday afternoon in their parents' bedroom.

The murder earlier that October morning had happened exactly five-hundred feet outside the Klail City city limits, and the distance made it a county crime.

And, where the crime had been committed was an interesting piece of business, too: the site was a gaudily-painted, cheaply-built, two-story apartment building constructed out of hollow cement blocks, which the absentee owner proudly called Rio Largo: A Complex for Young Marrieds. The first floor was known as Rio Largo I and the second as Rio Largo II. There had been plans for Rio Largo III and IV and for V and VI, too, as well as plans for an outdoor theater, maid service, and resident plumbers and electricians; all of this was still on the drawing boards and in someone's imagination other than that of the owner who had gone on to bigger and better things. As it were.

The five-hundred feet location was no accident. The two to three hundred souls who lived there did not vote in city elections, did not, then, pay city taxes, but then neither did the forward-thinking developer of Rio Largo I and II.

The Young Marrieds did have a minor inconvenience: since R.L. I and II were outside the city limits, the Klail City Fire

Department could not be called upon for assistance. No, this wasn't exactly true. The F.D. *could* be called upon, but would not respond, such calls being outside of its jurisdiction.

Most of the tenants held low to mid-level jobs in various Valley and Klail City businesses and accepted the shoddy plumbing, wiring, and construction uncomplainingly. But then, they were just as quick to move out as they were to move in. A halfway house, then.

Rafe Buenrostro continued his typing amid fitful stops and starts as he fiddled with the ribbon which would jump out of its holding bar from time to time. A stupid murder, he muttered, for the third or fourth time, as he attempted to bring a sense of order to a senseless occurrence.

It had begun as one of those harmless domestic disputes, so called. Husband I had a girlfriend who also had a husband. Husband I also had a wife, of course, and it was she who accosted the girlfriend, before two witnesses, in the laundry room of the apartment building. A regular punch-up.

Husband II was bringing in some additional laundry for his loving wife when he saw her being pummeled by Wife I. Husband II separated them and upon learning the reasons for the fracas, flattened his straying spouse, ran to their room, grabbed a gun, and went on the hunt.

Result: The building superintendent, in no way connected, was splattered by three slugs from a nasty-looking .38 S & W Master.

The super had been repairing a bathroom leak in Husband I's apartment and was walking out of the apartment when Husband II unloaded on him. A case of mistaken identity: Husband I, thirtyish and six-feet tall; the super, in his fifties, stood five-feet four inches tall.

Idiots.

Husband I, at poolside, heard the screaming and yelling, and ran for the laundry room. When he heard the shots, however, he sprinted across the parking lot, jumped in his VW, drove the twenty miles to Jonesville at top speed, parked the car in a shopping mall lot, ran across the International Bridge of Amity (El puente internacional de la amistad) to Barrones, Tamaulipas.

Damned fool.

Within a few minutes of the shooting, the two women made up on the spot; they also had a good cry, and then Wife I drove her newly-found friend to Small's Medical Clinic where they swore to stand by their mates.

The bonds of friendship.

Husband II, in the meantime, had called an attorney in Klail City who promptly advised his client to turn himself in to the arresting officer. He, the attorney, would then meet his client at Judge Hearn's court.

Rafe Buenrostro had taken the telephone call from an excited neighbor who proceeded to report three, possibly four, murders at Rio Largo II.

County Patrolman Rudi Schranz accompanied Lt. Buenrostro who instructed Schranz to arrest Husband II (Andrew Billings) on suspicion of murder and to present him before Municipal Court Judge Robert E. Lee Hearn for arraignment and hearing.

The photographer and the lab personnel arrived within minutes of Buenrostro; thirty-six photographs were taken for evidentiary proof and the various rooms were then powdered for prints.

Husband II handed the gun to Lt. Buenrostro who then tagged it and placed it in a plastic bag.

The victim, too, was identified and tagged and then driven to River Delta Mortuary, Inc., as per contract with the Belken County Commissioners Court. The owner of the mortuary was a brother-in-law to the County Judge and this, too, was no accident.

A search of the victim's room revealed three open cartons of cigarettes: Camels, Pall Malls, and some filter-tipped Delicados. Buenrostro found two picture albums of old-time movie stars: Banky, Bara, Bow, Naldi, Negri, Swanson, etc. . . . A grocery bag stuffed in the bottom of a laundry hamper revealed a small Kodak camera and thirteen envelopes containing two-hundred and thirty-five prints of youngsters ranging from six to fourteen years of age; the youngsters were naked and stared rather gloomily at the camera.

There were other personal effects in the superintendent's room: two pairs of brown shoes, two pairs of khaki pants, two blue chambray shirts, one dress shirt, five pairs of socks, an Army web belt, two new and unused nylon shorts in plastic bags, as well as two grimy jockey straps draped over the shower rod. Buenrostro found some assorted toilet articles in shoeboxes which contained two boxes of unused Sheik condoms and a plastic wallet. The identity card was made out to J. Thos. West; this proved to be the name of the superintendent as identified by the name plate on his bloody khaki shirt.

The wallet was empty save for some more pictures of young children similar to those found in the hamper.

The two laundryroom witnesses and four other apartment residents were cooperative, although none "actually saw the shooting, sir," but all of whom "heard the shots, yessir."

How many shots?

One. Two. Three. Four. Five. Six. Seven.

Names of Husbands I and II and their wives?

Phillips, I think. Brown; no, not Brown. Something like that, though. Can't recall just now. Don't know.

Typical.

A thorough search of the apartment cleared this up, of course.

Rafe Buenrostro telephoned the Mexican counterpart across the Rio Grande. Within twenty minutes, Captain Lisandro Gómez Solís reported that one Perry Pylant had been picked up at Alfonso Fong's China Doll Club rather "drunk and somewhat disruptive of the public order." (The last phrase covered everything from arson to spitting on the brick sidewalks.)

Señor Pylant, said Gómez Solís, was then escorted to the Jonesville side, warned not to recross the bridge and held there until he was picked up by the Jonesville police who, in turn, had already called the Belken County Patrol; Perry Pylant was held as a material witness and his car impounded for storage by Lone Star Salvage and Garage.

Patrolman Schranz drove to Jonesville, took a preliminary statement and drove the witness to the Klail City Court House. A second statement was then taken; since no charges were filed, the witness Pylant was released.

What arrangements he made to take his car out of storage were up to Mr. Pylant.

Husband II, Andrew Billings, had his bond set at $25,000 by Judge Hearn; Billings' attorney was accompanied by a friend who made bond. And so, Billings's attorney and both wives drove back together to Rio Largo II after the arraignment.

Assholes.

**The week begins with a dead man
in an abandoned car.**

2

Monday morning.

The car was a new one, he could see that all right. And, it was all white, and right in the middle of a cotton field on the Osuna farmland. The field had first been stripped by the insecticide and then the cotton picking machines had gone on to finish the job. That done, the lands had been plowed under, and there the car stood, bang center in the cotton field.

The black man walked around the car for the second or third time, being careful not to touch it. He didn't know who had driven such an expensive car—a Buick, as it turned out—but at least one fact was absolutely certain: the middle-aged white man sitting in the front seat wasn't going to drive it out. He was dead, and the old black man could see some of the dried blood around both ears, on the man's lower lip, and around his nose. The tie had been twisted around the man's neck, and the blank eyes stared dully at the rear view mirror.

The flies had gotten wind of this somehow and were already buzzing outside like dinner guests who've not yet been asked to sit and enjoy the feast.

The black man, John Milton Crossland, was eighty-five years old, and there remained a bit of a spring in his step as he began the climb to the top of the levee where he had parked his pickup truck.

Winded a little, he opened the door to the cab, sat down, and began to write on a scrap of paper: a new white car, four doors, white side walls, Lic. Pla. Tex. Dec. 72, AFT 348.

As he started the engine, he looked at the car again and said to himself: "No reason for me to hurry, 'cause he sure ain't going no place."

As he drove toward young Santos Osuna's ranch house, he

said aloud: "I'll call the police; the County Police; yeah, that's what I'll do."

John Milton Crossland, a former cavalryman, had been dishonorably discharged from the United States Army in 1907 by order of his Commander-in-Chief, Theodore Roosevelt. Crossland had been discharged along with two dozen other black soldiers, veterans all of either the Philippine or of the Cuban Campaigns in the War of '98.

In Cuba, Crossland and some of those black men who had been discharged with him fought on the same ground where their future Commander-in-Chief was supposed to have led a charge on a hill defended by Spanish regulars.

Also, it was entirely possible that descendants of the Old Bull Moose had brought some of Crossland's own descendants to these shores some two-hundred years before Crossland's bad discharge, as he called it.

But that had been a long time ago, and it had been a different world, too.

"Better not think a-that," he said rather loudly.

The number of those who remembered what had happened in '07, what had led to the so-called rebellion—what had led, in fact, to the shooting—that number was small and getting smaller. Crossland had outlived his Commander-in-Chief in addition to many of the leading citizens of Jonesville-on-the-Rio, and those of Barrones, Tamaulipas, who, in many ways, had been equally responsible for the shooting. They were also responsible for the bad discharge.

It rankled.

Crossland had started to work for the Osuna family as a farmhand in 1907. In the early Nineteen-Thirties, Santos Osuna Senior carried him on the payroll as a grocery clerk in Klail City, although Crossland continued to work as a farmhand.

"This'll qualify you for a pension, Mr. Crossland; it'll be your retirement. The Social Security, Mr. Crossland."

Santos Senior had then said, "You've got it coming. Man

who works like you work ought to have something to show for it."

And now, Crossland thought, I've been drawing my penny since Fifty-two.

That too was the year Santos Osuna Senior died and reminded his family—again—that John Milton Crossland, *Don Melitón*, was to be buried on the Osuna-Buenrostro-Landín cemetery near San Pedro. So now, Crossland also knew where he was to be buried.

His thoughts went back rather suddenly to Nineteen-Oh-Seven, and he shivered involuntarily. "I know what I'll do. I'll call young Buenrostro, or Sandy Junior can call him for me. Yeah; Sandy'll call El Quieto's boy for me, and that boy'll know just what to do."

He slowed the pickup, looked up and saw the long front porch to the Osuna ranch house. Aloud again, but speaking to himself, he said: "I wonder who that Anglo man was back there?"

And then: "That sure was a spiffy suit he had on. Yes-*sir*."

Names, names, names.

3

The dead man was quickly identified, and the contents of his billfold listed and initialed by Culley Donovan. He ordered the car be left in place under twenty-four hour guard until it could be transferred to the County Motor Pool for further search if necessary.

The photographers at the site did what they had to do and left the field for the lab assistants who exclaimed, rather gleefully, that "there were fingerprints inside that car like crazy."

Donovan nodded at them and looked on as the front and back seats were being removed under the personal direction of The Lab Man; among the first objects found were six bottles of mouthwash and two half-empty containers of hand cream.

The Lab Man, called that, although not to his face, was named Henry Dietz; the man was meticulous and cranky, but there were no complaints from the Homicide Squad in either regard. Also, Dietz could prove to be fractious on occasion, but as Sam Dorson said, "He's very good at his job."

The highest compliment.

The dead man had been buried by River Delta Mortuary after the identification process which included a week-long telephone search for relatives (none) and for some people whose names appeared in the man's appointment book. None showed up. This done, the County Coroner certified identification to the dead man's creditors (they were issued death certificates at the Court House) and this then allowed them to close their accounts. The certification also permitted the creditors to lard up their debit columns somewhat. This operation, however, required reason and restraint since IRS could come calling in cases of a too-creative piece of accounting.

The folder on the dead man, Charles Edward Darling,

began with an original birth certificate bearing a faint notary public's seal from Sedalia, Missouri (Pettis County), which attested that Charles Edward Darling had been born on February 3, 1919, in Sedalia, Mo., to Clark and Celia neé Griffin Darling.

The folder also held a wallet-sized photostatic copy of an honorable discharge from the U.S. Army, and another photostatic copy of his discharge issued by the Pettis County Clerk; this last confirmed parentage, the family's address, the time of induction (January 3, 1940), the date of discharge (9 October 1946), and the place of discharge (Fort Leonard Wood, Missouri).

The discharge certified that T/5 Charles Edward Darling, Jr. had accrued 60 days of furlough time which was then added to his mustering out pay, plus travel and per diem to Sedalia.

Rafe Buenrostro read the certificate again; he then glanced at the discharge photostat and wondered why the late Charles Edward Darling had used *Junior* after his name since his father's name was Clark.

It probably didn't mean a thing, he thought, but he went ahead and made a note of it from force of habit.

On the Tuesday morning following the murder, Molden, Hauer, Sam Dorson and Rafe Buenrostro drove to Darling's studio apartment across Klail City on the Jonesville road.

The four men began to compile separate lists of the personal effects. From the beginning it became evident that at least two men had shared the studio part of the time.

This was again confirmed when Buenrostro examined the clothes and went through the pockets of the suits, jackets, shirts, slacks arranged neatly but separately on the wall closet. Aside from the clothes, and various pairs of shoes and house slippers, he found two identical Japanese kimonos. Two pairs of short pajamas were hanging on nails; one of the pajama sets appeared to be Darling's size, the other was for someone taller, obviously enough.

In the bathroom, Dorson had counted four more bottles of mouthwash similar to the ones found in the Buick, three jars of petroleum jelly, a giant sized jar of hand cream, two separate sets of toothbrushes, shaving cream, razors, a steptic pencil, and various bottles of after-shave lotion. He also counted two bottles of aspirin and half a dozen plastic bottles containing pills of different colors and sizes. Dorson was convinced that the fingerprints would be unreadable. He then opened the doors to the washstand and picked up the neatly folded towels. He shook them, found nothing, and refolded them before returning the towels to the washstand.

Molden reported there were no newspapers or personal letters. The reading material consisted of five copies of three-year old *Reader's Digest*. Shaking the *Digests* produced some receipts signed by a Sara Allgood and addressed to a Michael W. Woodall. The slips were dated as recently as the previous Monday back to the first week of February of the same year. Someone had written *Thank you* in a small, neat hand at the bottom of each receipt.

Molden also found two library cards in the top drawer of Darling's dresser; each one had been renewed within the past month for an additional two years. One of the cards had been issued by the Klail City Public Library, and the other by the James T. Phelan Library in Flora, nine miles away.

The Klail City card had been issued to C. Ernest Griffin, the Flora card to C. Edward Pennington.

Names, names, names, thought Molden.

The clothing on Darling's side of the wall closet was plentiful, but decidedly on the trendy side. And cheap, or so stated Hauer who knew about such things. There were, however, two expensive *guayabera* shirts. One was long-sleeved, black on white, and it was handmade. The short sleeved *guayabera* was navy blue, and it, too, was handmade and handsomely embroidered. Nice, said Hauer to himself.

A search of the wide pockets in the navy blue *guayabera* uncovered four more receipts from Sara Allgood to Michael W. Woodall; the writing was the same; all four were dated and signed for the month of June.

Dorson poked around in the refrigerator but found it nearly

empty save two bottles of inexpensive varietal red wine.

He opened the small freezer compartment and picked up an empty ice cube tray. Frozen in it were fourteen keys; he put the tray and the keys in an individual plastic bag.

They had worked steadily for another hour but turned up nothing new after the first thirty minutes; Rafe Buenrostro went to the dinette table, took out a tablet, and began to set down the list of contents. When he finished, they looked at each other and Dorson led the way. Buenrostro sealed the door with the regulation yellow tape and Dorson stapled warning labels to each side of the door.

After this, the four men piled into Hauer's Volvo and drove back to Donovan's office.

Some keys to go with some names;
Sam Dorson is rewarded with a story.

4

The Lab Man had sent down a sarcastic note describing the keys as ordinary safety locker types; found *anywhere*, he emphasized. With that, Hauer had driven to the Klail City bus depot and after an hour or so, he found that six of the keys did indeed fit.

He opened the lockers; empty. But, there remained a fairly strong odor of marihuana. That meant nothing; how old were the keys, anyway? And, who used them last? There was nothing of Darling's there; that much was certain.

Dorson and Donovan began making phone calls at the same time, and hit the jackpot on the fourth call: The Jonesville airport. Same brand, according to the woman in charge of the lockers; but of different fit from those found in the bus terminal, she explained.

Dorson signed out a two-door Ford from the County Motor Pool and drove the twenty miles to Jonesville to talk to the woman, a Miss Loring.

Would she mind checking the boxes with him, please?
A frown, but she opened the lockers anyway; empty.
Have new keys been issued? No. Why should they?
Have they been in use long? Yes, daily. Why?
The woman would answer each of his questions with one of her own.

Sam Dorson thanked her and decided on the spot to stay at the airport the entire afternoon. It was not yet two o'clock, and the last flight would leave Jonesville at nine o'clock that evening.

He went back to the lockers, looked inside and smelled each one rather closely. No grass. A passenger stopped and gaped in astonishment as Dorson sniffed inside the lockers. The passenger took another look at Dorson and hurried away talking to himself.

Dorson checked each locker again; he ran his hand inside the lockers this time. Nothing. Curiouser and curiouser, but perhaps not; there's a reasonable explanation for everything, thought Dorson. Even for murder; no, especially for murder.

Sam Dorson had overdone it on the coffee; and, as foul as it tasted, the woman behind the cash register smiled and accepted the cash and the baleful look on Dorson's face with equal cheer.

Patience being its only reward was enough for Dorson, and it came in the shape and form of an elderly woman. Dorson was standing directly in front of the lockers, reading or pretending to be reading *The Jonesville Herald* when he saw the woman deposit four quarters in each of the lockers on Sam's list.

He followed her to the airport exit, saw her board a city bus, and he did the same. She alighted an hour later at the corner of Fifth and St. Francis in Jonesville, she walked to the middle of the block, trodded up the stoop, reached down into her purse for a key, and entered a recently painted two-bedroom home of the kind built immediately after World War II. The front door opened again, and he saw her checking the mailbox; the screen door was latched and this was followed by the closing of the solid-wood door at the head of the stoop.

Dorson walked up the stoop and read the name on the mail box: Sara Allgood.

Well!

He wrote down the address, walked to the nearest telephone booth, and called the Jonesville P.D. to request some I. & A., information and assistance.

Yes, the woman was named Sara Allgood, and she was 67 years old; yes, she lived at 515 E. St. Francis; phone number? Right here: 432-4164.

A bachelor woman, the desk man had said, and a former

schoolteacher. The desk man wanted to know what Old Lady Allgood was up to.

Dorson thanked him, and he, too, wondered what a sexegenerian was doing pumping quarters into empty safety lockers at the Jonesville airport.

Always a reasonable explanation somewhere, right?

Right.

Dorson rang the doorbell, identified himself, and was admitted by Miss Allgood who was to treat him to a remarkable story.

She allowed that she had retired from teaching at age 66, a little over a year and a half ago, in fact. A few months after her retirement, she had placed a personal services ad in *The Jonesville Herald.* She had listed her education, her background, and promised to produce three letters of recommendation attesting her character, credentials, etc.

She had run the ad for three weeks although she had almost decided to drop it after the first two. She had made the mistake, she said, of including her phone number in the ad.

The first week produced no less than twenty calls most of which asked if she were a model, a masseuse, or if she had an interest in working as a personal traveling secretary.

Innocent, but not completely, of the ways of the present world, Miss Allgood explained to some of the callers that she could type, read to the blind and the live-in, babysit on weekends, and that she was prepared to run errands for items such as mail, small grocery orders, laundry pickups, and the like. She would explain her fees for each service adding that transportation by bus would be an extra charge and not part of her hourly rate. Her time, she said, was worth five dollars an hour.

A mite steep for the Valley, thought Sam.

No, she couldn't remember why she had decided to run the ad a third week; it might have been because they were at reduced rates, for instance; but no, she couldn't remember why. She had done it and was surprised to receive a visitor on a Sunday morning of the third week.

A cultured gentleman's voice, she said. Dorson thought of his own flat, expressionless voice developed after fifteen years on the force and rediscovered to no surprise, that that was his actual voice: flat, expressionless. Monotonous, even. No, not a gentleman's voice; definitely not.

And not by Miss Allgood's definition, at any rate.

Miss Allgood had smiled when she said the word *gentleman*. The caller had been pleased, she went on, to learn that he was speaking with a former schoolteacher; oh, yes, he was. His own mother had been a schoolteacher, you see.

I'll bet.

Would she describe the man as short or tall? Tall, about as tall as you; five-ten, thought Dorson.

Brown hair, did you say? No; balding, as a matter of fact. And blue-eyed.

About forty-five, she'd guess.

Yes?

Oh, yes, and a businessman, too. Suit, tie, and brightly shined shoes; she'd noticed these, yes. Nice hands, too.

A gentleman with clear, blue eyes.

A tall, blue-eyed, bald man. Forty to fifty. Was there a name for the gentleman?

Oh, yes: Michael W. Woodall.

Ah-hah. Different from Aha!

The upshot was that Miss Sara Allgood was offered one hundred dollars a week for personal services which consisted of depositing four quarters Monday through Friday into airport lockers nos. 4, 9, 11, 16, 18, 25, 30 and 31, at the Jonesville airport; and that was all she was required to do.

If, for any reason, she was unable to do so by four o'clock in the afternoon, of any given day, she was to call him at 444-3631, his home.

Sam: "May I have the number again, please? Thank you."

Had she called that number?

No, she had not called the number; no need to, you see. She hadn't missed a day.

A nod from Dorson.

Miss Allgood said that the gentleman, Mr. Woodall, had come by taxi and that he had kept the taxi waiting during the visit. He called on her here, in person.

She was impressed.

After the introductions, she said, he informed her that he was looking for a reliable person who would perform personal services discreetly and for a reasonable fee. The gentleman considered one hundred dollars a week reasonable. He also said that he was convinced that he found the perfect person for the job.

They then talked of this and that and the other (Miss Allgood here). They also talked of the young and of the teaching of the young. He loved the young, he said, but unfortunately, he went on to say, he had found them not to be as reliable as "us older folk."

Some chuckling followed this, thought Dorson.

Yes, she understood what he meant and intended to mean, as well; she, too, loved the young, and a lifetime of trying to teach them responsibility had been as rewarding as it had been heartbreaking.

Mr. Woodall had also left a card.

Oh?

"Here, Mr. Dorson, I'll go get it for you."

Bless you!

The blue-eyed man had also said he'd phone in other instructions in a week or so, and he had. Before he left, it was agreed again that she was to receive one hundred dollars a week for her services, five days a week, weekends excluded.

Hmph.

"Pardon me, Mr. Dorson?"

"Sorry, Miss Allgood; I didn't mean to interrupt."

Yes; she could do the service, and she would work from Mondays through Fridays; would Monday next be all right?

It would be perfect. The gentleman also said it was customary for the first employer to pay for the cost of the ad, and he had handed her a fifty-dollar bill.

Miss Allgood was delighted, of course.

Of course.

But, she had protested: the ad had only run to twenty-seven dollars for the three weeks.

Mr. Woodall (that was his name, Mr. Dorson, and I'm sorry about the card, but I can't find it anywhere), Mr. Woodall said that he wished he could stay and chat some more, but that business was pressing at the moment.

Of course.

"But no work on weekends?"

"Pardon me?"

"There was to be no work on weekends?"

"Yes; that was the arrangement."

Oh, Miss Allgood remembered what the card said: "The Woodall Group. Imports."

Oh, where *is* that card, Mr. Dorson?

Yes, agreed Dorson, silently. Where?

The gentleman had left the first week's salary on the table, in an envelope; no, the envelope had been thrown away as well. Was it important?

No. Kindly.

Well, yes, after he left in the taxi . . . the cab waited for him as I said, and Mr. Woodall waved as he was being driven away.

And she was paid promptly?

Oh, yes. And in cash, too.

Of course.

And how did she receive the money?

The salary? By registered mail; every Saturday morning, and that included the expense for the lockers and transportation.

One of the envelopes?

No, I'm sorry; but I'll have one next Saturday.

I wonder, thought Dorson.

Would he want one?

Oh, yes.

She had been employed by Mr. Woodall since February, yes. Was she doing anything wrong?

And then: "Oh, how silly of me, Mr. Dorson."

Yes?

"The receipts, Mr. Dorson; I have the carbons; I keep them."

Bless you, Sara Allgood.

Dorson smiled for the first time, and she smiled, too.

No, no crime as far as he could see. It was perfectly normal; she performed a service and was paid for it. He called on her, yes, as a policeman, but he was also planning to call on other people who were regular users of safety lockers.

Really?

Oh, yes.

A survey, then?

Yes, something like that.

But she wasn't doing anything illegal?

Dorson played with his tie and collar, and, in his best manner, and looking at the former English teacher, he said there was no need to broach (Broach! ho-ho!) the visit to Mr. Woodall, but should Mr. Woodall bring it up, why, she was to give her employer all the facts and details of Mr. Dorson's visit.

That'll set him to thinking, thought Dorson.

With that, soft and pleasant goodbyes from both sides of the door and with assurances that he would return the original receipts to Miss Allgood.

"Oh, Mr. Dorson."

"Yes?"

"I'm a Mormon."

"A what?"

"A Mormon. I'm a member of the Church of Latter Day Saints. We don't drink coffee, you know. Would you care for a glass of ice-cold water before you leave?"

Smile. "Yes. Thank you."

Sam Dorson walked to the phone booth again and made another call to the Jonesville P.D. A check on Mr. Michael W. Woodall. Where? Well, try Vice. Larceny. Fraud. Grand Theft-Auto. Homicide. Everywhere.

Could he wait?

Wait? Happy to.

Fifteen minutes later: Nothing on Michael W. Woodall.

Nothing?

At all.

He was about to ask: "Are you sure?" but he checked himself. He knew better than that. He also knew what the answer to *that* would be.

He merely said, "Thanks."

He then returned to the Jonesville airport and checked the lockers again. All locked and in use, meaning they were empty, and that was that.

But what was that all about?

**With Sara Allgood identified,
the question remains: What is
her relationship to the dead man?**

5

Donovan looked up and watched as Dorson set the two cups of coffee on Donovan's desk.

"Does it taste anything like the coffee at the airport?" Knowingly.

"God, no. You'd think they made bad coffee on purpose, wouldn't you? Like a form of prohibition, to discourage coffee drinking."

Donovan said, "I was out there on the Peggy Mack thing, remember? I finally brought my own in a thermos."

"Peggy Mack," Dorson repeated. "She couldn't stop bragging about how she had hacked up 'My Norman,' could she?"

"Lucky for us she did brag, and lucky too that we got her before the American flight to Mexico City."

"I'll say . . . Ah, did you get a chance to read about my afternoon tea with Miss Sara Allgood?"

"Oh, yes." And then: "What's she like, Sam? Really?" Laughing the while.

"Grandmotherly." The straight man.

"Ah-hah; know what you mean. Rafe's got the main folder right now, and I just ran off a copy of his report. Here."

Dorson set his cup down and pointed to the cup: "Good coffee, Cull."

Donovan handed him the stapled sheets and said, "I sent Joe Molden to see The Lab Man."

"That was brave of you." Grinning.

"I should have sent Hauer, I know, but I've got him checking fingerprints."

"Quite a few from what I hear; and aside from the dead man's, only one set, right?"

"It's crazy, Sam. The inside of that car was covered with them. There were prints all over the place: the dash, the glove box, the windows, all four of them, and that doesn't include the windshield or the back window. Covered with them; clear prints, too.

"So now, Hauer's been calling here every fifteen minutes saying he can't locate 'the perpetrator's prints' on file."

"He actually say that? *Perpetrator?*" Incredulous.

"Oh, yeah, and he likes the sound of the word *alleged*, too." Resigned.

"Oh, Lord . . . Well, let me see what you've got."

Sly. "By the way, Sam . . ."

"Uh-huh."

"Rafe found Michael W. Woodall."

"What?" Excited now. "Now how did he do that?"

Just then Joe Molden walked in, nodded to both of them, and began to write some notes on a legal-sized pad.

Donovan looked at Molden, frowned, and said: "He took the Valley-wide telephone book, looked under the 'W's' and bingo! Man has a business in Jonesville. Out in the open. He has an office at Cooke First National, and he's listed in the Yellow Pages: The Michael W. Woodall Group. Imports."

Molden: "Which corroborates Miss Allgood." An interruption.

Donovan and Dorson looked at him, and Molden went back to his writing.

Donovan: "That's *right*." And looking straight at Molden: "But read Rafe's report anyway, Sam."

Sam Dorson held up his right index finger, pursed his lips, and shook his head slightly. Culley Donovan nodded and in turn pursed his lips, too.

Turning to Molden, who was poring over a report from The Lab Man, Donovan said: "What did Dietz come up with?" Sighing.

**Rafe Buenrostro makes an appointment
and is invited to coffee and pound cake.**

6

Rafe Buenrostro had, in effect, looked up Woodall's name in the Valley-wide directory, and there it was, in plain sight. He had then checked the Yellow Pages; an eighth of a page ad. Nothing fancy. He then opened the folder and looked for the number Miss Allgood had given Dorson. The numbers didn't match.

Rafe Buenrostro went back to the directory, looked for Woodall's residence number but found none. The numbers in the white pages matched the Yellow Pages, but these were business phones.

Unlisted home phone!

He'd have to drive to Jonesville, he decided. He dialed the number in the phone book, and a woman's voice, bright and clear said, "The Woodall Group, Miss Landero speaking."

"Miss Landero, my name's Rafe Buenrostro; I'm a lieutenant of detectives for the Belken County District Attorney, and I'd like to make an appointment to see Mr. Woodall; I'd like to see him today, please." Nicely.

A slight gasp, and then: "A detective? You're not making a business call then?"

Rafe: "No, I'm not. It's a police matter."

A police matter, he thought. A police investigation. Police business. Jee-sus. Well? What else *could* he say?

He plowed on: "Is he there? And, is he free this afternoon?"

Brightly again: "Oh, yes; he's always here."

Always? An expression of habit, most likely.

"And you'd like to see him this afternoon?"

"Yes; how does three o'clock sound to you?"

"Three. Oh. Clock. I'm writing this down. Yes. That's fine. And, how do you spell your name again?"

Again? A cutie, that secretary.

Rafe spelled it out, hung up, and wrote down the information for the file. He then buzzed Culley Donovan.

"Yeah, Rafe."

"I found Woodall, and I got an appointment in a couple of hours. Anything on the prints yet?"

"Not yet."

"Sam in yet?"

"No, but he'll be happy to hear you found a Michael W. Woodall, Rafe."

"Any news from Dietz?"

"I sent Molden out again, and I have it on good authority that he'll be in sometime before the end of the year."

Chuckle. "Patience and forbearance, Culley."

"Yes, Dad."

And yet, thought Rafe Buenrostro, Molden would probably wind up as a good cop; a decent cop. Still, it wasn't either Donovan's fault or Molden's that the younger man was related to Sheriff Parkinson.

Patience and forbearance, indeed.

**Rafe Buenrostro learns of Maimonides'
Eight Ways of Giving. He remembers
his Lamb and is rewarded with a smile.**

7

A series of small surprises awaited Rafe Buenrostro, and he walked right into them. He had no idea, of course. "Check it out" was the universal motto, as was "only doing his job."

The first surprise was Miss Landero: she stood five-feet-one atop some three-to-four-inch heels. The young, clear voice over the phone didn't match the face: old; the hair: light blue. She was fingering her blue-shaded sunglasses held by a chain and clip. She wore a flowered-print dress; it wasn't cheap. Rafe Buenrostro guessed her age to be anywhere from sixty to seventy-ish, but wouldn't have been surprised to find himself wrong. He often was when it came to guessing people's ages.

This was Rafe Buenrostro, the keen observer.

He learned later that morning that she was eighty years old. Alert, too.

The clear, youngish voice again. "You're Lieutenant Buenrostro?"

"Yes." Smiling slightly.

"Mr. Woodall just stepped out."

He nodded. Was there mischief in that smile of hers?

"He went to buy us all some pound cake." Smiling. It *was* mischief.

"That's his office; the coffee's in there, by the way. Won't you go in?"

"Thank you. Very much." Funny old thing; but, a cutie-pie, as Dorson would say.

Rafe Buenrostro walked in and faced an old desk, some three feet high and close to eight feet long. Massive. In fine shape, too. Two desk trays: one empty, the other held a newspaper. Today's *Herald*. Two windows to the right overlooking busy Oreana Boulevard, six stories below. Behind the desk: a high-back chair. Both the chair and the desk were highly polished. Teak? Why not? The Woodall Group was in the import business, after all.

A brilliant deduction. One in the long line . . .

An easy chair. Brocade and green; an old Morris, Rafe thought. A Davenport, too. Everything's old, but not gone. Admiringly.

He glanced around and saw two more matching high-back chairs in a corner on the right wall of the room.

To Rafe Buenrostro's left, on the opposite corner, a half-open dressing screen, and a handsome coffee table standing in front of the screen. It too was highly polished. Nice. Coffee pot, tray, spoons, knives. All silver. He picked up a cup. The real stuff.

Very nice.

The telephone sat on a smaller table immediately to the right of the desk. Was Michael W. Woodall a southpaw?

The telephone was definitely pre-World War II; the receiver weighed a pound, no less. He picked up the base and read the manufacturer's name: Monotone, Chicago, Ill. By the heft, he guessed it weighed three pounds, minimum. It looked indestructible. Probably had never needed maintenance, either. They built them for talking in those days, he thought.

Except for the trays, the top of the desk was bare. No paper clips, no pencils; he then noticed an absence of filing cabinets in the office.

No business, then?

But this was Jonesville-on-the-Rio. A city of 67,000, an international seaport and landport. The files must be in another room. Behind that door, he thought. A mahogany beauty.

Directly behind the eight-foot desk, Rafe Buenrostro found himself staring at two black-and-white group photographs. He walked over and saw some young faces in each.

The picture on the left showed ten young men in World War II flying gear. In the immediate background: a B-24, Liberator. He read six of the legible signatures; one of them belonged to Arthur M. Woodall, but Rafe couldn't tell which one of the aviators was Arthur M.

On the righthand side of the group photograph, the date: March 4, 1943, and below that, a fading note in typescript and held there by a thin strip of white adhesive tape: 359th Squadron; and, below that, an inscription: "Love, Artie." And, to the right of that, in a small neat backhand: A.M.W., Capt., USAF, 1916-1943.

The other black-and-white showed still another group of earnest young men, some kneeling and some standing on a carrier deck with a body of water as a background.

Of the fifteen, Rafe Buenrostro counted seven who were smiling; a bit sheepishly, it seemed to him. The others were serious enough and had looked straight into the camera. An India ink inscription on the left side bottom, read: "Ensign Robert Gray, lone survivor of this torpedo bomber squadron, Task Force 17. Battle of Midway; May, 1942."

Rafe looked for the Woodall name and found it written in the same neat backhand: Maurice A. Woodall, Lt. (JG), USNR, 1916-1942.

Twins?

Arthur and Maurice Woodall; neither brother had survived the war. Were there other Woodall brothers and sisters?

The thought of the war took him to Korea briefly. He was about to rub his left eye but thought better of it. It would swell slightly from time to time, and rubbing would bring temporary relief. He dropped his hand.

He then remembered he was scheduled for his yearly visit to the William Barrett V.A. Hospital next January 4.

Mentally he was halfway between Korea and World War II when he heard a rather hoarse but pleasant: "Hello, there."

An old man; probably as old as Miss Landero, he thought. The hair was white, but thick, and sitting atop a pinkish head. No liver spots, he noted. The man was standing some twelve feet away in the ample office, and Rafe Buenrostro caught a glimpse of Miss Landero closing the door behind her. He hadn't heard it open.

The second surprise: "I'm Michael Woodall."

But, he wasn't bald, or balding, and he certainly wasn't middle-aged. This man was *old*, and even Rafe Buenrostro was certain of that. Tall? Mr. Woodall was only slightly taller than his secretary.

"Looking at the group pictures, I see." Smiling.

Rafe nodded and watched as the man who introduced himself as Michael Woodall walked to the coffee table, unwrapped the coffee cake, and began to cut and measure out some half-inch slices around the circular tray.

Looking up. "But you haven't had your coffee, yet; Miss Landero said it was ready."

Slightly off-balance, Rafe Buenrostro said, "It is, but I, ah, I was admiring the pictures."

"Ah, yes; those old things." His voice dropped slightly. And then: "My sons."

He looked down for the briefest moment and then smiled again.

"Were you in the War?"

"No." And then Rafe Buenrostro was surprised to hear himself say: "Not in that one, no."

"No, I can see that, now. You were much too young for that one. Korea, perhaps? Yes?"

"Yes; two winters." Half-grin. A smooth questioner, Mr. Woodall.

And then, from out of nowhere: "Ah . . . I'm eighty-one, Lieutenant."

"Pardon?" Had he been staring at him as obviously as that?

"My age, Lieutenant: I'm eighty-one; Estelle and I adopted the boys; they were twins, you see. We adopted them on my thirty-fifth birthday, a Monday, October 23, 1916.

"They were a week old then, and we tried to raise them with everything two boys would want: love, intelligence, understanding, and with a fine sense of humor.

"Do you, Lieutenant? Do you have a sense of humor?"

Rafe Buenrostro didn't know what to say off hand, but he supposed that he did and said so. A bit disconcerted, too. He looked at Mr. Woodall's eyes again; they were brown.

Hmph.

Will the real Michael W. Woodall please rise?

"But what am I doing? Sit down, Lieutenant, please. Sit down; no, don't use that arm chair. I'm afraid it only *looks* comfortable. Here, I'll get one of those high-backs. There. Well, now, and how can The Woodall Group be of service to you?"

Rafe Buenrostro smiled and wondered which one of the two was supposed to be asking the questions.

"It's a fairly involved story, and I've come to see you to clear something up for us."

True.

"I'm with the County Police, and I live and work in Klail City." Gold badge, and picture i.d.

The door.

"He doesn't have his coffee yet, Jimmy." Mild reproof, but smiling the while. Rafe Buenrostro felt as if he were being smothered by kindness, being laid to rest in a pool of lotus blossoms, he thought.

Cynical young man; naughty young man. They're old, and I'm company; this isn't a business call.

But she had called him Jimmy. And Michael?

"One slice or two?" Miss Landero. Smiling.

"Two. Please." A nice little boy. Feeling increasingly diverted, he tried to relax somewhat, to get himself on some sort of course.

Miss Landero smiled happily. "Two it is."

Miss Landero was pleased. Miss Landero approved. "You won't be sorry; will he, Jimmy?"

Mr. Woodall smiled, and he too accepted two slices of the pound cake. "Bon appetit, Lieutenant."

"Aussi." Automatically.

"What's that?" Mild surprise.

"Oh. It means, 'you, as well,' or 'likewise,' ah, 'you, too.' "

"Ah, you speak French, do you?"

Embarrassed. "I only know a few words."

Smiling. "Is that true?"

He admitted he knew more than a few words, and heard Mr. Woodall say, "You're a frank young man, aren't you?"

"Yes." Ordinarily, he thought.

"And you'd like for us, for me, to clear something up, yes? Is 'clearing up things' what you do?"

Rafe Buenrostro considered that for a moment and nodded in agreement. "Yes; police work is mostly clearing things up."

How true.

"Is it dangerous work, police work?"

"No, not particularly."

Also true.

"Been involved in many shootings, ah, shoot-outs?"

"No." Neutral.

"And in Korea?"

"Oh, yes." Back to that again.

A shift in gears. "Well, what can I clear up for you?" Smiling and meaning it. And then Michael W. Woodall raised his hand to stop Rafe Buenrostro; the old man picked up the two cups, walked to the coffee pot, and served his guest and himself.

"I'll not go into all of the particulars, Mr. Woodall, since we don't know where we—the police—are at the moment. It's still a preliminary, as we say, and I'll begin with some questions and see where we go from there. Fair enough?"

"Fair enough." Mr. Woodall was enjoying himself. But all business, just the same.

"Do you know Miss Sara Allgood?" Brass tacks.

"Yes; she's one of our projects." All business now.

"Would you explain that for me." Not a question.

"Certainly." Emphasis on the *cert*.

"Sara Allgood is a retired schoolteacher of English. She receives what is most certainly a niggardly retirement pension from the State's teacher retirement fund and that after some forty years at hard labor. We felt she was deserving of more; she must've been having some difficulty when she placed the ad."

"The ad." Encouragingly.

"Yes. A personal services ad in the *Herald*."

Rafe Buenrostro listened, made no assumptions, and knew better than to hurry his host.

"And so, Estelle and I—Estelle is Miss Landero—and my wife, too—(Ah!)—decided to help her financially. Not a dole, no, nor anything resembling a gift, either. That would have proved embarrassing, you see. Embarrassing all around, I daresay, and, most importantly, not in keeping with what we wanted to do."

Is he English? European of some sort? Wake up, Buenrostro.

"And so, as luck would have it, Estelle spotted the personal services ad placed by Sara Allgood, and we concocted the project on the spot."

Mr. Woodall stopped on a dime, looked directly at Rafe and said, "You're dying to hear what the project is, aren't you?"

Fake punt?

"It's very simple. Really. But, it's what I suspect part of your police work may be: a tidying up of accounts. I'll begin at the beginning."

Pleasant little man. And pink. A Kris Kringle sans beard.

"Artie, up there, (pointing) who died on takeoff from an English airfield—Estelle and I have been there and have made the trip several times—anyway, he was one of Miss Woodall's favorite students.

"We've never met her, by the way."

Oh?

"Artie wanted to be a writer, and Maurie (pointing), he wanted to join me in the business, and both looked upon their courses in English as the most indispensable tool for business."

A set phrase?

"Both of the boys were hard and willing workers, and Miss Allgood fell in love with them. And she worked them to death, too, but they always came back for more. She piled the work on, really. Staggering amounts of it, but they merely thrived the more. Compared to English, they said, their other subjects were a snap, a breeze."

The boys probably called them 'crips' in those days, thought Rafe.

"When Maurie was killed in Midway and when Artie followed him less that a year later, Miss Allgood suffered what was then called a nervous breakdown. Simply put, she was interned in the Flora Asylum.

"She was released a year-and-half later, cured, and the war was mercifully winding down by then. She must've put up with cruel and childish taunts, but in time people forgot about her illness or accepted it, I guess. Anyway, she continued to work until her retirement dinner a year or so ago.

"We did not attend, of course. Estelle and I—" He stopped. And then: "We're Jews, Lieutenant."

"Pardon me?"

"We're Jews, Estelle and I. She's Sephardic, and hence the Spanish name."

Where are we headed now?

"My name was Udoff, Lieutenant, Meyer Udoff. But, we chose *Woodall* years ago. And, when we came to the Valley, we learned that being Jewish here meant very little. *We* were classified as Anglos. A funny term, isn't it?"

Hmmmm.

"The point, Lieutenant, is that we were at loose ends, and we had the money. And, too, we only had each other after Nineteen-forty-four. We're Orthodox, and Maimonides, Lieutenant, a Spaniard, well, he explains about charity, and this is what we are doing. Maimonides explains the eight ways of giving. I won't go into all of them, but Miss Allgood falls under number one.

"Number one is the highest degree, you see. It's giving a gift or a loan or taking one as a partner or finding employment by which the person can be self-supporting."

Hmmm.

Smile. "I'll begin again. Some six months ago, Estelle read the ad we spoke of, and we decided to give her some work."

"The lockers."

"Yes, exactly. She was to check them for us. A ruse, you understand. But, this would get her out of the house, she'd enjoy the bus ride, she'd see people, and she'd receive her money. She would have a job; something to do."

Very proud of himself.

"I see; and who called on her?"

"Our attorney; or perhaps someone from his office staff."

Waiting.

"Jerem Pratt of Pratt and Hoskins. He made the arrangements, and . . ."

"How is she paid?" Rather smoothly, that.

"By registered mail, Lieutenant. All of this was *arranged* beforehand." Disappointed in the young man. And then: "More coffee?"

Press on, Buenrostro.

"And (carefully now) and, what about the lockers at the Klail City bus depot?"

"And what lockers are those?" Genuine surprise.

Rafe Buenrostro leaned back and decided it was time to let out more line.

"In the course of our investigation (watch that officialese) we ran across some keys similar to the airport locker keys."

"And?" Very interested.

"We were checking out why someone would pay money to maintain empty lockers; it's not a crime, obviously, but our particular interest concerns the man who last held the airport keys and the bus keys, as well."

Nod.

"He's dead."

"Dead." Bland.

He knows about death, too. Buenrostro to himself.

"Yes. By strangulation, we think; but, also as a result of a series of blows to the head. Severe concussions, then."

Nod.

Buenrostro decided it was Mr. Woodall's turn now. He smiled at him and waited.

"Well, yes, the projects give *us* something to do, Lieutenant.

"Estelle and I retired from active business in Nineteen forty-six. We could have gone on, but when Artie and Maurie died . . .

"Well, we kept the company name, the office, the telephones, our agent number, the export licenses, everything. Everything but actual work, Lieutenant.

"We travel some, come to the office from Monday through Friday. We maintain a charade, but it gives us something to do."

"And Miss Allgood?" Yes, back to that again.

"One of our projects." Sadly.

"Does Mr. Pratt handle that? Does he do the leg work?"

"Goodness, no; he heads a law firm of some ten to twelve attorneys here in Jonesville. If anyone, it'd be some young attorney or Mr. Krindler, his business and office manager."

"That's Kindla?"

"Krindler. K-ah-i-n-d-l-e-ah. Otis." Hesitation.

Nod from Rafe Buenrostro.

Full hesitation stop from Mr. Woodall, until:

"He's one of those."

"Those." Neutral.

"Yes, you have a saying in Spanish: *es de los otros.*" Speaking to a child. "A homosexual, Lieutenant."

"Another question. Why Monday to Friday only?"

"You do stick to the subject, don't you? Well, it's a work week."

The most natural answer. Still . . .

"Yes, but what if she found something in storage at those boxes after the weekend? What then?"

Smile. "At the Jonesville airport? Not hardly. But, knowing Miss Allgood, she'd keep track of the account and report it."

Carefully: "Does she have a telephone number to call? For directions or instructions?"

"I imagine she does."

An answer for everything.

"You find it strange, Lieutenant? Someone helping someone else?"

Got you there, Buenrostro.

The truth, now.

"Not strange, no. Surprising, perhaps. Exemplary, even."
My, my, you really should consider going into politics,
Buenrostro.

And that was about it for the day's meeting.

"Thank you for your time, Mr. Woodall; and for the coffee, of course."

"Is that it?"

"For now."

"All cleared up, then?"

"In part, yes." Smiling.

Miss Landero entered at the right moment; probably had
heard every word said.

She gave them each her best smile; Rafe Buenrostro rose
from his chair, shook hands all around, repeated his thanks,
and added: "For everything." Meaning it, too.

"Thank *you*." In chorus and happy as larks the Woodalls.

"One more thing, please."

Smiles in place.

"Miss Landero calls you 'Jimmy' . . ."

"Yes, my name's Meyer or Michael, but my old friends
call me Jimmy. No (softly) . . ." He stopped.

He hesitated and looked at the younger man. "Do you read
Lamb, Lieutenant?"

"I have, yes."

"Good. I was about to say 'I have none to call me Charley,
now.' Do you know it?"

"A letter, isn't it?"

"Very good. Yes, Eighteen-twenty-seven, to his friend
Robinson."

Rafe Buenrostro nodded, turned to go, and then stopped in
his tracks. He said: "The letter to Robinson was dated on the
20th of January, on the Eve of St. Agnes."

The Woodalls smiled wider still.

"*Very good!*"

"Bye, now. And, thanks."

Rafe Buenrostro stepped outside into some very bright sunshine. Surprise number four: He had a vague notion of night-fall, and the stars out, and the lights flashing off and on in downtown Jonesville. He glanced at his watch: 4 o'clock.

He brought the watch to his ear: four o'clock was right. An hour at the Woodalls? Was that all?

He thought of Donovan and Dorson; they're going to love this, he sighed.

Rafe Buenrostro walked to a corner telephone booth and looked up the numbers (there were three) for Pratt and Hoskins' offices. None matched Miss Allgood's number given to Sam Dorson.

Why not call her? Why not, indeed?

Introductions; yes, she remembered Lieutenant Dorson. Was this about the same thing? Yes? Happy to cooperate . . . No, she had not called the number; no need to. Not up to now, no.

Thank you.

He reached for another coin; why don't *you* call the number yourself, Dummy? Why not, indeed?

Four-Four-Four Three-Six-Three-One.

A male voice. A recording. "Four-Four-Four Three-Six-Three-One. I'm out just now. At the tone, please leave a message. When you hear the tone, you'll have exactly one minute."

No, thank you.

Another call to Miss Allgood. Apology for the time taken and could she do him a favor? Of course. And then: "I'll call you back in ten minutes, Miss Allgood. Thank you."

He jay-walked across Citriana Boulevard, entered the nearest restaurant, and ordered some iced tea.

He looked over some of his notes, finished the tea, ordered a second glass, and looked at his watch. Time to call Miss Allgood again.

Yes, she had dialed the number, and yes, she had remembered the voice, but no, she didn't say a word, just as the Lieutenant had asked. But, yes, she was sure; the voice belonged to Mr. Woodall, to the gentleman who had called on her.

He assured her that all of this was but a mere formality, and he appreciated her cooperation very, very much.

She had made the voice. So?

One more call, this one to Pratt and Hoskins.

"No, Lieutenant, Mr. Pratt won't be in until tomorrow. Is it important?" Nippy; ice forming round the edges.

"Mr. Hoskins, then."

Frost on the periphery. "He's dead."

"What time does Mr. Pratt come in, please?"

"I couldn't say." You are wasting our valuable time.

"What *time*, please?"

"Ooooooooooh, tennish, I'd say." Tres relaxed.

Firm. "I'll be in at eleven o'clock, Miss. What's your name?"

"What?" Shock and horrors! Her *name*?

"Name. What do you *go* by?"

The big wilt.

"Sylvia; ah, Miss Howard." And rattled, too.

I bet you're a bully, Sylvia Howard. Let's try you out.

"I'll be there at eleven, Miss Howard. You tell him it's a police investigation, and you can tell him we expect his full cooperation as an officer of the court."

Gasp.

"Bu . . ."

"Thank you, Miss Howard."

Bit abrupt there, Buenrostro. But that's the way it goes: Civility from the Woodalls and snot from the Catch-alls.

"Ye-es."

"I'll be there at *eleven*."

The Homicide Squad receives a telephone call from the insane asylum.

8

Culley Donovan had waited for Rafe Buenrostro's return from Jonesville. He listened to the tale of the Woodall projects, the Pratt-Hoskins connection, the mention of the office manager's homosexuality, and then asked:

"Is that last important?"

Buenrostro: "*Who* knows? It's just one more piece of cardboard for the puzzle."

"Okay; I'll talk to both Pratt and Krindler tomorrow."

"I leaned on the receptionist a bit."

Laugh from Donovan.

Buenrostro: "Let's send Joe Molden to the Flora asylum today . . ."

"I'm all for it."

". . . to check on Mr. Woodall's story about Sara Allgood."

"Ah; what do you expect he'll find there?"

Rafe shook his head and said, "I don't know."

"Well, we're all going to have to talk on this sometime, and everyone's agreed for tomorrow afternoon."

"How's the folder, Culley?"

Buzz. Dorson.

"Is Rafe there?"

"Yeah, Sam."

"Something just came in over the phone; I'll be in as soon as I can."

Culley walked over to the coffee pot, shook it, peeked inside, and didn't like what he saw. "Damn thing's almost empty; better unplug it."

Rafe nodded absently, sat on the long bench, and waited for Dorson.

"Sam was surprised how easily you found the Woodalls."

Buzz. "You guys still there?"

Donovan pressed the voice button:

In chorus: "Yeah."

"Well, just hold on a sec, I'm still on the phone out here." Click.

Rafe left the bench and said, "I'll go ahead and make us some coffee."

"Right."

And then Dorson came in: "Got a phone call from the Flora asylum, and . . ."

Rafe Buenrostro and Donovan looked at each other; looks of surprise.

Dorson: "What's that all about?"

"I'll tell you in a minute; what've you got?" Culley.

"Some guy there (reading from a pad), Sonny Rollins is his name; he's an intern, he says. He sounded nervous and said he wanted to talk to us. It's about a murder, he said. And he *was* nervous, you guys."

Donovan said, "That's a matter for the Flora police; a city matter."

"I was about to tell him that when he hung up on me."

"Just like that?"

"Well, he then said, *Jee-sus, I'll call you back*; and that was it."

"What do *you* think?"

Dorson shook his head, shrugged, and shook his head again. An idea: "I'll call the Flora P.D., let them handle it."

"They'll probably laugh, too. They'll say it's a crank call."

Culley: "But I'd check it out anyway."

Smiles all around, and Culley Donovan then said: "You're just doing your job."

"*Is* there any coffee?"

Rafe said, "I was just about to make some; Culley'll fill you in on the Woodall Group. By the way, tomorrow's afternoon meeting is all set. Leave notes for Molden and Hauer."

"Good, looking forward to it. Where're you going, Rafe?"

"Up to see Dutch Elder on the apartment building murder; see you guys later."

Dorson: "Some of the Lab Man's stuff is in, but nothing from pathology. And, no i.d.s as yet. But, we do have some stuff to work on. Folder's getting a little fat, looks good."

Donovan smiled at Sam and agreed. A good part of the answer was in the folder; it usually was. One just had to get it out.

Easy as pie, to coin yet another phrase.

Donovan: "We'll do it this way: I'll brief Molden, send him out to Flora; and then I'll have him do a special errand or two." Looking at Dorson: "To check out Woodall's statement on Miss Allgood's illness, for starters."

"Good."

Donovan went on: "I'll tell Molden to talk to this Collins guy."

"Rollins."

"Rollins. Just a check, okay? Molden will also report on the car seats and whatever it is we have on the sketchy medical report, the shoe tracks, and whatever else he can come up with.

"Young Mr. Hauer will read the entire folder, break it down, step by step, and we all five have us a little talk; he's coming in at eight, and we meet at two, sharp. I've got Molden working on a couple of other things, too."

Nod.

"I heard that Big Foot Parkinson wanted to know how we were coming along on this." Dorson.

"When did he learn to read?" Donovan.

Molden, the Golden Nephew, wasn't there to hear this, but Donovan would have said it anyway. Unfair, of course, but what the hell, right?

Donovan again: "Sam, I'm going to Jonesville tomorrow morning; going to talk to a law firm that handles the Woodalls' affairs."

"Business affairs?"

"No business at all," said Donovan. "Rafe learned they stopped doing business in Forty-six; they go to the office everyday, sit there, drink coffee, eat pound cake, quote Charles Lamb, and conduct some private charities once in a while."

Dorson shook his head and said, "Takes all kinds, doesn't it?"

He sat down, pulled out a cigarette, lit it, and poured himself a cup of coffee. He scratched his head some, thought on Sara Allgood, on Rafe's locating the Woodalls, and pondered on time, the great ally. This'll be cleared up, too. In time.

**Wherein the Homicide Squad meets to
sit and talk about what it is they
have in the folder.**

9

Art Benavides, the day man, had been instructed to hold all
calls starting at two o'clock; one exception: The Lab Man.

"And if Big Foot calls, I mean, if Sheriff Parkinson
calls?"

"Tell him we've gone fishing."

"Did you say *fishing*, Captain?"

Click.

A call for Rafe Buenrostro came in ten minutes after two,
and Benavides wrote: "Lt. B., call Milden Croftland; the
Osuna Ranch. A. Benavides, Sgt. 2:10 p.m., Oct. 16, 1972."

Rafe Buenrostro was to take notes. He was, then, "building
the case," as Culley Donovan called it.

Peter Hauer gave the first report:

"The Buick was a car rental from the Jonesville airport.
That was Dorson's assignment."

Cough.

"The Lab Man identified the blood; it's A positive and it
corresponds to the victim's blood group. The blood was ana-
lyzed and taken from the victim's face, clothing, and inside
the car." (And perhaps from the killer's clothes when we find
him and them, Dorson to himself.)

"The Lab people found some threads of Stevens Twist
Twill on both the front and back seats, on both the front and
rear floor boards, and on the right-hand doors, front and
back, and some threads mixed with and stuck, again front and
back, to the velvet of the door panels.

Donovan: "What's Twist Twill?"

Hauer, keeping his eyes on his notes: "The Lab Man says it's a brand name of a fabric manufactured by a textile mill in Roanoke, North Carolina. Famous mills, according to him."

"They had some union trouble in times past." Dorson, by way of explanation.

Rafe looked at Dorson; he wasn't surprised. Sam spent much of his free time reading everything he could get his hands on. No TV watcher, he. As to work, Dorson came early and left late. Sam's wife, Effie, liked it that way, and Sam loved it that way. Bliss.

Donovan: "What's so special about the fabric?"

"You see it every day; it's high-grade stuff, too. They use it for uniforms: forest green for the old Sinclair stations, taupe for Mobil, light-blue for Humble and now brown for Exxon . . ."

Interruption. Molden, "How do you know all that?"

Dorson: "He's reading it."

"This particular Twist Twill is white, but not Gulf white, 'cause that's got . . ."

"Blue pin-stripes." Dorson.

"The Lab Man says white's usually worn by some laundry delivery men in the Valley. Here's a partial list he gave me: Home Service and Lone Star both in Klail; Broadus Cleaners in Jonesville, Lone Star in Edgerton, and White's Big State Cleaners in Ruffing.

"Ahhhhh, The Lab Man also says that the state of Texas' Department of Corrections has used white at times; last contract for that was two years ago."

"For the guards?"

"For the inmates."

"Huntsville's what? Four hundred miles?" Dorson.

"Close to that." Molden.

"So that's out," said Sam Dorson looking blankly at Molden.

"And?"

"Part of that particular two-year old purchase also went to several mental institutions."

Hello?

Hauer stopped to see what the silence was all about.

Donovan: "Is the Flora asylum included in that two-year old list?"

"Let's see . . . . no."

Rafe: "Did Henry Dietz happen to mention if the Flora asylum had used white at any time?"

"Yes; the last time was six years ago, according to him."

Back on course.

"Go on." Donovan patted his left shirtpocket looking for non-existent cigarettes; he had stopped smoking five years before. He looked down at his pocket and shook his head.

Dorson smiled and winked at him.

Donovan nodded.

"No luck on the prints; and we've checked with the brethren at the F.B.I."

Donovan snorted at the use of the word *brethren*.

Molden: "They've probably got them somewhere. Shits just can't find 'em, is all."

Donovan, mild look of surprise, looked at Molden. And, he agreed with him. Silently. He then thought there might be some hope for him yet. To be fair, Donovan remembered that Joe Molden had asked some good questions on occasion.

Hauer: "Well, yes. The F.B.I., ahhhhhh. Well, it's happened, yes. A couple of times."

"Go on."

"The foot prints away from the car go every which way. Around the car a couple of times, too. The crew found some white Twist Twill on the ground; as if the perpe—*person* had gone to sleep or something. The tracks then went on for a fairly straight course. The dogs lost them on the highway."

"They'd find 'em if this were a movie." Dorson.

"I'll say." Molden.

Hauer again: "The dogs were paraded up and down for a quarter of a mile on both sides of the road; the tracks stopped on the right hand side of the road."

"That's Highway Eighty-three out there." Dorson.

"Yes."

"Going north, then." Molden.

"Most likely." Donovan.

"Probably hitched himself a ride." Molden, archly.

Dorson: "A short while after he'd clobbered a guy to death."

Molden: "Jee-sus!"

Dorson: "Let that be a lesson to you, Joe. Teach you to pick up people."

Laughter all around.

Donovan asked: "Anything else?"

"The Lab Man's having the complete physical and path. report typed for us. He said he'd have it ready before five-thirty, today."

"*Before* five-thirty?"

"That's what he said, yeah."

"That it, Peter?"

"That's it."

Donovan turned to the others and said, "Joe Molden's next."

"I also started off with the prints, and I didn't get any-where either. The Lab Man said he counted over two-hundred of 'em; it's crazy. Like somebody didn't care."

Hauer: "Or like somebody pushing the windows and the windshield trying to get out."

Molden: "Or like somebody . . ."

"Go on," this from Donovan. Gently.

"Miss Sara Allgood was admitted to the Flora facility, ah, asylum, on 17 July 1943; she was released in January, 1945. On *12* January 1945; sorry.

"She taught English to some of the teachables there. She was quiet, cooperative, spent most of her time reading or weeping silently or writing long letters, none of which she mailed.

"Eight months later, March of Forty-four, she stopped her letter writing and joined the office staff. Very efficient. She was pronounced cured the following November but begged to stay on a while longer.

"This is against State regs., but a Dr. Anthony Sturmer, Head of Psychiatry, held on to the release forms and, legally then, she was allowed to remain a few more months.

"An informal arrangement. Dr. Sturmer died on 16 June 1957."

Rafe looked up from his notes and said to himself: "Very good, Joe."

"When she did leave, she was re-hired by the Jonesville Independent School District at her old job, but this time at the new Jonesville High. She taught there until the Spring of Seventy, after which she retired.

"I checked her for priors . . ."

"Ha!" from Dorson. (Rafe: Don't over do it, Joe; not too much zeal, now . . .).

". . . and she's clean."

Laughter all around.

Molden did not look up.

Just doing his job, said Rafe to himself.

"It *was* funny, Joe."

Molden looked at Dorson and nodded.

"Go on." Donovan.

"I also talked to one James Rollins; he's a temporary there; been on the job some five to six weeks."

"I know him."

Buenrostro, Dorson, and Donovan looked at Hauer. "Went to college with him; he's a social worker or something like that."

Molden: "He finally got a degree in hotel management, and he's at the asylum as a management trainee. On-the-job training, sort-a."

Dorson: "Talk about symbolism. The Crazy Hotel."

"And?" Donovan, gently again.

Molden: "Rollins said one of the inmates leaves or goes AWOL on a regular basis. He said that the man's been doing that for some time. He comes back on his own after a day or two, three at the longest. There's never been a written report or anything like that."

"Well, shit." Dorson left his desk, stood by the door, face

to the wall. Half-turning, he said: "They've got a nerve; no goddam reports on something like that."

"Tell them the rest, the way you told me."

They all looked at Donovan this time. "Late last night, Joe called, and we talked on this."

Nods.

Molden: "The inmate's been there for some eight years, and although they can now wear clothes from home, if they want to, he still wears whites. He has three complete sets; or he did. Rollins says the man now has two pair. When Rollins inquired about the other pair, for inventory purposes, he told him, the inmate said that he had thrown the third pair away. It was old; worn out, he said.

"His name's David McKinlow, and I checked him for prints here. None."

"None." Dorson.

Molden: "I, ah, called the two garbage disposal companies in Flora, and García-Treviño Removal has the contract for the asylum."

Hesitation.

Good for you, Joe Molden. (Dorson to himself.)

"The Flora facility uses white plastic bags for trash, and it's collected once a week; on Thursdays. Patrolman Bobby Bleibst got the number of the truck, the time of the garbage pick up, and he was out there by ten a.m. yesterday. He found the shirt, but he couldn't come up with the pants.

"He swears they weren't there. *Any place.* Bobby spent eight hours out there; at the garbage dump."

"Boy deserves a month's leave for that duty." Dorson.

Pause.

Molden: "There was some blood on the shirt's left sleeve and on the right cuff."

Very quiet.

Evenly. "I tagged it, stuffed in an envelope, and hand-delivered it to the lab. I told Munson to give it to The Lab Man, and to no one else. Right after that, on my way here, Art Benavides said that The Lab Man would call us at six. He said six 'cause he's got some other stuff to hand in this afternoon."

"That's the physical and path. reports he's doing for us. Your stuff's next, obviously."

"Can Rollins name the days the man left and came back to the asylum last week?" Rafe.

"No."

Hmph.

"Rollins himself was on sick leave for a couple of days, so he doesn't know *when* the guy left or at *what* hour he came back."

"But the guy did leave, and he did come back." Hauer.

"And there's the shirt." Dorson.

"Right." Molden.

"How does the guy spell his name." Dorson to Molden.

"McKinlow. *Mc* and then a *K*."

"Rollins just read about the murder out at the Osuna Ranch a couple-a days ago, and he thinks this guy's capable of murder. The man's a trusty, but Rollins says he isn't fooled by this McKinlow guy."

"A hunch, then." Dorson.

Rafe: "And a missing pair of pants and shirt."

Culley Donovan: "Peter, call Rollins right now and tell him we need McKinlow's fingerprints. That shouldn't be too hard, not if he's a trusty. Wait up, Peter, send a uniform and tell him to wait there until Rollins gets the prints."

Hauer left the room and was back within a minute or so. He sat next to Molden. Rafe moved from the bench to his desk and pulled out another legal-sized pad.

Rafe: "Culley read my notes on the Woodall couple and drove down to Jonesville this morning to see their attorneys and a man named Otis Krindler; he's the office manager for the firm."

Buzz. The phone. An internal call, then.

Rafe said, "The Lab Man." He picked up his phone. Dorson and Donovan listened on Dorson's phone as Molden and Hauer listened on Donovan's phone.

A bit testy but full of triumph, too. The Lab Man.

"The blood on the shirt Molden brought in matches the blood spots on the front seat, on the victim's face, hands, and shoes, and clothing. No mistake."

The Lab Man hath spoken.

And then: "Rafe, I'm having the physical and path. typed up right now. The shirt was no sweat, by the way, and it took Doug Gault but six minutes for assessment, corroboration, and assignation of blood type."

Rafe wondered if that were a world's record. "First-rate job, Henry." And it was, too.

"Ah, I understand you all are meeting on this right now, that right?"

Rafe smiled and asked: "What else you got?"

"The late Mr. Charles Edward Darling, his right name, by the way, had a specialized infection in his eyelid."

Specialized? Was that a medical term?

"Oh?"

"Yes; I won't bother *you* with the name, it'll be on the path. report, but the victim was a homosexual; the infection proves it. An active participant is what my learned colleagues (snort) in psychiatry call it (snort)."

"Anything else, Henry?"

"Yes; there were traces of semen in all three of the mouth-wash bottles in his apartment and on the sheets and on the bottle in the trunk of the car."

"In the trunk, did you say?"

"You deaf or something?"

"Anything else, Henry?"

Beside himself now. "The strangulation was botched; the tie was used some, sure, but the hands did the work. Big mothers, Rafe."

Mothers? Henry?

"He still had some life in him, and he must've thrashed around some and that's how he broke his left wrist. On the steering column. The boys here report that the steering column had some of the victim's blood on it.

"But! What killed him were the head blows. Vicious blows, Rafe. No iron pipe; no rock in a sock. The killer used his hands, Rafe."

And then: "You got a bad one out there somewhere."

Rafe: "Peter Hauer says you found foot prints all around the car, and evidence of a body lying down not far from the car."

"Ha! The man probably took a nap."

"What do *you* think, Henry?"

"It's all in the report, son; don't get greedy."

"One more thing, Henry?"

"Go ahead."

"Did the victim leave the car, walk around?"

"No trace a-that."

Rafe: "We'll be sending you some additional prints in about an hour."

"Okay."

Dietz coughed and said, "They were chopping blows, Rafe. He's a bad one."

Pause.

"Toodle-ooh." And with that, Dietz hung up.

Well!

Donovan: "Mr. Krindler is a homosexual, too."

Hauer and Molden: "Who?"

"Otis Krindler, the office manager for Pratt and Hoskins, the Woodalls' attorneys."

Ah.

Hauer: "Why'd you ask if the victim left the car?"

"Henry mentioned the semen in the mouthwash bottles and he said they found them in the trunk. Since there's no trace of the victim stepping out of the car and since the keys were in the ignition, the argument, if that's what it was, must've started and ended inside the car."

Nod.

**Donovan and Dorson present their facts,
and the facts refuse to go away.**

10

"Pratt is a contract attorney; Hoskins was too, but he died fifteen years ago. Three of the senior partners handle the maritime law section, two junior partners are estate planners, two are in gas and oil, and they've also got four younger attorneys who go out and drum up business for the firm; as you might suspect, they also do a bit of lobbying up at Austin. Not one minute of *pro bono publico*, by the way. And, they are not, most emphatically, not available for criminal law, according to Jerem Pratt. He's *the* Pratt of Pratt and Hoskins.

"The business for the Woodalls on the Allgood matter and two other projects, the Woodalls' word for it, are done as a personal favor. The firm also manages the Woodall estate, by the way. No surprise there.

"Lawyer Pratt says he knows of Otis Krindler's predilections, his word, and that Otis is discreet."

"How broadminded of him." Dorson.

Knock on the door. Dorson opened it: Irene Paredes; smiling and wearing her green smock.

"Mr. Dietz says I'm to give this to Lieutenant Buenrostro. Is he in?"

Dorson, out to prove that chivalry was not completely dead, opened the door and bowed.

"Hi, Rafe."

"Irene."

"The Lab Man sent this. For *you*, he says."

And then: "I saw your cousin. Again." Smiling now; pretty teeth and meant to be shown.

"Which one?" Grinning right back and knowing full well whom she was talking about.

Rafe Buenrostro's teeth were there and all his, but a trifle too big for some people's likes and dislikes.

"Your cousin Jehu. We went across last night. To Barrones, I mean."

General laughter; she laughed too. An old border joke.

"How's he doing?"

"Pretty good; we're going to the dog races in Barrones on Sunday. Can you get away?"

Rafe looked at Culley. "Not for a while; we're kind-a busy right now." Too true.

"My cousin Leah's on vacation. She was in town, and she's now back in Jonesville. But, she's got two more weeks left."

Well? Buenrostro?

"I'll call Jehu. Really."

"*Okay*; see you Sunday, right?" Wink. "By-e y'all."

General byes all around.

"Well," said Dorson, "that was a nice break."

Culley Donovan grinned and said, "She got a fifty-year-old cousin, too?"

Laughter from everyone but Hauer.

Donovan looked at him and said friendly-like, "What's the matter, Peter? I'm a widower, just like Rafe; I'm just a little older, that's all."

Rafe broke in: "I'll ask her. You speak Spanish?"

Donovan laughed and deflected that one: "Make us some coffee, Sam."

Hoots and laughter all around again.

"Coming up."

"Okay, where were we?"

Rafe: "Krindler."

"Right. Pratt knows about the homosexuality, and doesn't care.

"Pratt and I waited in Krindler's office until lunch time, and when the typists and receptionists left for noon lunch, I discovered that Pratt had catered lunch for the three of us.

"Right off, Pratt cut in and told me he would act as Krindler's attorney during the questioning. I reminded him that his office manager was not charged with anything. A bit of fencing; nothing personal.

"He's a little banty rooster, is Mr. Pratt. He calls Otis

Krindler, O.K., and I understand the lawyers do too, but not the help, of course."

"Of course," said Dorson.

Donovan grinned. "*Vurry* chummy lunch."

"What did Pratt order for lunch?" This from Peter Hauer.

"Rabbit food and some of the best damn lemon meringue pie I've *ever* had. I swear."

"The Plaza."

"What?"

"The Plaza. The Plaza Hotel caters for some downtown execs in Jonesville, and they make a hell of a lemon meringue."

"How do you know shit like that?" Dorson. Pleasantly.

"I'm a cop."

And one, Rafe thought, with a sense of humor. You'll need it in Homicide.

"Is this going to take all day?" Molden.

Donovan: "You going somewhere?"

"I guess not."

Donovan chose to ignore that, and there was Joe Molden, winding his way to the doghouse again.

But Molden's going to be a good cop someday, thought Rafe. If he sticks it out. Donovan's a good guy to work for; *with*, really. He's loyal, and he's tough. And honest, thought Rafe.

And Donovan was also right. Where was the fire? It's plodding work, but it had damn well better be accurate or, as Dorson says: "There'll be shit on the can, the fan, and the man." Slow but sure was good, accurate was better; and all three together were best.

That wasn't Lamb; it was a man named Canfield out at the Police Academy.

Donovan: "I began with the keys, and we went straight to business, as I said. Krindler and Darling were friends; had been friends. And, they had been close at one time. Intimate, even. It was said matter of factly, and 'we're all grown-ups here' was the attitude.

"Around three months ago, Krindler discovered that some of his pocket money was missing; not much, he said. But some little things, too, like the Woodall receipts signed by Sara Allgood. It happened on a regular basis and usually when he was with Darling. A pattern.

"He asked his friend about the missing money, and Darling admitted it right off, claimed he was a bit short. Krindler delivered a kindly lecture, and the matter was patched up until the key incident."

Pause. No comments.

"Krindler said he brought the business of the airport keys to Darling's attention. In a *nice* way, he said. Not accusatorily at all.

"Here's Krindler: 'Thank *God* we were not at a public place.'

"Darling became angry; accused Krindler of accusing *him* without proof, and then Darling ran out of the bedroom, dressed in the kitchen, slammed the door to the apartment and left. He was back in a minute: it was his own studio apartment, you see."

"It's a goddam movie." Dorson.

"Well, when Darling came back, they both enjoyed a good laugh and made up. Krindler now says he was seriously considering breaking the relationship around this time."

All eyes were on Donovan who flipped a page and went on:

"Krindler upped Darling's allowance at that point, though, and Darling continued working as a waiter at *The Blue Hat*."

"I know the place. Expensive, great service, and bad food." Hauer, of course.

Molden: "Who talked to the people at *The Blue Hat*?"

"Rafe did, when he went to see the Woodalls. Nothing there." Sam Dorson.

"The break came when Krindler discovered *two* keys, quite by accident, he says. He was fluffing out the living room cushions, and he found them. Quite by accident, he repeated. He faced Darling with them, Darling claimed the keys were his, not Krindler's, and then Darling took him by the hand, Krindler said, led him out of the flat, and straight to the Klail bus depot.

"A depressing place, according to Krindler."

"Oh, *I've* been there," Dorson brightly with Hauer averting his look.

Darling opened the lockers, pointed to them, and quickly shut them. He was triumphant, said Krindler.

"Krindler also says he made up his mind to break the relationship right then and right there. Not one moment later.

"One of the lockers contained marihuana, you see."

"Ho-ho." Molden.

"And, Krindler said that *that* did it for him. He spoke with his employer, gave him the facts, and was advised to say nothing. It was then recommended to Krindler that he discontinue the relation. Discreetly, of course."

"Of course." Dorson, deadpan.

"And that was it; oh, a series of bothersome calls from Darling, but the receptionists had been instructed personally and beforehand, and they handled that end of it.

"Darling didn't *importune* him at the office, but he did mail Krindler a letter."

Pause. "I read it, and it's of no importance to us here."

Raised eyebrows all around.

"Krindler says he did not bother to answer the letter."

"Now, a week ago, Darling tried to call Krindler again, but with no success. After this came a telegram."

Pause.

"I took it down: 'Am leaving town; need one-hundred dollars. Please. For old times. Lied about keys. Please forgive. Keys in freezer. Send money to Hat. Please. Love. Edward.' "

Molden: "Who's Edward?" And then Molden again: "Oh, Charles *Edward* Darling. Sorry."

An impassive Culley Donovan: "Krindler did not bother looking for the keys; he considered the one-hundred dollars a cheap enough farewell gift, and that was it."

"On the day of the murder, Krindler, Pratt, and Krindler's assistant, Pam-Ella Carmela Tisdale . . ."

"What a *name*!" Young Mr. Hauer.

". . . spent five hours, seven including dinner, on staff evaluations, considerations of raises, bonuses, and new accounts brought in by the four musqueteers."

"A Saturday, right?" Dorson.

"Yes; they meet at the office, they work, and then finish it off with dinner at the America in Barrones. Once a month, on a regular basis.

"I called Polito Sandoval at the America, and he confirmed it."

"Check it out," Hauer, laughing. Donovan smiled.

Dorson: "He's got an alibi, and that clears up the voodoo of the names, the receipts, and the keys in the freezer. We get rid of the Woodalls and Sara Allgood. Agreed? Fine. So, what do we have? We have a dead man, but no killer. And, if I may add something to Culley's at this point, the marihuana was no longer at the depot; there had been some grass at one time, and it stunk up the place."

Rafe looked up from his notes, and Dorson then said: "I talked to Culley last night, and then I came in here, got Ronnie Aguilar from the lab. He was working late, and on the way home, I asked him to go to the bus depot with me."

Nods.

Dorson again: "I'll follow Culley."

"Darling, calling himself C. Ernest Griffin and showing enough i.d. to satisfy the car rental clerk, rented the Buick at the Jonesville airport that Saturday. He walked up to the rental counter with a carry-all bag and an overnighter, and the clerk thought he had just gotten off a plane. Natural enough assumption.

"Griffin paid by check. However, he first produced an American Express card, he then pretended to change his mind, made a little drama out of it, see, and then said something like 'Oh, what the heck, I'll go ahead and pay cash.'

"He wrote out the check *on a local bank*, but he used *out of-state i.d.* Shows the type of help they hire nowadays.

"He rented the car for the one day, and the mileage records show a total of thirty-three miles. He checked the car out at one that Saturday afternoon.

"Now, I drove from the Jonesville airport to Darling's flat here in Klail, on to Highway Eighty-three and then to Farm Road 906, and from there to the Osuna Ranch. That's a distance of twenty-eight miles."

No comments.

"From the Osuna Ranch, I returned to Jonesville airport, and that's a distance of twenty miles. I by-passed the flat. Okay?

"I then drove from the Jonesville airport to his flat, to The Blue Hat, he had the Krindler check there, got to Highway Eighty-three, crossed to Farm Road 906, and then on the levee overlooking the cotton patch; thirty-three miles."

Hauer and Molden stared at Sam Dorson.

"He probably picked up somebody along the way. A hitch-hiker, let's say. A chance he took.

"Old Crossland found the body early Sunday morning; he wrote down the time as 7:02 a.m., as we all know."

"Narrowing the time," Hauer.

Dorson: "I checked Darling's record with Vice. Three arrests, no convictions. One of the arrests was for trespassing—a peeping tom incident—and the other two came as a result of Vice's periodic harrassment of homosexuals around election time."

Nods all around. The most natural thing in the world, of course. And Vice hiked up its arrest records, too.

"I also checked with the Klail City Library where he had a card made out to C. Ernest Griffin. One woman clerk remembered him, and then another one joined in. Their stories coincide. Mr. Griffin, they said, would spend his time reading magazines, not books. Four or five hours at a time.

"And, sometimes he left alone and sometimes with a friend.

"When I asked if the friends were men friends or women friends, the clerks looked at each other until one of them blurted out: 'Men friends, yes; now that you ask.' "

Pause.

"Probably trolling a bit. The descriptions given of his library friends do not coincide with Miss Allgood's description of Mr. Otis Krindler."

"Whom she knows as Woodall." Hauer.

"Whom she knows as Woodall, thank you. I then went to the Phelan Library in Flora. He used the name Pennington there. But it was the same routine. He read no books, instead he passed his time in the magazine section. Four or five hours at a clip. Trolling there, too, I suspect."

Hauer: "They call it cruising."

"Yes, and I call it *trolling*." Evenly.

"One difference. He usually showed up at the Klail City Library in the daytime, and at the Phelan only in the evenings. Till closing time, poor thing."

No sarcasm on Sam's part.

"A young clerk at the Phelan remembered him; the kid's a high schooler, and he said that Pennington tried to pick him up a couple of times. They mostly talked about model trains, he said. He also said Pennington was a walking encyclopedia on 'em. Could tick them off, he said. Oh, and photography, too. The kid said Pennington was a whiz at that."

"Whiz," repeated Dorson.

"The boy laughed when he told me about the attempted pickups. The boy said *he* liked girls.

"And that's it," said Dorson. "A lot of facts, but no killer."

"We've still got Joe's peripatetic inmate." Hauer.

Dorson looked at him. "Sticky."

"That's right; he's *already* crazy." Molden.

"If he's the man." Donovan.

"If he's the man." Dorson.

"And, if he *is* the man, we'll have to prove it even more so for him than for anybody else. Won't we?" Molden here.

Sighs all around.

Donovan broke it up: "Let's plan to meet for lunch tomorrow, everybody."

Hauer: "A working lunch, then?"

Dorson turned to Rafe and asked, "Where're you off to, pardner?"

Rafe grinned. "I'm going to make a phone call."

"To Jehu?"

"To Jehu is right."

With that, the Belken County Homicide Squad, like Lord Ronald's horse, rode off in all directions.

**Less of a working lunch,
and more of a digestion of facts.**

11

At noon the next day, a Saturday, Rafe Buenrostro was the last one to arrive at the Busy Bee Restaurant.

Dorson looked up and asked: "All set for the dog races tomorrow afternoon?"

Grin. "Yeah, unless something else happens 'round here. Go on, scoot over."

Donovan raised both eyebrows in mock surprise: "And what could possibly happen in peaceful Belken County, in the Magic Lower Rio Grande Valley of Texas?"

Groan from Joe Molden.

Donovan smiled at him. "You're right."

A youngish waitress came over; bored *and* stiff. She rested her eyes disinterestedly on Rafe Buenrostro.

Hauer: "Try the dark beer; it's Montalbán from Yucatán, and it's good."

"Yeah, I'll have one of those. Could I have some *barbacoa*? *Mexicana*, please. And some brains, if you have 'em."

Another old border joke, but this time it was no joke.

"Any tortillas to go with that?"

"Please."

"Corn or flour?"

"Corn, please."

She looked straight at Rafe again and nodded. On her way to the cook's window, she counted the *pleases*. Three. And he's a cop?

Hauer giggled. "No brains."

And Molden broke in: "Great legs, though."

Dorson leaned over and said, "I'm going to tell your wife, Joe. And as for you, Young Mr. Hauer, I'll remind you that you're a servant of the people, and that makes the waitress your employer."

"God!"

She was back in a minute or two, laden with iced-down beer mugs.

"You're Lieutenant Buenrostro, aren't you? I saw your picture in the paper at Christmas time. Peggy McDougall; the Hatchet Queen, at the airport."

Rafe nodded and pointed to Culley Donovan. "Captain Donovan made the arrest."

Interested. "Really?"

Dorson: "All by himself." Grinning.

"Wow." And off she went.

"Wow," repeated Hauer.

Donovan shook his head. "I'll ask her if she has an aunt or something." Smiling. "Well, now that we're all here, how about a spot of business?

"The uniform Hauer sent to the Flora asylum brought back two ashtrays to the lab last night. The prints match those found in the car."

Looks all around, and then Dorson said quietly, but with conviction, "Looks like we got 'im."

Nods.

Lunch was followed by another beer with Dorson sticking to coffee. The first cup was pronounced *good*, and he said so. The second was *not bad*. The third one, trying to convince himself and the others, was *pretty good*.

"That stuff's going to kill you someday."

"Nah."

At the office.

"After the lab called me on the prints, I drove to *The Blue Hat*, talked to the owners, the chef, and to some of the waiters. Nothing. Some waiters didn't even know Darling. They were new. From where I sit, everything points to McKinlow." Culley.

Rafe nodded.

Culley Donovan said: "Bring 'im, Rafe; take Sam and Peter with you."

Molden frowned but said nothing. Donovan turned to him and said, "Joe and I can build the case here."

A signal honor.

Sam nudged Rafe and winked at him. To Hauer: "Get your gun, Peter."

Joe Molden brightened up considerably; Rafe Buentrostro usually built the cases for them, and Molden was now in charge.

Donovan, however, had other plans in mind. Molden needed the experience, but Rafe Buenrostro was also an attorney and less likely to foul things up in a legal sense. The arrest, after all, was to be made at a mental institution, and this called for a softer touch.

Donovan picked up the phone and said, "I'm calling Jim Lee in Flora; I'll let him know we've got the County Wolfpack working in his town."

Molden turned to the three and asked, "You going out to see Rollins right now?"

Dorson: "We'll call to see if he's on duty first."

Molden nodded.

"He is," Rafe Buenrostro said. "I had Art Benavides check it for me before I went to the Busy Bee. Rollins is at the asylum, and he's waiting for us." And then: "I checked with the lab myself to see if the prints were in." By way of explanation to Donovan.

Dorson grinned at Culley Donovan and pointed his finger at Joe Molden. He then led Peter Hauer to the door and said: "I drive."

**Three needs in the McKinlow arrest:
discretion, cooperation, and six
huge policemen.**

12

The plan was for Sam Dorson to identify himself, ask for
Rollins, and bring him out to the car.

With Hauer sitting in the back seat and Rafe in front, Dorson turned to them and said: "Look at the sign there." It
read: The Flora N. Klail Institution for the Insane. No bones
about what the place was all about.

Dorson parked in the visitors' zone; he got out without a
word and walked to the twenty-foot gate holding an eight-foot
sign reading: ENTRANCE/ENTRE. "Good thing I can
read," he muttered.

Rafe glanced out the windshield. Seven three-story buildings and each a depressing green.

Was green the cheapest paint the State could buy? It was
certainly the dreariest, he thought. He then looked at the iron
bars in each of the buildings; all on the third floor.

Personal violence there. Sadly.

Hauer tapped him on the shoulder and said, "I like Dorson, Rafe. Really."

"What brought that on?"

"Well, he, ah, he calls me Young Mr. Hauer and Young
Peter, you know; but I don't mind. And, I don't really think I
get on his nerves as much as he says I do or as much as he
lets on. What do you think?"

Rafe half-turned but kept his eyes on Sam who was cutting
across the grass and gravel path to the guard gate.

"Sam's okay, and he's a hell of a cop. And, he's honest.
I'm not talking about graft, here. There's a lot of character in
Sam Dorson."

Hauer didn't react.

"You can learn a lot from him, Peter." A moment later

Rafe Buenrostro said, "I still do."

"Well, I've been on the force for six years and a detective for eighteen months, and . . ." Hauer stopped and then, in a rush, said, "And with you guys since April, in Homicide, and in this team, you and Sam and Culley and Joe . . . you know." Rambling.

Rafe followed Sam's walk to the office building; he half-turned again and nodded. "It'll be okay; as Culley says, it's a matter of time."

"Does, ah, does Sam resent the fact that . . . I mean, well, you went to college, and *law* school, and Joe and I, we went to college, too."

Rafe watched Sam ring the doorbell; the door opened from the inside and Sam walked in. "He's in."

"What? Oh, Sam? Yeah. Good."

Busy with his own problems was Young Mr. Hauer.

"What were you saying about college?"

"I was saying how you and I, how we, the younger guys, how we all went to college."

Rafe turned his head toward the office again, and then said, "So did Sam." Neutral.

"Really?"

"Oh, yes. And, he reads history, he likes his music, and he reads *The New York Times*." Chuckle. "He also knows about plays, but he prefers operettas. I guess he knows the lyrics to every Gilbert and Sullivan piece there is."

"No kidding?"

"He reads Housman, Hardy, Synge . . ."

"Who are they?"

"And, he quotes poetry."

"Sam *Dorson*?"

Rafe Buenrostro threw his head back and laughed, but not in ridicule of the sensitive Hauer. "And, he went to a good school; Northwestern."

"In Chicago? Illi-noiz?"

"In Evanston; by the Lake."

"What lake is that? Oh, yeah; Lake Michigan, right? Well, I wouldn't have figured him for that. Me? Well, I went to

Trinity up in San Antonio and that's where I met Sonny Rollins; he's from Ruffing."

Rafe held his breath for a moment. Either the beginning or the end of confession time; like waiting for the other shoe, although Rafe wasn't interested: What if the guy upstairs only had one foot?

Besides, his interest lay in Sam Dorson, and there he was coming down the walk accompanied by a man wearing a suit and a tie.

"Here they come."

"Yeah; that's Rollins, all right."

Rafe noticed that Rollins was clenching and unclenching his fists. Nerves.

Introductions.

"The supervisor's in, Rafe. We'll see him in a minute or two, but I want you to listen to Mr. Rollins first; it's a good story."

Peter Hauer stuck his head out the window:

"Hi, Sonny."

"Hullo, Peter. Mr. Dorson said you were part of the team."

'Part of the team!'

Rafe looked at Dorson and grinned at him. Dorson looked away, but Hauer didn't see this. He couldn't; he wasn't there at the time. At that moment, Peter Hauer was some 40,000 feet above Flora, Texas.

Rollins' story was interesting. His boss, a stone bureaucrat with thirty-five years in, spent his time picking his nose, scratching his behind, and taking stuff home once in a while.

This is new? To Hauer and Rollins it was.

Man's name was Alpha Ogden, and he had been pilfering State property for years: some food, a lawnmower or two, some drills and drill bits, shoes issued to inmates whose families couldn't provide any, light bulbs (a case here and there), a box of soap (here and there) a box of detergent (cleanliness is next to godliness), some pencils (by the crate), ball points, etc. Nothing major.

Quite a long list, though, and according to Rollins, it had been going on for years.

Rafe and Dorson said, silently, "Centuries, my boy."

Mr. Ogden, then, was not greedy; Dorson said that Ogden had a touch of the Goethe in him: "Ohne Hast aber ohne Rast,"—without haste, but without rest.

Hauer wondered who Gerda was; but, he knew better than to ask Sam Dorson.

A little gold mine and some foul things going on, according to Rollins. (Dorson, to himself, "Wait till you start running those hotels, kid. What are your ideas on illicit fucking? Of little boys? And B J specialists waiting in your room before you and your wife open the door? Hotel *management*, indeed.")

Rafe watched Dorson's eyes, and if he didn't know exactly what his partner was thinking, he wasn't too far off. They both looked at James Rollins who needed a little guidance here:

"About David McKinlow, Mr. Rollins." Rafe.

"What? Oh, yeah."

Yes, he was sure Alpha Ogden knew of McKinlow's periodic unauthorized leaves, slipping easily into the b'cratic jargon. And, for his part, McKinlow knew about, and helped, too, most likely, in Alpha Ogden's systematic looting.

Not necessarily blackmail, more of a marriage of convenience.

As for David McKinlow, Rollins then said he was (hesitation) a, a, a, a, a brute. He was six-feet eight inches tall, and he weighed some two-hundred and twenty pounds. A brute.

Not in basketball, thought Rafe, but a frightening son-of-a-bitch, nevertheless.

Rollins looked down and said, "A big, black motherfucker."

Dorson winced visibly, and Hauer swallowed and blinked. Hauer couldn't believe his ears: "A *Trinity* man, for Christ's sakes!"

Rafe Buenrostro said, "We're going to need proof which will serve as evidence against Ogden if we're going to get him to talk about McKinlow."

"That's going to be hard." Rollins.

"Why is that?" Dorson.

"Well . . . I've checked. Some of the files are missing. A lot of the paperwork, too; he's been culling it for years. Everybody knows it, though."

Dorson cut in. "The State."

"Wha?"

"The State records: sealed bids, dates; requisition numbers, dates; purchase orders, dates; vouchers, dates; model numbers, registration numbers. We can have that checked."

Relieved, Rollins said, "It'll be easy, huh?"

"No." All three in chorus. And all three policemen thinking of the six-feet eight-inch McKinlow who weighed in at two-hundred and twenty pounds.

"Oh."

"But we *can* do it," said Rafe Buenrostro. "Let's see if we can scare Mr. Ogden first."

"Oh."

"We need your help a bit."

Rollins shook his head. "He's tough."

Rafe Buenrostro and Sam Dorson looked at each other, and Dorson then said, "Good. Let's see how tough he is."

But, as Thurber once said, "It was like stealing thunder from a baby."

Ogden started to cry from the beginning. He had cancer, he said. And, he had a year to live; maybe two. And, he was counting on his State retirement and his Social Security for his wife, ah, widow.

It was in the bag from the very start.

Ogden sat in a corner of his office and Dorson picked up the phone to call for help from the Flora P.D.; Donovan, he discovered, had been way ahead. Jim Lee, the Flora chief, was waiting for Dorson's call.

"I need six. Big ones, too."

"They're on their way," said Lee. Dorson put down the receiver. Turning to Ogden, he asked: "Where's McKinlow?"

"In the laundry room." Dejected. "I'll call him for you." Resigned.

"Not yet. We'll wait for the Flora police to get here first. We'll wait here, in your office.

McKinlow, unsuspecting, of course, entered Ogden's office and the Big Six jumped him on the spot. The first thing that happened was that the inside door broke in half. The screen door was then torn off its hinges and landed some fifteen feet away.

McKinlow was finally subdued, but two of the uniforms paid a price: two broken noses, some teeth loosened or lost somewhere in the gravel path after which David McKinlow went catatonic on them. He stretched out in a dead faint.

Too much excitement. Sam Dorson, in a grunt.

Lifting him and carrying him to the EMS ambulance became the chore. The ambulance guys (Dorson here) strapped him the tightest they could, and would've sat on him had he, Sam, not been there with them.

After the preliminary paper work, Hauer and Molden were feeling proud as punch, to coin another phrase.

Donovan called the Woodalls, Jerem Pratt, and more importantly, The Lab Man.

"We really ought to have a beer one of these days, Henry."

"Who's buying?" The Dietz pennon read: "Nothing like straight talk."

Culley: "I'll buy the first round, Rafe the second, and Dorson the third."

Humor from the Lab Man. "Well'p, three's my limit, you know, but I'll go ahead and buy the fourth. When is it we're doing all this drinking?"

"What's wrong with six o'clock this afternoon?"

"Why, nothing at . . . just a minute, Culley. Is Young Buenrostro there? Put him on."

"Young Buenrostro? I heard that."

"What? What did you hear?" It was Irene Paredes.

"I thought it was Henry."

"No, silly. So. It's set for tomorrow, right? Jehu and I've already talked to Leah, and she said she's seen your picture in the paper."

Picture? Paper? "Is she a waitress at the Bee?"

"Leah? No. She lives in Jonesville, you know that. She's a buyer for Gillete and Whitman; G and W, Rafe. Veddy nice."

Rafe: "Sounds like a winner, "I": See you Sunday."

With that, both hung up; he picked up a message stuck to the message holder and squinted at some of the worst example of handwriting he had ever seen.

Art Benavides, the desk man. Call came in yesterday. But who's Milden Croftland out at Sandy Osuna's ranch?

Oh. Milton Crossland.

Donovan: "Sticking around a bit?"

Receiver in hand, "Call from Old Man Crossland."

"Oh?"

Nod. He dialed his cousin, Sandy Osuna.

Donovan waved and said he was on his way to see The Lab Man.

"Sandy? Rafe."

"Yeah. You get my message? I called there yesterday and again this morning. I said it was about Mr. Crossland." Rafe looked at the handwriting: Milden, Milton, Mister.

"He died, Rafe. Died last night."

"Too bad; he was a fine old man. Ah, when's the funeral?"

"Tomorrow morning; at the families' cemetery. It'll be at ten; you'll be there, right?"

"Sure. Sandy . . . has anyone called Jehu?"

"I did; he'll be there."

"Okay. He and I'll drive up together then; early."

He replaced the receiver and went to join Dorson and Culley and The Lab Man. It wasn't going to stop at four beers tonight; a lot to talk about; the old soldier, for one.

John Milton Crossland was dead, and according to Santos Junior, he had died a happy man, a vindicated man. Crossland had received news that his bad discharge, thrown at him before World War I, had been rescinded. Replaced by an honorable one signed by still another Commander-in-Chief, another Great White Father in Washington.

The work of some professor, according to Sandy Osuna.

Someone who kept plugging away at the truth.

So, John Milton had been able to smell some of the roses, if only for a brief time.

As he walked out, Art Benavides handed him another message. Rafe stopped, looked at the desk man, decided against saying anything, and tried to read the chicken marks. He gave up.

"Read it for me, Art."

Beaming. "Yes *sir*. It says, 'I'm at the KBC.' "

"When did it come in?"

"Just now, Lieutenant. You was on the phone."

"Thanks."

"The caller didn't leave no name, Lieutenant."

"I know."

He turned around, smiled, and headed for the door.

Sammie Joe Perkins was back in town. Back home, at the Klail-Blanchard-Cooke Ranch; the KBC.

**A banker with back trouble
discovers a potential pain in the neck.
Saturday, 9:00 a.m.**

13

Jehu Malacara was in his office, sitting on a swivel chair, with hands extended some four feet apart, and hunching his sore shoulders up-down, up-down, one-two, one-two.

The exercise was intended to ease the tension in his neck, or so Irene Paredes had recommended. She, in turn, was given this piece of medical advice by The Lab Man.

It worked, somewhat, although the pain refused to go away completely. A botheration, Jehu Malacara puffed.

The second light on his telephone started to blink off-on; off-on; and he went on one-two, one-two until:

He picked up the receiver.

"Hello." A statement, not a question.

"Mr. Malacara?"

"Yes, this is he." You English major, you.

"Good."

Oh?

Pause.

Jehu looked at the receiver, and thus he missed hearing part of what the voice said.

And the voice seemed different from the first one, too.

"I didn't hear you."

It *was* a new voice now. ". . . and because of that, I had asked if you were going to record our conversation."

"Who's this, please?" No annoyance in his voice; all business.

"You may not know me, but this concerns the bank."

Finality and self-assurance in this voice.

The bank?

"Oh?"

"The information is *not* for sale." Hurt.

Pause.

"Mr. Malacara?"

"Yes, I'm still here." Neither bored nor expectant.

"Are. You. Interested?"

"If it isn't some sort of joke, yes; I'm interested."

"Curious, then?"

"No." Truth and sincerity.

"My . . . my *associate* and I have some information, and it concerns you, or it will when you hear it."

"Does it concern me or the bank?"

If it's blackmail, don't lean on this tree, doggie.

"Something that's going on already in the other two banks in town, in Klail, and yours may be next."

Pause.

"All right." Neutral.

"What I'm saying is true; remember that, please. Okay?"

"Yes, I will."

"Can I call you back this afternoon?"

Why not?

"Yes, of course." Watchful waiting.

"I've also got your home telephone number."

Who doesn't? It's in the directory.

"But I'll call at the bank; we, ah, I'm at work, too. Ba."

Ba?

Had they been cut off? The caller sounded rushed. And the first voice sounded hesitant. No, that's not the word. Unsure? No, not that either.

He *had* recorded it, of course. He recorded every call; not a mania, purely record keeping. No mystery, either. A sound business practice, if anything. Besides, it *was* business.

He rewound the cassette, pressed the play button, sat back and listened to the conversation.

The first voice was a younger voice. Female, definitely. The second voice was older. A Valley woman. Anglo voices, most probably; but in the Valley, one couldn't always tell about accents and intonations.

He reversed the cassette again and played it back a second time.

79

Older woman. Definitely mature. Younger woman: unsure of herself. No, that's not the word. Timid? Diffident? Come on! *Diffident*! Was it a joke? Too elaborate. Level of sincerity? High. Younger woman. Rushed. Insistent.

Nature of call? *Bank* business.

"Something that's going on already in the other two banks in town, in Klail, and yours may be next," the voice had said.

The voice had said *Klail*, not Klail City. A native? He straightened up, rose to his feet, and discovered that the pain had disappeared. Nothing like a mysterious phone call to cure all your troubles, he humphed.

He'd thank the caller at a later date, he said, but for now, he was going to see his boss, Arnold 'Noddy' Perkins; the President of the Klail City First National Bank.

He pushed himself away from the desk and checked for pain again. It was gone. Ah.

The phone light again.

Jehu Malacara looked at the phone as if he'd never seen it blink before. He hunched his shoulders and picked up the receiver.

The voice said, "Jehu."

That was fast. Who?

"Noddy here. You busy?"

"Morning, no; I was coming over to see you, right now as a matter of fact."

"No, that's okay; I'll come over myself."

Jehu Malacara pressed the dial-tone button and set the phone on no-calls. He studied a recent acquisition to his office: a wide-angle photograph of Klail City, dated July 4, 1921. A mass of Klail Citians posing in front of the first Klail City High School.

Some of the kids in the picture were close to sixty-years old by now; and, some could have been killed in World War II; Korea, even. Most of the older folk were dead; had to be. Oh, a few of them left, but not many; not in Nineteen Seventy-two, they weren't.

The photograph was a clear, clean piece of work. Fine detail on the faces, too; and great contrast. The photographer was a man named Leopoldo Ramírez; he had died sometime last year, he recalled. His sons, Leo and Fred, owned and operated four camera shops up and down the Valley. This bank's financing; his recommendation, too.

No Malacaras in that picture; nor Buenrostros. And no mystery, either. They had simply chosen not to pose, that was all.

Vanitas, vanitas.

Noddy Perkins' outline appeared vaguely on the mottled-glass part of Jehu Malacara's office. There was also a side office, a smaller one for the steno and for his secretary.

As always, an unlit cigar clenched in Noddy's left fist; Jehu had never seen Noddy light one, and he'd known the man for a dozen years or so.

"Jehu, you been out of the office in the last half-hour?"

Vintage Noddy. All business, with none of that 'good morning' claptrap. Time is money, Zeit ist Gelt.

A shake of the head.

"Well, I got two phone calls in the last thirty minutes, Jehu. The first one hung up on me, and then the second call some woman with a mousy voice called . . ."

That was the word: Mousy.

". . . and said something about the Bank, this bank, and about the other banks in town. Kind-a garbled. Wanted to know if I wuz interested. And, right before I could even ask who it was, or go to hell, or I'm fine, doc, how're you, she hung up on me. Again!"

"Hmph."

Noddy: "And what's that supposed to mean in English?"

Jehu Malacara walked to his desk top, inserted the cassette, and said: "Listen to this. I got a call just a few minutes ago."

They listened in silence. Noddy shook his head, pursed his lips outward, and took his glasses off. His right hand went up, and Jehu Malacara said,:

"Don't start rubbing your eyes, Noddy."

The older man nodded and said, "Thanks, Jehu."

The man's eyes were easily strained these days and rubbing them did nothing but make them redder still. It was a habit anyway; they didn't itch, he said.

Jehu walked to the phone; it was blinking, but it was the last light on the series: inter-office call.

"Yes." Noddy looked at Jehu Malacara who said, "Okay, Esther, show him right in."

"Someone coming in to see you, that it?"

"Sam Dorson from County Homicide."

Noddy grinned and said, "What have you been up to?" With that he started for the side door, stopped, and said, "Any ideas about the calls?"

Jehu Malacara looked at him and said, "They'll call back."

"Right." And with that, Noddy stepped into the smaller office.

Sam Dorson had taken part in a baptism earlier that morning. A recent convert to Catholicism (his wife didn't attend any church), he had served as a *padrino* to three-year old Paulino Anciso. This had been Dorson's first baptism as a sponsor.

He was wearing a tailor-made, tan-colored, summer-weight gabardine suit that had *Made in Mexico* stamped all over it. The shoes were wing-tipped Cordovan bluchers, highly shined; he was wearing a light-blue buttoned-down oxford cloth shirt tied by a soft Paisley which Effie Dorson must have picked out for him. A gardenia in his lapel.

At that moment, Noddy Perkins stepped in again from the side door, and the two men looked at each other. Jehu Malacara then realized that Dorson and Perkins had not met before.

After the introductions, Noddy Perkins said, "You got your picture in the *Enterprise*, didn't you? That woman, around New Year's; the Machete Queen, as the papers called her."

Sam didn't bother to say the arrest had been made on Christmas Day; it was unimportant now at any rate.

Sam smiled and amended that to "The Hatchet Queen."

Noddy agreed and in his usual abrupt-but-business-matter said to Jehu Malacara: "Let me know when they call again; I plan to be in all day, just about."

And then: "Mr. Dorson, we're in the business of making

money around here, so I'll leave you to Jehu. A pleasure."

He left the door open and Jehu Malacara went up to close it when Esther Bewley, his secretary, was about to do the same thing.

"No calls, Esther."

"Right." Smile.

Jehu Malacara walked to the front of his desk, pulled up a chair and invited Sam to sit at the chair next to his.

"What's up, Sam? Who died?"

"You're looking at Paulie Anciso's *padrino*, Jehu."

"Congratulations. First time?"

"Yeah; feels good, too. But, I'm here on something else . . . Who do I see about buying a car and getting a loan around here?"

"Came to the right bank," grinning.

Sam gave a low chuckle and asked, "What's your title now, Jehu?"

"Vice President and Cashier."

"Is that pretty good?"

Jehu Malacara laughed and said, "Well, it sure beats picking citrus."

Buzz. "Esther? Need a small-loan form."

"Small loan?" Sam Dorson.

Jehu Malacara said, amiably, "To this bank, it's a small loan, Sam. Ah, when we're through here, I'd like to show you something. I want you to listen to it."

"A police something?"

"I think so. And probably Federal, too; it usually turns out that way with us; some regulation or other."

Dorson straightened up from his semi-slouch, nodded a bit, and then said, "Rafe got a phone call this morning about a bank in town. The call came in around eight-fifteen this morning. I went straight to the Court House from church and then came here. Rafe made a note of it and routed it through for comments. Procedure."

Jehu looked at the friendly, intelligent face before him. "Are you really interested in buying a car, then?"

Sam, surprised, and laughing aloud, said: "Oh, hell yes.

That's what I came in for; Effie and I've been reading up some . . . Maybe we can combine business with business." Grinning.

Light knock. Short-thin-but-trim Esther Bewley walked in with the loanpaper forms in hand.

"Hello, Mr. Dorson."

"Hello, Esther Lucille."

She flinched.

Three needs in the McKinlow arrest: discretion, cooperation, and six huge policemen.

12

The plan was for Sam Dorson to identify himself, ask for Rollins, and bring him out to the car.

With Hauer sitting in the back seat and Rafe in front, Dorson turned to them and said: "Look at the sign there." It read: The Flora N. Klail Institution for the Insane. No bones about what the place was all about.

Dorson parked in the visitors' zone; he got out without a word and walked to the twenty-foot gate holding an eight-foot sign reading: ENTRANCE/ENTRE. "Good thing I can read," he muttered.

Rafe glanced out the windshield. Seven three-story buildings and each a depressing green.

Was green the cheapest paint the State could buy? It was certainly the dreariest, he thought. He then looked at the iron bars in each of the buildings; all on the third floor.

Personal violence there. Sadly.

Hauer tapped him on the shoulder and said, "I like Dorson, Rafe. Really."

"What brought that on?"

"Well, he, ah, he calls me Young Mr. Hauer and Young Peter, you know; but I don't mind. And, I don't really think I get on his nerves as much as he says I do or as much as he lets on. What do you think?"

Rafe half-turned but kept his eyes on Sam who was cutting across the grass and gravel path to the guard gate.

"Sam's okay, and he's a hell of a cop. And, he's honest. I'm not talking about graft, here. There's a lot of character in Sam Dorson."

Hauer didn't react.

"You can learn a lot from him, Peter." A moment later

Rafe Buenrostro said, "I still do."

"Well, I've been on the force for six years and a detective for eighteen months, and . . ." Hauer stopped and then, in a rush, said, "And with you guys since April, in Homicide, and in this team, you and Sam and Culley and Joe . . . you know." Rambling.

Rafe followed Sam's walk to the office building; he half-turned again and nodded. "It'll be okay; as Culley says, it's a matter of time."

"Does, ah, does Sam resent the fact that . . . I mean, well, you went to college, and *law* school, and Joe and I, we went to college, too."

Rafe watched Sam ring the doorbell; the door opened from the inside and Sam walked in. "He's in."

"What? Oh, Sam? Yeah. Good."

Busy with his own problems was Young Mr. Hauer.

"What were you saying about college?"

"I was saying how you and I, how we, the younger guys, how we all went to college."

Rafe turned his head toward the office again, and then said, "So did Sam." Neutral.

"Really?"

"Oh, yes. And, he reads history, he likes his music, and he reads *The New York Times*." Chuckle. "He also knows about plays, but he prefers operettas. I guess he knows the lyrics to every Gilbert and Sullivan piece there is."

"No kidding?"

"He reads Housman, Hardy, Synge . . ."

"Who are they?"

"And, he quotes poetry."

"Sam *Dorson*?"

Rafe Buenrostro threw his head back and laughed, but not in ridicule of the sensitive Hauer. "And, he went to a good school; Northwestern."

"In Chicago? Illi-noiz?"

"In Evanston; by the Lake."

"What lake is that? Oh, yeah; Lake Michigan, right? Well, I wouldn't have figured him for that. Me? Well, I went to

Trinity up in San Antonio and that's where I met Sonny Rollins; he's from Ruffing."

Rafe held his breath for a moment. Either the beginning or the end of confession time; like waiting for the other shoe, although Rafe wasn't interested: What if the guy upstairs only had one foot?

Besides, his interest lay in Sam Dorson, and there he was coming down the walk accompanied by a man wearing a suit and a tie.

"Here they come."

"Yeah; that's Rollins, all right."

Rafe noticed that Rollins was clenching and unclenching his fists. Nerves.

Introductions.

"The supervisor's in, Rafe. We'll see him in a minute or two, but I want you to listen to Mr. Rollins first; it's a good story."

Peter Hauer stuck his head out the window:

"Hi, Sonny."

"Hullo, Peter. Mr. Dorson said you were part of the team."

'Part of the team!'

Rafe looked at Dorson and grinned at him. Dorson looked away, but Hauer didn't see this. He couldn't; he wasn't there at the time. At that moment, Peter Hauer was some 40,000 feet above Flora, Texas.

Rollins' story was interesting. His boss, a stone bureaucrat with thirty-five years in, spent his time picking his nose, scratching his behind, and taking stuff home once in a while.

This is new? To Hauer and Rollins it was.

Man's name was Alpha Ogden, and he had been pilfering State property for years: some food, a lawnmower or two, some drills and drill bits, shoes issued to inmates whose families couldn't provide any, light bulbs (a case here and there), a box of soap (here and there) a box of detergent (cleanliness is next to godliness), some pencils (by the crate), ball points, etc. Nothing major.

Quite a long list, though, and according to Rollins, it had been going on for years.

Rafe and Dorson said, silently, "Centuries, my boy."

Mr. Ogden, then, was not greedy; Dorson said that Ogden had a touch of the Goethe in him: "Ohne Hast aber ohne Rast,"—without haste, but without rest.

Hauer wondered who Gerda was; but, he knew better than to ask Sam Dorson.

A little gold mine and some foul things going on, according to Rollins. (Dorson, to himself, "Wait till you start running those hotels, kid. What are your ideas on illicit fucking? Of little boys? And B J specialists waiting in your room before you and your wife open the door? Hotel *management*, indeed.")

Rafe watched Dorson's eyes, and if he didn't know exactly what his partner was thinking, he wasn't too far off. They both looked at James Rollins who needed a little guidance here:

"About David McKinlow, Mr. Rollins." Rafe.

"What? Oh, yeah."

Yes, he was sure Alpha Ogden knew of McKinlow's periodic unauthorized leaves, slipping easily into the b'cratic jargon. And, for his part, McKinlow knew about, and helped, too, most likely, in Alpha Ogden's systematic looting.

Not necessarily blackmail, more of a marriage of convenience.

As for David McKinlow, Rollins then said he was (hesitation) a, a, a, a, a brute. He was six-feet eight inches tall, and he weighed some two-hundred and twenty pounds. A brute.

Not in basketball, thought Rafe, but a frightening son-of-a-bitch, nevertheless.

Rollins looked down and said, "A big, black motherfucker."

Dorson winced visibly, and Hauer swallowed and blinked. Hauer couldn't believe his ears: "A *Trinity* man, for Christ's sakes!"

Rafe Buenrostro said, "We're going to need proof which will serve as evidence against Ogden if we're going to get him to talk about McKinlow."

"That's going to be hard." Rollins.

"Why is that?" Dorson.

"Well . . . I've checked. Some of the files are missing. A lot of the paperwork, too; he's been culling it for years. Everybody knows it, though."

Dorson cut in. "The State."

"Wha?"

"The State records: sealed bids, dates; requisition numbers, dates; purchase orders, dates; vouchers, dates; model numbers, registration numbers. We can have that checked."

Relieved, Rollins said, "It'll be easy, huh?"

"No." All three in chorus. And all three policemen thinking of the six-feet eight-inch McKinlow who weighed in at two-hundred and twenty pounds.

"Oh."

"But we *can* do it," said Rafe Buenrostro. "Let's see if we can scare Mr. Ogden first."

"Oh."

"We need your help a bit."

Rollins shook his head. "He's tough."

Rafe Buenrostro and Sam Dorson looked at each other, and Dorson then said, "Good. Let's see how tough he is."

But, as Thurber once said, "It was like stealing thunder from a baby."

Ogden started to cry from the beginning. He had cancer, he said. And, he had a year to live; maybe two. And, he was counting on his State retirement and his Social Security for his wife, ah, widow.

It was in the bag from the very start.

Ogden sat in a corner of his office and Dorson picked up the phone to call for help from the Flora P.D.; Donovan, he discovered, had been way ahead. Jim Lee, the Flora chief, was waiting for Dorson's call.

"I need six. Big ones, too."

"They're on their way," said Lee. Dorson put down the receiver. Turning to Ogden, he asked: "Where's McKinlow?"

"In the laundry room." Dejected. "I'll call him for you." Resigned.

"Not yet. We'll wait for the Flora police to get here first. We'll wait here, in your office.

McKinlow, unsuspecting, of course, entered Ogden's office and the Big Six jumped him on the spot. The first thing that happened was that the inside door broke in half. The screen door was then torn off its hinges and landed some fifteen feet away.

McKinlow was finally subdued, but two of the uniforms paid a price: two broken noses, some teeth loosened or lost somewhere in the gravel path after which David McKinlow went catatonic on them. He stretched out in a dead faint.

Too much excitement. Sam Dorson, in a grunt.

Lifting him and carrying him to the EMS ambulance became the chore. The ambulance guys (Dorson here) strapped him the tightest they could, and would've sat on him had he, Sam, not been there with them.

After the preliminary paper work, Hauer and Molden were feeling proud as punch, to coin another phrase.

Donovan called the Woodalls, Jerem Pratt, and more importantly, The Lab Man.

"We really ought to have a beer one of these days, Henry."

"Who's buying?" The Dietz pennon read: "Nothing like straight talk."

Culley: "I'll buy the first round, Rafe the second, and Dorson the third."

Humor from the Lab Man. "Well'p, three's my limit, you know, but I'll go ahead and buy the fourth. When is it we're doing all this drinking?"

"What's wrong with six o'clock this afternoon?"

"Why, nothing at . . . just a minute, Culley. Is Young Buenrostro there? Put him on."

"Young Buenrostro? I heard that."

"What? What did you hear?" It was Irene Paredes.

"I thought it was Henry."

"No, silly. So. It's set for tomorrow, right? Jehu and I've already talked to Leah, and she said she's seen your picture in the paper."

Picture? Paper? "Is she a waitress at the Bee?"

"Leah? No. She lives in Jonesville, you know that. She's a buyer for Gillete and Whitman; G and W, Rafe. Veddy nice."

Rafe: "Sounds like a winner, "I": See you Sunday."

With that, both hung up; he picked up a message stuck to the message holder and squinted at some of the worst example of handwriting he had ever seen.

Art Benavides, the desk man. Call came in yesterday. But who's Milden Croftland out at Sandy Osuna's ranch?

Oh. Milton Crossland.

Donovan: "Sticking around a bit?"

Receiver in hand, "Call from Old Man Crossland."

"Oh?"

Nod. He dialed his cousin, Sandy Osuna.

Donovan waved and said he was on his way to see The Lab Man.

"Sandy? Rafe."

"Yeah. You get my message? I called there yesterday and again this morning. I said it was about Mr. Crossland." Rafe looked at the handwriting: Milden, Milton, Mister.

"He died, Rafe. Died last night."

"Too bad; he was a fine old man. Ah, when's the funeral?"

"Tomorrow morning; at the families' cemetery. It'll be at ten; you'll be there, right?"

"Sure. Sandy . . . has anyone called Jehu?"

"I did; he'll be there."

"Okay. He and I'll drive up together then; early."

He replaced the receiver and went to join Dorson and Culley and The Lab Man. It wasn't going to stop at four beers tonight; a lot to talk about; the old soldier, for one.

John Milton Crossland was dead, and according to Santos Junior, he had died a happy man, a vindicated man. Crossland had received news that his bad discharge, thrown at him before World War I, had been rescinded. Replaced by an honorable one signed by still another Commander-in-Chief, another Great White Father in Washington.

The work of some professor, according to Sandy Osuna. Someone who kept plugging away at the truth.

So, John Milton had been able to smell some of the roses, if only for a brief time.

As he walked out, Art Benavides handed him another message. Rafe stopped, looked at the desk man, decided against saying anything, and tried to read the chicken marks. He gave up.

"Read it for me, Art."

Beaming. "Yes *sir*. It says, 'I'm at the KBC.' "

"When did it come in?"

"Just now, Lieutenant. You was on the phone."

"Thanks."

"The caller didn't leave no name, Lieutenant."

"I know."

He turned around, smiled, and headed for the door.

Sammie Joe Perkins was back in town. Back home, at the Klail-Blanchard-Cooke Ranch; the KBC.

A banker with back trouble
discovers a potential pain in the neck.
Saturday, 9:00 a.m.

13

Jehu Malacara was in his office, sitting on a swivel chair, with hands extended some four feet apart, and hunching his sore shoulders up-down, up-down, one-two, one-two.

The exercise was intended to ease the tension in his neck, or so Irene Paredes had recommended. She, in turn, was given this piece of medical advice by The Lab Man.

It worked, somewhat, although the pain refused to go away completely. A botheration, Jehu Malacara puffed.

The second light on his telephone started to blink off-on; off-on; and he went on one-two, one-two until:

He picked up the receiver.

"Hello." A statement, not a question.

"Mr. Malacara?"

"Yes, this is he." You English major, you.

"Good."

Oh?

Pause.

Jehu looked at the receiver, and thus he missed hearing part of what the voice said.

And the voice seemed different from the first one, too.

"I didn't hear you."

It *was* a new voice now. ". . . and because of that, I had asked if you were going to record our conversation."

"Who's this, please?" No annoyance in his voice; all business.

"You may not know me, but this concerns the bank."

Finality and self-assurance in this voice.

The bank?

"Oh?"

"The information is *not* for sale." Hurt.

Pause.

"Mr. Malacara?"

"Yes, I'm still here." Neither bored nor expectant.

"Are. You. Interested?"

"If it isn't some sort of joke, yes; I'm interested."

"Curious, then?"

"No." Truth and sincerity.

"My . . . my *associate* and I have some information, and it concerns you, or it will when you hear it."

"Does it concern me or the bank?"

If it's blackmail, don't lean on this tree, doggie.

"Something that's going on already in the other two banks in town, in Klail, and yours may be next."

Pause.

"All right." Neutral.

"What I'm saying is true; remember that, please. Okay?"

"Yes, I will."

"Can I call you back this afternoon?"

Why not?

"Yes, of course." Watchful waiting.

"I've also got your home telephone number."

Who doesn't? It's in the directory.

"But I'll call at the bank; we, ah, I'm at work, too. Ba."

Ba?

Had they been cut off? The caller sounded rushed. And the first voice sounded hesitant. No, that's not the word. Unsure? No, not that either.

He *had* recorded it, of course. He recorded every call; not a mania, purely record keeping. No mystery, either. A sound business practice, if anything. Besides, it *was* business.

He rewound the cassette, pressed the play button, sat back and listened to the conversation.

The first voice was a younger voice. Female, definitely. The second voice was older. A Valley woman. Anglo voices, most probably; but in the Valley, one couldn't always tell about accents and intonations.

He reversed the cassette again and played it back a second time.

Older woman. Definitely mature. Younger woman: unsure of herself. No, that's not the word. Timid? Diffident? Come on! *Diffident*! Was it a joke? Too elaborate. Level of sincerity? High. Younger woman. Rushed. Insistent.

Nature of call? *Bank* business.

"Something that's going on already in the other two banks in town, in Klail, and yours may be next," the voice had said.

The voice had said *Klail*, not Klail City. A native? He straightened up, rose to his feet, and discovered that the pain had disappeared. Nothing like a mysterious phone call to cure all your troubles, he humphed.

He'd thank the caller at a later date, he said, but for now, he was going to see his boss, Arnold 'Noddy' Perkins; the President of the Klail City First National Bank.

He pushed himself away from the desk and checked for pain again. It was gone. Ah.

The phone light again.

Jehu Malacara looked at the phone as if he'd never seen it blink before. He hunched his shoulders and picked up the receiver.

The voice said, "Jehu."

That was fast. Who?

"Noddy here. You busy?"

"Morning, no; I was coming over to see you, right now as a matter of fact."

"No, that's okay; I'll come over myself."

Jehu Malacara pressed the dial-tone button and set the phone on no-calls. He studied a recent acquisition to his office: a wide-angle photograph of Klail City, dated July 4, 1921. A mass of Klail Citians posing in front of the first Klail City High School.

Some of the kids in the picture were close to sixty-years old by now; and, some could have been killed in World War II; Korea, even. Most of the older folk were dead; had to be. Oh, a few of them left, but not many; not in Nineteen Seventy-two, they weren't.

The photograph was a clear, clean piece of work. Fine detail on the faces, too; and great contrast. The photographer was a man named Leopoldo Ramírez; he had died sometime last year, he recalled. His sons, Leo and Fred, owned and operated four camera shops up and down the Valley. This bank's financing; his recommendation, too.

No Malacaras in that picture; nor Buenrostros. And no mystery, either. They had simply chosen not to pose, that was all.

Vanitas, vanitas.

Noddy Perkins' outline appeared vaguely on the mottled-glass part of Jehu Malacara's office. There was also a side office, a smaller one for the steno and for his secretary.

As always, an unlit cigar clenched in Noddy's left fist; Jehu had never seen Noddy light one, and he'd known the man for a dozen years or so.

"Jehu, you been out of the office in the last half-hour?"

Vintage Noddy. All business, with none of that 'good morning' claptrap. Time is money, Zeit ist Gelt.

A shake of the head.

"Well, I got two phone calls in the last thirty minutes, Jehu. The first one hung up on me, and then the second call some woman with a mousy voice called . . ."

That was the word: Mousy.

". . . and said something about the Bank, this bank, and about the other banks in town. Kind-a garbled. Wanted to know if I wuz interested. And, right before I could even ask who it was, or go to hell, or I'm fine, doc, how're you, she hung up on me. Again!"

"Hmph."

Noddy: "And what's that supposed to mean in English?"

Jehu Malacara walked to his desk top, inserted the cassette, and said: "Listen to this. I got a call just a few minutes ago."

They listened in silence. Noddy shook his head, pursed his lips outward, and took his glasses off. His right hand went up, and Jehu Malacara said,:

"Don't start rubbing your eyes, Noddy."

The older man nodded and said, "Thanks, Jehu."

The man's eyes were easily strained these days and rubbing them did nothing but make them redder still. It was a habit anyway; they didn't itch, he said.

Jehu walked to the phone; it was blinking, but it was the last light on the series: inter-office call.

"Yes." Noddy looked at Jehu Malacara who said, "Okay, Esther, show him right in."

"Someone coming in to see you, that it?"

"Sam Dorson from County Homicide."

Noddy grinned and said, "What have you been up to?" With that he started for the side door, stopped, and said, "Any ideas about the calls?"

Jehu Malacara looked at him and said, "They'll call back."

"Right." And with that, Noddy stepped into the smaller office.

Sam Dorson had taken part in a baptism earlier that morning. A recent convert to Catholicism (his wife didn't attend any church), he had served as a *padrino* to three-year old Paulino Anciso. This had been Dorson's first baptism as a sponsor.

He was wearing a tailor-made, tan-colored, summer-weight gabardine suit that had *Made in Mexico* stamped all over it. The shoes were wing-tipped Cordovan bluchers, highly shined; he was wearing a light-blue buttoned-down oxford cloth shirt tied by a soft Paisley which Effie Dorson must have picked out for him. A gardenia in his lapel.

At that moment, Noddy Perkins stepped in again from the side door, and the two men looked at each other. Jehu Malacara then realized that Dorson and Perkins had not met before.

After the introductions, Noddy Perkins said, "You got your picture in the *Enterprise*, didn't you? That woman, around New Year's; the Machete Queen, as the papers called her."

Sam didn't bother to say the arrest had been made on Christmas Day; it was unimportant now at any rate.

Sam smiled and amended that to "The Hatchet Queen."

Noddy agreed and in his usual abrupt-but-business-matter said to Jehu Malacara: "Let me know when they call again; I plan to be in all day, just about."

And then: "Mr. Dorson, we're in the business of making

money around here, so I'll leave you to Jehu. A pleasure."

He left the door open and Jehu Malacara went up to close it when Esther Bewley, his secretary, was about to do the same thing.

"No calls, Esther."

"Right." Smile.

Jehu Malacara walked to the front of his desk, pulled up a chair and invited Sam to sit at the chair next to his.

"What's up, Sam? Who died?"

"You're looking at Paulie Anciso's *padrino*, Jehu."

"Congratulations. First time?"

"Yeah; feels good, too. But, I'm here on something else . . . Who do I see about buying a car and getting a loan around here?"

"Came to the right bank," grinning.

Sam gave a low chuckle and asked, "What's your title now, Jehu?"

"Vice President and Cashier."

"Is that pretty good?"

Jehu Malacara laughed and said, "Well, it sure beats picking citrus."

Buzz. "Esther? Need a small-loan form."

"Small loan?" Sam Dorson.

Jehu Malacara said, amiably, "To this bank, it's a small loan, Sam. Ah, when we're through here, I'd like to show you something. I want you to listen to it."

"A police something?"

"I think so. And probably Federal, too; it usually turns out that way with us; some regulation or other."

Dorson straightened up from his semi-slouch, nodded a bit, and then said, "Rafe got a phone call this morning about a bank in town. The call came in around eight-fifteen this morning. I went straight to the Court House from church and then came here. Rafe made a note of it and routed it through for comments. Procedure."

Jehu looked at the friendly, intelligent face before him. "Are you really interested in buying a car, then?"

Sam, surprised, and laughing aloud, said: "Oh, hell yes.

That's what I came in for; Effie and I've been reading up some . . . Maybe we can combine business with business." Grinning.

Light knock. Short-thin-but-trim Esther Bewley walked in with the loanpaper forms in hand.

"Hello, Mr. Dorson."

"Hello, Esther Lucille."

She flinched.

Theo Weaver's Kum-Bak Place
and the Man Without a Face.

14

Harvey Bollinger, the Belken County District Attorney, let out a groan as he read the *Klail City Enterprise News*. After the groan, a moan followed by a Christ-a mighty.

It was "those guys downstairs," again; they had arrested and charged with murder a man who was certifiably insane. A man who was in the Nut House (sic), for Christ's sake, and what did he, Gus Elder, think of that?

"Don't they know what they've *done*? Don't they *care*? he pleaded with Elder.

Dutch Elder, Bollinger's office manager and the most experienced prosecutor, looked at the man, turned his back and pretended to read the Status of Progress and Case Assignment Log. He was also smiling. Homicide wouldn't send this case up for another week or so, and besides that, Elder had other worries, other cases on hand.

Elder could hear Bollinger's voice and protestations now and then, but he refused to hear the anguish. In a minute or two, Elder stopped hearing the voice altogether. Looking intently at the Assignment Log, Dutch Elder couldn't believe his eyes: Bucky Chapman, easily the top prosecutor on the young staff, had been assigned to prosecute the forger Robert Simpson who was also known as:

> Robert Sampson
> Russell Simpson
> Russell Sampson
> Sam Roberts
> Bert Simpson
> Bert Sampson

and on and on through other variants as repetitive as they were unoriginal.

If cases can be called simple (and they can't because one doesn't know just-what-in-the-hell juries are ever going to come up with), the Simpson case was simple, and Bucky Chapman was too good to be wasted on it. God.

Grand Theft-Larceny, another group of "those guys downstairs," had built an absolutely airtight case. Simpson, a well known petty and bothersome forger, had stepped out of his league on this one: counterfeiting, and he was now charged with uttering a $100.00 bill to the teller Mary Lozano at the Klail First National Bank.

So, if Simpson wanted a jury, that was fine. If he did not, then that was fine, too. The camera, the teller, and the other two counterfeit $100.00 in Simpson's possession would be enough for conviction.

He'd be out of their hair for five years. Easily. Thus, when Elder read Chapman's name, he stopped smiling. What a waste of talent.

He was about to turn around to the screaming Bollinger but decided against it almost immediately. Relax now. One. Two. Three. Four. Five. Six. Seven. Eight. Nine. Ten.

"I need more numbers," he sighed to himself.

Harvey Bollinger, who ran for District Attorney every two years, also ran for other state offices at every available opportunity; with no success up to now, this had neither dissuaded nor stemmed the man's ambition.

Elder managed the office, prosecuted some of the top cases and was evenhanded in the distribution of the case loads. A brick. Another plus: he read the evidence carefully, and he knew which attorney or attorneys would be better suited for what kind of case. A worker, then.

Oh, Chapman would win all right; no doubt on that. But it also meant a minimum of two or possibly three to four days in court. Almost a week away from the office and this would keep him from working on the good stuff; the meaty kind.

It *was* Attorney Robert A. Chapman's job to be in court, wasn't it?

Yes. Sure. But! Why *not* the upcoming McKinlow case, dammit? *That* was something. Elder lost his concentration for a second, but it was enough and he heard Bollinger's voice whining, bitching, and bouncing off the walls and circling somewhere around the room. Relax, now.

Elder stopped thinking on Chapman and Sampson and on Bollinger, as well. And then, for what must have been the hundredth time that year, he stopped to consider on the *why* of Bollinger's seemingly erratic behavior. But Elder already knew why.

It was all too evident, really; Bollinger was not best pleased to have too much young intelligence on the staff.

But the cost, dear Lord! Bucky'd be bored; he'd lose his edge for a while, and then, one day, unannounced and from out of nowhere: out! Out into private practice, and God help us if he went into Criminal Law. Why, he'd yank the pants and socks off just about everyone in the office and show us for the asses we really are . . .

Hell! Taking a deep breath, he said to himself: "Fifty-four's too young to die of a heart attack." He sat down, took another deep breath, and tried to settle down a bit. The trial for Simpson was three days away. "I'm just going to have to convince Harvey to assign that case to one of the younger guys; Dub Bailey, for one."

Elder was edgy, and he knew it. And, he knew why, too. Overwork. But that was his own fault. His wife, that very morning, had said he had to leave the office for a full ten days.

"Go fishing," she had said.

He had looked up from his cereal, smiled, and then promised: "Next week, Mim; I mean it."

Elder had forty-five days of accumulated leave, something that Miriam Elder would remind him of gently, from time to time.

"I want a husband, not some burned-out case, Gus." And then they laughed thinking about the previous night.

"Was I that bad last night?" "No," she had said. And she meant it.

"But will you go fishing? You promised." Mim Elder then put her arms around her husband and said: "Why don't you come home for lunch?" A giggle.

And she wasn't a giggler. He kissed her, ran his hand down her backside, and said: "I'll knock off early today . . . I'll be here at three. Scout's honor."

"And just for that, you get a kiss. Here."

Gus Elder had no possible way of knowing that four hours after the breakfast chat with his wife that he, Ambrose Gustave Elder, would punch Harvey Bollinger in the office, just above the left eye, knocking the man on his ass, sprain two knuckles in the process, and that instead of ten, he would take forty days of the forty-five to wait for things to cool down.

And if they didn't cool down?

He had a ready answer for that one: "Fuck it."

Almost immediately after he knocked Bollinger down, he regretted it. "What I did was *dumb*," he said to himself as he drove home. But Mim had laughed out loud. "He's an asshole, Gus. Look at me: Who loves you?"

The two had met as orphans in Austin some thirty-five years before and had been married for the last twenty-eight years. Elder had been delivered to the Austin state orphanage at age eight and lived and worked there until his seventeenth birthday. He left the place, worked for a year as a laborer, and then joined the army for a four-year stint.

Miriam had been taken to the state school at age six, and she remained there until age seventeen as well. Unadoptables, they were called.

On Miriam's seventeenth birthday, twenty-two year old Pfc. Gus Elder proposed marriage and after the three-day waiting period, they married in an army chapel at Fort Ben Milam in William Barrett. Five years later, with his army discharge papers in hand, Gus Elder did what thousands of others were doing at the end of 1945: he enrolled in college. Miriam saw him through law school and he saw her through college as well.

"Three degrees and two kids between us, Dutch. And now they're gone. Go fishing, like you promised me you would."

"I was dumb, Mim."

"Yes, but I love you anyway."

Smiling again, he said: "I'm home earlier than I expected . . ."

She looked up and laughed. "I'll beat you to the bedroom," she said, and, she was off upstairs before he began taking off his tie.

It may very well be that no one deserves to be knocked ass-up by a colleague, but it happens. Wives don't deserve to be beaten up by their husbands, either; and daughters don't deserve to be raped by their fathers; and some poor jerk doesn't deserve to be killed by some out-and-out drunk who happens to have seven speeding violations hanging on him. But it happens.

This last didn't happen to Gus Elder, of course, but he wound up just as dead.

Many false trails and assumptions (the hazards of the trade) and too many pet theories and some pat ones, and too much help at times almost botched the solution to Elder's murder. But, in the end, the solution came with a swiftness that proved ironic since it was also unexpected.

And, the solution was also due to many hours of honest plodding work, and to the culling of facts until only a fool would refuse to see the end of it. And the end came because as Eustace Budgell said over one-hundred years ago: Facts are very stubborn things; they refuse to go away.

To help itself along, the Belken Homicide Squad dealt in facts. They used some imagination, and they relied on memory too, but on the whole the squad preferred facts. The squad was comfortable with facts; and both the squad and the facts refused to go away.

To be sure, there was never any question that it was murder; the causes, too, were based on those reliable and inevitable circumstances: time and place.

Elder had walked into something, and he never knew what it was that hit him.

On the ninth day of his enforced vacation, with the incident "forgiven and forgotten" at the office, and with routine there falling apart, and with everything else "going to hell and staying there," according to Bucky Chapman, Elder decided that that day would be his last one off the job.

With that in mind, he left the house at ten o'clock that Tuesday morning, pointed his pick-up truck toward Denman's Catfish Pond for one last round of sweetwater fishing; he had planned to pick up a bag of ice and some beer along the way at Weaver's Kum-Bak Inn, located ten miles southeast of Klail City on Farm to Market Road No. 906.

The owner of the Kum-Bak, Theo Weaver, was off that Tuesday, and his day man, twenty-five year old Kenny Joe Bunton, was manning the place.

At the corner booth, next to the broken-down Wurlitzer, Bunton and a local farmer named John Schultz, were huddled together, drinking beer, and grumbling about 'too much water' almost ruining the cotton last August, 'but not enough' for the second tomato crop coming up.

Two other men, Mexican nationals from the looks of them, and wearing suits and ties, were working on their second beer and on some peanuts Bunton had served them. They were strangers to the place.

The fifth patron that morning was Gus Elder; he walked in, asked for a cold bottle of Pearl, and headed for the men's room. He stopped some two feet away from the Men's door, turned around and said to Bunton: "The beer's to go, Kenny Joe. Put the can in a paper bag, will you? And go ahead and ring up a six-pack of Pearl; I'll be right back."

John Schultz watched him go into the men's room, and he later stated and swore that less than a minute later, top, three other Mexicans came in, armed with machine guns.

**That Tuesday morning
a perfectionist finds no satisfaction
in a job well done.**

15

Joe Molden was having difficulty finishing the write-up of
the McKinlow Case. Rafe Buenrostro had read it and pronounced it clear and succinct; he'd even said 'well done.' But,
Molden remained unassured; he was afraid the case would
topple over; it didn't seem sturdy enough, he said.

Understandably, it was his first case.

Rafe had been a help; a big help. But to bother him again?
Molden sighed, and Rafe looked at him across the room.

"Need some help, Joe?" Noncommital.

Joe Molden nodded, bit his lower lip lightly, and waved the
McKinlow papers at him. He motioned for Rafe to come over.
"I'd appreciate it," he said.

"Be there in a couple of minutes." The early morning mail
had included some material Rafe was waiting for. The Lab
Man had sent him a rather slim but complete autopsy report
on the dead superintendent at Rio Largo I. He inserted The
Lab Man's report to his own file folder. He then drew out a
routing slip, marked it READY, initialed it R.B., and placed
it in his OUT tray.

That closed the case on the building superintendent as far
as Homicide was concerned.

It's up to Dutch Elder now, and he'll be back on board
tomorrow, he thought. This was followed by a *humph*, but this
was meant for Harvey Bollinger. Rafe looked across the lawn,
across the palm trees, and out into the parking lots where he
spotted Sam Dorson's new car, a flame-red VW. Rafe
Buenrostro wondered why the Germans had not bothered to
include gasoline indicators in the first models years ago. The
crap I carry around in my head, he said to himself.

His eyes went to the OUT tray again, and he noticed that he

had forgotton to red-stamp HOM. SQ. on the front of the folder. He did so and returned it to the tray.

He glanced toward Joe Molden who was staring at the paper work in front of him.

The McKinlow Case. A second *humph*, and this one too was for Harvey Bollinger.

Rafe Buenrostro could hear Bollinger now, "Those guys downstairs . . ." But Bollinger would first check with Dutch Elder before assigning cases willy-nilly from now on. Rafe shook his head again, and again looked at Joe Molden who had his eyes fixed on the McKinlow file.

Rafe opened the left drawer, drew out a blue Frankoma coffee mug, and served himself a full one. A new coffee pot. "Who bought the new pot?"

Silence from Molden.

If you don't know, don't say anything, right?

Rafe wrote a note for Sam Dorson: "Nice pot; how much do I owe you?"

Joe Molden looked up again as Peter Hauer came in and said, "You guys bring raincoats or something? There's something blowing out there, and it looks like half-a West Texas is going over right now. I think it's part-a that weak norther that blew in last night. When it stops, you guys, we're going to get some chilling rainwater 'round here."

Late October rains. That meant slightly cooler mornings for a while, and this would bring some moaning from the farmers: "Too much water's gonna ruin the tomato crop." Or, "If we don't get rain now, then say goodbye to the citrus crop." Always something.

Rafe Buenrostro smiled as he thought of his brothers Israel and Aaron. They had farmed all their lives and planted 'just right.' It wasn't luck, they said.

As Rafe Buenrostro glanced toward Joe Molden's desk, Molden jumped up and asked in a higher voice than usual: "Is it really raining, already?"

Hauer: "No, just a lot a-dust right now, but . . ."

Molden sat down, blushed a bit, and said: "My car's not even here; it's in the shop."

That kind of day.

Rafe nodded, pulled up a chair, and waited for Joe Molden to put the report sheets in order.

Softly: "Thanks, Rafe."

A nod and then: "I took over from Dorson seven years ago; let's hope I'm as good a teacher . . ."

Hauer stood up, announced that *he* was going to work on the files, and he was deep at it when Sam Dorson came in from the lab with another weather report. (It *was* that kind of day).

"Getting a bit dark out there." He looked at his watch: "It's eight-thirty, you guys. Has Culley come in this morning yet?"

Hauer looked up and said, "Not since I've been here."

Rafe Buenrostro didn't hear Dorson's question; he was reading Molden's evidence report and Molden was looking at him for signs of approval or disapproval.

Dorson: "Ho, ho! Who brought in this beauty?" He poured himself a generous mug, lifted the paper weight, read Rafe's note, and dropped it in the basket.

Sam looked at the pot closely and noted that it was new; brand new, he thought, although the style was old somehow.

Twelve cups; nice.

He walked to Rafe's desk, noticed the little super's file on the OUT tray, and decided that *that* was that. He walked to his desk, pulled the writing tray on the right of his desk, sat down, stretched his legs, and let his feet rest on the tray and the desk. He'd just finished talking with Jehu Malacara at the Klail First again.

Neither Jehu nor Noddy Perkins had heard from the mysterious callers; not since that first day, they had said. A week after the calls, Sam had called on Jehu again asking if there were anything to report.

And again, no. Nothing new. Nevertheless, Sam Dorson wrote his first memo to Chris Colunga, the man in charge of Grand Theft-Larceny, informing him of the phone calls received by Noddy Perkins and Jehu Malacara.

Colunga acknowledged first by telephone, and a day later,

through a short note via inter-building mail.

It wasn't Sam's nor Chris Colunga's business yet; and, if anybody's, it could wind up as a Fed job, for all they knew.

Jehu had called the locals. Logical, thought Sam; you go around screaming *wolf*, and even the Fed sheep-shearers won't show up. Still, Sam saw no harm in checking with Chris Colunga with a written note that took him less than two minutes to set down in a Read and Route memo.

For his part, Chris Colunga had sent a memo to Graham Donaldson, the Klail City police chief. Donaldson, in turn, thanked him and later on sent him a memo of his own. And that, too, was that.

These weren't 'cover your ass memos' either; the dates and times established a record of purpose. If *anything* developed later on, it was helpful to know when, whatever *it* was, had surfaced for the first time.

As the old guys kept saying: "You can't beat procedure, but first: get it down on paper."

Culley Donovan was not feeling well that Tuesday morning, but he walked into his office at six o'clock as planned. With Elder scheduled to return on the following day, the division chiefs were reporting on the files at hand. Culley knew that Rafe Buenrostro would have the Andrew Billings matter ready by that morning, and if Joe Molden asked for help, then Homicide would have two cases for Dutch Elder bright and early Wednesday morning.

Culley was meeting with "the upstairs guys," and had been with them since six forty-five. And, it was he who had brought the silverplated coffee pot to the office.

Culley Donovan and his late wife, Corinne, had received three coffee pots, numerous towels, bed sheets, a set of every-day dishes, cloth napkins, among other household items as wedding presents twenty-five years before.

A childless Catholic couple, Donovan and Corinne had devoted their married life to each other and had accumulated their share of private jokes during their twenty-one years of marriage. That had come to an end four years ago, in 1968. On the first of Lent of that year, Corinne, over coffee, told

Culley she wasn't feeling well. A bit weak, she said. She had lost weight in the early part of the spring and during the previous winter; but there was nothing to worry about; their doctor had said:

"You're just off your feed, Corinne; it happens."

By Good Friday of that same Lent, and after two five-day stays at Travis Medical, the illness was diagnosed as uterine cancer. A month after Easter, she was down to eighty pounds, and she was dead by the middle of May.

Mercifully dead some people said, but Culley and Corinne had not thought in those terms. They had had each other, and then she was gone. Nothing merciful in that, Culley reflected.

There was a second widower in Homicide: Rafe Buenrostro. He had married at eighteen and widowed at nineteen when his wife, Conce Guerrero, drowned during a family Easter picnic on the south bank of the Rio Grande.

He had managed to repress Conce's death for a good part of the time a year later during his service in Japan and in the Korean Peninsula, but it wasn't until he returned to Klail and its familiar surroundings that the finality of Conce's death set in.

On his return, he would find himself thinking where he had been two months before, or the three months before that, and so on, and what the winters in Korea had been like. And, as always, what the dying in Korea had been like.

And then, after his junior year at Austin, Rafe Buenrostro decided to enter law school upon graduation. He borrowed additional money from his farmer brothers, finished his law studies, prepared for the bar, passed it, and then to everyone's surprise, he decided to become a County Patrolman.

His transfer to Homicide came as a result of a written report Rafe Buenrostro turned in outlining the evidence on a rural murder. Sam Dorson had brought the report to Culley Donovan and although neither man knew the County Patrolman, both recognized a methodical, logical mind at work. Later on they discovered that he was also hard-headed enough not to give up or to be discouraged or disappointed when disappointments came.

Six years later, Rafe was promoted to Lieutenant of Detectives first grade after solving a bloody homicide involving the school superintendent at Bascom High School, the man's secretary, and a graduating senior; the three had been stuffed in the trunk of the secretary's car by five mannish-looking senior girls during the school's Senior Day celebration. Rafe was also wounded in that case; one of the girls had re-opened a war wound over his left eye, and this had put him on limited duty during the summer of Sixty-four.

For his part, Culley Donovan had mended slowly after his wife's death. Rafe Buenrostro called on him regularly, but even Rafe had to admit that the visits 'were deadly.'

Careful, frugal, save-a-penny Corinne had catalogued and listed each of their wedding presents; she had been careful, too, and after those twenty-five years, some of the presents had gone unused, some boxes unopened; two extra coffee pots among them.

After the first one broke down, the Donovans switched to instant coffee; since Culley was an indifferent coffee drinker, the change had meant little to him.

When Culley returned to their home, he unpacked some unfamiliar boxes; boxes which had been in the garage and taken for granted because they had, as he said, 'always been there, part of the place.'

He had found two coffee pots: the Westinghouse coffee maker and a General Electric model as well as a toaster, a counter cooker, and a Sears blender. Dorson, he knew, would appreciate the Westinghouse 12-cupper. As he unwrapped the box, a well-wish card fell out; it was signed "The Williamsons" and Culley Donovan had no idea who they were; office friends of Corinne's, he supposed.

He rinsed the pot carefully, repacked it, and set it on the table next to his service revolver. Drinking his last cup for the morning, he heard the Bennie Tolar Early Weather Report on KCTX, the local station: ". . . and with cloudy skies, the precipitation probabilities are now up to forty-percent, Klail Citians, or so says the U.S. Weather office in Jonesville-on-the-Rio . . . Brrrreak out your winter clothing, everybody, it'll be in the fifties by tonight, and now . . ." Click.

Precipitation probabilities . . .

"Whatever happened to rain?" he said aloud. He placed the cup in the sink and picked up the coffee pot and the gun. He looked at his watch: five forty-five a.m.

The office was four lights and fifteen minutes away.

**Miss Williger and Miss Tarver
pay a business call.**

16

The two women in Jehu Malacara's office were wearing what he considered a poor idea that had been forced down someone's throat: uniforms for bank tellers. Poorly paid to begin with, this additional expense was another illustration of Edward Moore's dictum about adding insult to injury. In this particular case, the women also paid for the cleaning: an additional injury.

The older of the two, a black woman named Elizabeth Tarver, wore an ill-fitting maroon-colored box suit draped around and across her tall, angular frame; she could have just as well been wearing a maroon-colored potato sack; poor thing.

Irma Williger's uniform was another failure since her Texas State Bank uniform was a replica of the First State Bank's worn by Elizabeth Tarver. To add to this, Damon Williger's youngest needed all the help she could get, and she certainly wasn't going to find it in what Jehu's secretary called 'those abortions.'

The women had called him on the telephone around closing time on the previous day. Could they see him the next day, during the lunch hour?

The Tarver woman coughed lightly to clear her throat, and said: "Irma and I called you a month ago. We also called Mr. Perkins; you remember that?"

Jehu Malacara looked at the maroon sights and said, "I remember. Did you call Lieutenant Buenrostro as well?"

Nods.

"Well, sir, (Irma Williger this time), there's something going on in my bank, and it isn't right."

The voice wasn't mousy at all; it was soft, yes, but there was some spine behind that sweet voice.

Something going on at the bank.

Thievery? Why not? They're all underpaid; Noddy thinks I'm a crank on this, but the job's a damn drudge, they handle most of the cash, and then we don't *pay* them enough.

Irma coughed to clear *her* throat. Jehu Malacara could see they were agitated, but they were managing to keep themselves in check. The story would come.

Gesturing toward Elizabeth Tarver, Irma Williger then turned to him: "And it's going on at Bessie's bank, too."

What? But, Jehu knew better than to interrupt. Asking a question is a form of interruption, he knew. The two had lived with whatever it was, and it had taken them an additional month to make up their minds before they set up the appointment. Patience, then.

Jehu nodded, seemed interested, and showed it by looking intently at Irma.

"Hm-huh." The echoic encourager.

Irma turned to Elizabeth Tarver again and then to Jehu: "I don't know if it's going on here at the First, but . . ."

The sentence was left unfinished.

"Oh?"

"Let me tell it, Irma." But Irma Williger shook her head and raised her hand to ward off her friend.

"This is what we think—no—this is what we *know* is going on over there: there are people who are paying off some of our tellers, and it's illegal."

You're damned right, thought Jehu. But what? Bribery?

Jehu raised his left hand. "I have a cassette recorder; with your permission, I'd like to make a recording of this."

No reaction.

"First of all," he explained, "it's for accuracy's sake, and, secondly, it'll be held in strictest confidence."

Jehu, who was not fond of repeating himself, nevertheless heard himself saying 'strictest' for the second time.

He looked at them; neither sensing nor seeing any opposition to his proposal, he added: "You'll know about it, of course; and Mr. Perkins, Mr. Cooke, and I will know. And, if it's as sensitive as you say—and I certainly see no reason not to believe either one of you—it may be a Federal matter. But first, I *have* to hear the story."

No gasps for air, no shuffling of chairs. They were reso-
lute; the month's wait had served its purpose, obviously.

"Any objections to the cassette?"

Stubborn and decided shakes of the head.

Bessie Tarver, evenly, and with no melodrama, said: "Go
on, Irm."

It had been quite a story, and it had been told sequentially,
too. The spare, lean narrative was deceiving, however. It was
a minefield, and there was earnestness in their story. Ah yes,
truth lies within a little and certain compass. He then finished
the quote: error is immense.

The Valley, as the southernmost land entry point to Mexico
is served by a fairly major inland seaport: Jonesville-on-the-
Rio. The mouth of the Rio Grande empties peacefully enough
less than twenty miles from Jonesville's city limits; and a
channel had been cut some fifteen miles to the north of the
mouth, and then on into Jonesville's inland port. Mexican oil
and Valley cotton had traditionally brought in much of the
revenue; in Nineteen Seventy-two, drugs and their artificial
affluence were forcing their way into the economy.

The Coast Guard, pitifully underfunded, did the best it
could. Under the circumstances, their public information officer cried out. It wasn't nearly enough; plainly speaking, then,
it was nothing.

But there was other money in the air that year of Nineteen
Seventy-two; there was money to be earned, and to be saved,
and as always, to be exchanged. Spent, people called it.

Jehu nodded to himself and said, "Money to be moved."

Yes, and there was money for hideous maroon-colored uniforms as well. Jehu decided that it was the uniformity of it
that he disliked, for Jehu Malacara was an uncommon banker,
and had come into banking in an uncommon way. And he
thought about that, and about money, and about the new
money in the Valley.

But, heading the list was Irma Williger's and Bessie Tarver's story. This called for Federal help. Definitely. An obvious Treasury violation. No question, but Jehu Malacara was also a borderer, first and last. And, as most borderers throughout the world, he had little confidence in central authority. Still, that's where the responsibility lay: with the Feds. In *them*, as Noddy Perkins called the Feds.

"They lack the human touch," Jehu said to himself. But, he had to act in a hurry; the two women had given him information that was at least two-three months old.

He listened to the cassette again. His concern did not rest solely with the Klail City First National Bank; his reasoning was one of a wider responsibility and concern for the law: if the other two banks in town are in trouble, *we're* in trouble. Indirectly involved, perhaps, but involved for all that. And, indirect involvement was close enough for Jehu Malacara in this case.

The women had left almost abruptly, and then he remembered they had seen him on their lunch hour. Prisoners of time.

Looking at the door long after they had gone, it dawned on him that Elizabeth Tarver was black; he had seen her, of course, but he'd seen her as a teller. Not as an individual. A black woman. It occurred to him that she was the only black teller in the three Klail City banks. In the Valley. Where she had come from was a fact he most certainly did not know.

Aside from some black soldiers he had met in the Army, the only black man he had known was John Milton Crossland at Sandy Osuna's ranch. And Crossland had been in the Army, too, he remembered.

He reached for the telephone and called Noddy Perkins.

Noddy Perkins and his brother-in-law, E.B. (Ibby) Cooke sat in Jehu's office paying close attention to the cassette. "Let's hear it again, Jehu."

Cooke nodded in agreement. It was replayed, and then Noddy said, "No *real* proof from what I hear . . ."

"At first blush." Ibby Cooke.

". . . but since it's about money, that's where we come in. Well, Jehu, what do you think?"

"A job for Treasury."

"Just like that?"

"Just. Like. That."

But Noddy Perkins, too, was a borderer. The Feds were strangers; *fuereños*, he said to Jehu in Spanish. No Blanche Dubois he, Noddy Perkins said he sure as hell wasn't going to rely on the kindness of strangers, of *fuereños*.

But, facing facts was also one of Noddy's strongest points. When Ibby Cooke began what he called "an imperative reconstruction" of the events, Noddy raised his eyebrows. This, then, signaled that the meeting was over. Cooke meant to repeat, point by point, what all three already knew.

Noddy Perkins raised his eyebrows a second time, and Jehu translated this correctly: "Let's get Ibby out-a here."

But there was something else in those eyebrows of Noddy Perkins.

There was genuine concern; Noddy would say later on, genuine economic concern!

"Someone's trying to fiddle with our money," Noddy muttered, and Cooke followed this with: "One can't ever be too careful. About anything."

The eyebrows went up a third time, and Jehu stood up and led them out the door.

**The Kum Bak Inn, the curious,
and the dead.**

17

The first County Patrolman to arrive at the Kum-Bak that Tuesday morning was an older man, a sergeant named Bowly Ponder; he arrived at 11:43 a.m., and he wrote the time on his pad. Right after that, Rafe Buenrostro and Sam Dorson pulled in, and Dorson stayed by the car radio.

Rafe knew Bowly Ponder; had saved him from an embarrassing situation a couple of years back: carrying a service revolver, off duty, inside a beer joint, in a neighboring county.

"Lieutenant, it's pretty bad in there, but I didn't go in, sir. I peeked." He then drew out his pad and wrote down the time again: 12:10 p.m.

Rafe nodded and told him to start directing traffic; Farm Road 906 was beginning to get congested, and the sooner Ponder had some help, the better.

Help was coming on the way, Ponder explained, and was there anything else he could do?

"Just keep the traffic moving; tell the people to go home."

"Right." And with that Bowly Ponder walked off and waved to Sam Dorson who was on his way to the front stoop at the Kum Bak.

It was bad. It was bloody, it was depressing, and it was going to be one hell of a mess.

"Got Culley at home; he said he still wasn't feeling well, but this sure got him up. I also got hold of Joe Molden. You?"

"Yeah, Hauer said he'd be here in twenty minutes . . ." Rafe Buenrostro's voice trailed off and then: "That's Dutch Elder's fishing truck over there."

Sam Dorson nodded and said, "I know." His voice was barely above a whisper. They looked at each other, nodded, and saw the Lab Man heading their way. The time was 12:20 p.m.

A friend had been murdered. And, in this case, a friend of the police, and no one was going to question the number of man-hours worked, the cancelled vacations, and there would be no minor complaints that would appear on Friday and disappear by Monday morning. A friend.

Sam Dorson pointed with his chin and said, "Here comes the rest of Henry's crew. I think I better warn Irene Paredes."

"No, don't. Let Henry do it, if he wants to." Evenly.

Dorson looked at his partner, was about to ask why, but he shrugged his shoulders instead. Another car, Hauer's Volvo, drove up, and he almost ran over some gawking farmer-types wearing overalls. The photographer had come in Hauer's car, and was now busily getting his equipment in order.

Dietz: "How bad, Rafe?"

"Bad enough; it's Dutch Elder."

Rafe Buenrostro walked down the stoop and said, "Sam, you and I'll go in later; Henry and his crew can lead the photographer around. Let's go run some of these people off; come on."

The newspaper reporters were buttonholing potential witnesses. The television people were also setting up their equipment and taking up all manner of space. Ponder was having his hands full, and he welcomed any help he could get. Dorson and Rafe Buenrostro managed to keep the traffic moving and did so until four County Patrolman came driving by and took over.

Dorson called one of the patrolmen over and said, "Get the TV people to move. Choose some place where they can park all that crap of theirs; across the highway. Run *everybody* else off, except the witnesses: Bunton and Schultz, you'll see them, they've got Belken County I.D. tags on 'em."

With that, Rafe and Dorson returned to the stoop and waited for The Lab Man who was working inside.

Henry Dietz poked his head out the door and asked, "Is Irene back yet? And then: "No, I guess not." He walked out, stood between Rafe and Sam Dorson and said, "A goddam mess. The boys are picking up .45 cartridge shells by the dozen in there; it's that bad. To crown it, whoever it was that did this, also used a shotgun. Tore Dutch's face off."

Later on, both Rafe and Sam Dorson would swear to Culley Donovan that The Lab Man had said, "Shit." Unheard of in Dietz's case.

Dietz walked over to his car, reached for a black bag, and walked back into the small building. After a while, Irene Paredes walked toward them. There was blood on the plastic bags covering her lab shoes. The rich farm dirt was clinging to the bloody plastic. She was trying, with little success, to appear calm, at ease.

Rafe Buenrostro walked down to meet her and not unkindly said: "Before you say anything "I," the answer is *yes*. You *can* get used to it. It's like anything else, it's like everything else." Brutal, but straight out.

He stepped aside and didn't try to prevent her from reentering the place. She looked up at him, and Rafe Buenrostro said, "It's up to you, Irene."

She looked at her shoes again, and with that he turned around and started to go inside when she reached out and touched his shoulder: "Rafe," she said, "are Sam and Culley used to it, too?"

Evenly. "Sure."

"I don't want to get used to it, Rafe."

He nodded, and she walked down the stoop, and half-ran to a group of lab people who were busy sorting out plastic bags, clear plastic covers for their shoes and slippers, plastic gloves, and fingerprinting kits. One of the technicians looked up and pointed at something that Irene Paredes picked up, folded, and laid next to the black bag. She started slowly at first, and then went on methodically, systematically, until she began to lose herself in her work.

STATEMENT BY WITNESS JOHN SCHULTZ. Taken by
Sam Dorson: 12:42 p.m. Tuesday. Oct. 24, 1972.

'They was all in black: coats, jackets, shirts, pants, and
hats. And their shoes; yeah.

'All three a-them was carrying them Chicago machine-
guns. They just walked in and didn't say a word; a little guy
motioned for me to go the door, and out I went, brother. A
chubby guy, he pointed his gun to Kenny Joe, and *he* went
right out-a there, too. Yeah.

'The third guy I don't know. I guess he was holding the gun
on the other two at the bar."

(Dorson: What kind of gun did *he* have?)

Schultz: The third guy? A machine-gun, like the others.

'Now, this couldn't've taken half-a minute, no sir. And,
like I say, they didn't say a word. And we didn't either.

'Kenny Joe and me was outside when the shooting started.
I *think* I heard a scream or somebody saying 'Hey!' or 'Hi!'
or something. Okay? One thing, they didn't fire till we was
outside. They must've been watching us, see.

'And I might's well tell you right off: I plain forgot about
the man in the john. He'd come in less'n a minute before the
shooting. Jee-sus . . .

'Now, when the shooting started, and it was loud, we just
lit out, and Kenny Joe, he was almost runned over by a car
passing by on the road, and I just ran the hell-out-a-there;
didn't know where I was going neither. I just plain kept running till Kenny Joe got me to come back.'

Marginal note by Culley Donovan. "From the evidence, at
least one of the men used a shotgun."

STATEMENT BY WITNESS KENNETH J. BUNTON:.
Taken by Rafe Buenrostro, 12:45 p.m., Tuesday, Oct. 24,
1972.

'I guess I'm the only one who noticed the car. It was a
four-door Olds; a solid cream-colored Olds. Kind-a new, too.

It had one-a them luggage racks, and the car was pointed to 906 road. Okay?

'The engine was running; yeah. And, the windows was up and they was dark, too. Black to green, but dark, and they was rolled up. And, the guy at the wheel, he was wearing a cap 'r a hat; he was wearing something. It wasn't no mask, though. A flat hat, kind-a.

'When I got behind a tree, I saw the car was headed on the way to Klail. I remember I looked at it for a while, then I started to run again, and tripped on that irrigation ditch over there.

'I didn't know what I was doing. Jee-sus. I then ran back to the place. It was terrible. Ah . . . the man there, Mr. Elder, he didn't have no face. Jee-sus. I just stood on the doorway, and I ran right back out; got sick then, by that pecan tree there. And then! I saw the Olds coming *back!* Yeah. It went tearing through here at a hundred-mile an hour. On the way to Jonesville this time. Yessir. He flat tore through here. I was on my hands and knees, throwing-up, but I saw it; it was the same car, all right; cream-colored, luggage rack 'n everything.'

**Rafe Buenrostro's close reading
of the witnesses' statements.**

18

On the morning following the triple murder, a Wednesday, the 25th of October, Rafe Buenrostro reached into the folder, sat down, and gave a third reading to the statements given by Kenny Joe Bunton and John Schultz.

He read them a fourth time. After this, he looked for Kenny Bunton's residence phone, found one Bunton on the River Road Crossing: William L., and dialed that number. Kenny Joe answered.

"Hello."

"My name's Rafe Buenrostro, and . . ."

"Hey, Lieutenant, it's me, Kenny Joe. How you doin'?"

"Hi. I need some help."

"Sure thing. What can I do for you?"

"Well, I'd rather talk there, at home; if that's okay. You got the time?"

"Yessir; you know how to get here, do you?"

Rafe Buenrostro replied that he did, thanked him and picked up the office copies of Schultz's and Bunton's statements, signed out for them, and inserted them in a manila folder.

He left a note for Sam Dorson, and then went to sign out for an unmarked car in the County Motor Pool.

Schultz, among other things, had said, "Kenny was almost runned over by a car passing on the road." But Bunton had made no mention of it; a natural omission given the excitement of the day. To add to this, Bunton had seen Dutch Elder's body, the man without a face, and he couldn't have been thinking clearly; given that circumstance.

When Rafe Buenrostro pulled into the driveway, he saw Bunton sitting under a palm tree working on a fishing net.

"Hi, Lieutenant."

"You doing all right?"

"Yeah . . ."

He's thinking about Dutch Elder and the other two. Rafe to himself.

"I guess you, ah, you sort-a get used to that work, right Lieutenant?"

Rafe Buenrostro made some sort of noncommital answer, and Bunton said he was going to "get us a couple of chairs."

When he came back, Kenny Joe Bunton turned to him and said, "Well, what can I do for you?"

Rafe Buenrostro explained he was looking for some help; he told him of Schultz's statement, the car incident, and of Bunton's unintentional but quite understandable omission.

"Let me think on that a minute." He got up and said, "How about a cold Coca-Cola?"

"Sounds good to me."

"Be right back . . ."

He was back in less than a minute, handed Rafe the cold drink, and took a longish pull from his own. Another swig was followed by a smacking of the lips. Rafe Buenrostro usually choked on cold Coca-Colas and watched in wonder as the twenty-five year old Bunton finished the Coke in three swallows.

"I remember now. Yeah. A convertible; it had the top down, hah, and that mild norther hanging on . . . A guy wearing sunglasses. Yeah.

"He wasn't speeding, I don't think, and he didn't come that close to me, Lieutenant.

"It was light-blue; two-door. But don't ask me for no license plates, un-hnh."

Rafe Buenrostro smiled encouragingly and said, "I won't."

"You want another Coke, Lieutenant?"

"What? Oh, no; thanks."

"Be right back," he said.

Rafe Buenrostro was writing what Bunton had said when the younger man came back, Coke in hand.

"I ran back to the same side-a the road, you know. I then headed for the place, got sick, went to the pecan tree . . .

yeah. Well, after a little-whiles, I went back to Theo's place, ducked in and out again. And I threw up. Again. Yeah; and it was then that I saw the cream Olds coming back.

"They was heading back, 'n doing a hundred, I betcha."

Rafe: "How far did they go toward Klail before they turned around, you think?" Careful. Don't lead him now.

"Couldn't say; but from the way they were going, it couldn't've been too long before they got to the city limits, right? And besides, these Farm to Market Roads are in good shape, and 906 is straight, too. It's good for race-draggin', sometimes."

Rafe Buenrostro smiled, and put his empty Coke bottle on the ground. "You remember anything else about the two-door, light-blue convertible with the man wearing sunglasses?"

He was drawing a picture for Bunton.

A shake of the head, and then he blurted out: "Jesus, yes. Hold up a bit, Lieutenant. The guy had a dog with him; a Labrador Bay retriever; it was sitting in the back, had his back to the wind. A black Labrador; full grown, too."

Rafe Buenrostro asked, "What kind of dog was it?"

"A Labrador Bay, Lieutenant. A retriever."

Rafe Buenrostro was not familiar with Labrador Bays. He wrote down the information. He looked at the words, thought on the second car and nodded. To himself: "It's possible that the driver of the convertible saw the Olds. But first things first."

Looking at Bunton he said, "Anything else?"

"Did Jay Schultz say the gunmen was all wearing stocking masks? And gloves?"

"No." Quietly.

Rafe had read the statements, had them in his car, in fact, and added to which, he knew them by heart.

"Are you sure?" Quietly.

"Oh, yeah. Except for the guy in the car. He was wearing a cap a-some sort 'r other."

"Mr. Schultz was pretty sure they were Mexicans." Neutral. Informative.

"Well, it's possible, but how could he tell that? They didn't say a word; nothing. They just pointed those guns at us." Kenny Joe Bunton looked at his empty Coke bottle, and said, "The guys that was killed were Mexicans; the two at the bar. I served them myself. You think that's what Jay was talking about?"

Rafe Buenrostro didn't say anything.

"No, Lieutenant. They didn't say a word. Nobody said a word. I just saw them two machine guns and that shotgun and I was glad to be out-a there."

"Shotgun." Quietly.

"Yeah; the third guy next to the booth, facing the john. He had a pump gun."

Rafe Buenrostro nodded to himself, looked at Bunton and thanked him again. He also asked for directions to Shultz's farm. "Here's the Coke bottle," smiling.

"You can't miss it, Lieutenant. There's a sign on the right-hand side-a the road, okay? Schultz's Farm. See you, Lieutenant."

Kenny Joe Bunton waved at him, and Rafe Buenrostro drove to Schultz's farm some four miles away.

Schultz couldn't confirm the stocking masks, and he vaguely remembered the car that "almost runned over" Kenny Joe Bunton.

"I wadn't drunk; I had had a couple of beers, but that was all."

And no, he didn't see no dog, either. Yep, he saw the cream-colored car going toward Jonesville all right. Must've turned around, 'cause they was first headed toward Klail.'

That much of it was right, reflected Rafe Buenrostro. He thanked John Schultz and headed for the Belken County Court House; he thought about what his report would look like.

And the convertible? Sunglasses, a dog . . . Was the driver headed home from the beach? If so, then the weak norther must've driven him away from Sandy Dunes Beach.

Whatever it was, it was going to take some digging, anyway he looked at it.

The driver could live in Klail City or in any point westward, if indeed he was going home. Eastward? Jonesville. But he was coming from that direction. Ruffing to the north, Relámpago to the south and west, and looking straight west: Flora, Bascom, and Edgerton in Belken County, and then came Flads, in Dellis County.

How many gas stations in Klail? Twenty? Thirty? He'd start there, he thought. He'd see if the sunglass wearing, dog-owning driver was a regular customer somewhere. The car was light-blue and a convertible; couldn't be too many of those.

He hoped.

First, write the report, put it in the folder, and *then* start the calls to the gas stations. After that, a visit to The Lab Man.

It was a start.

Captain Lisandro Gómez Solís
and a day in the life of young Mr. Hauer.

19

The day following the murder found Hauer on the telephone. First, to The Lab Man's assistants to ask the age-old question: "Got anything?" The answer to this was: "We'll call *you*." The second call was to confirm his early morning appointment with Captain Lisandro Gómez Solís of the Barrones, Tamaulipas, *Cuerpo de policía estatal*; *Sección del orden público*. This is a special section of the Tamaulipas State Police charged with overseeing public order in the city of Barrones and the surrounding area.

Public Order meant exactly what the state government in Victoria, Tamaulipas wanted it to mean: Drunk and disorderly? A disruption of public order, Section this. A hold-up? A disruption of public order under Section This and Section That. A bank robbery? A major disruption of public order according to Sections These, Those, and Those Over There.

"Some charge," said Hauer, after listening to an explanation by fifty-five year old Captain Gómez, the man in charge of the Barrones *municipio*.

"Yes," Gómez smiled back; "it is that." And then: "Look at this scar, Sergeant Hauer."

A whitish, five to six-inch jagged line beginning below the left nostril and extending to the left ear lobe, a small piece of which was missing.

"That," he smiled, "was a personal disruption of public order." He smiled again and wound up laughing at his own joke. He was not above laughing at someone else's, by the way.

Hauer nodded and wondered to himself how deep the scar had been. Gómez continued smiling and said, "It was deep enough, and it was bad enough."

Hauer looked at the man closely and thought that Gómez

Solís's English was flawless, but he didn't say so. A breach to have done so, most likely.

Gómez then pushed away some folders on top of his desk; he made some room, opened a drawer, closed it carefully, opened another, reached down, and produced a picture frame. He turned it over and slid it toward Hauer.

It read: "By authority of the Board of Trustees of the University of Illinois and upon recommendation of the University Senate at Urbana-Champaign LISANDRO GOMEZ SOLIS has been admitted to the degree of Bachelor of Fine Arts and so entitled to all rights and honors thereto appertaining."

There were some signatures and the Seal of the University of Illinois on the left-hand side of the diploma.

Gómez Solís said, "Sam Dorson mentioned your interest in American university diplomas. Do you collect them? A hobby, perhaps?"

There was neither guile nor malice in the question.

Hauer tried to shrug it off, and was saved by a knock at the door. A man entered without any apparent word or signal from Gómez Solís; he too was wearing civilian clothes and turning to Hauer he said in English, "How do you do?"

Hauer answered automatically: "Fine, thank you." And then, "And you?"

The man smiled and said, "Likewise." He turned his attention to the captain and said in English for the benefit of their guest, "This is what we've been able to come up with so far; anything else turns up, I'll let you know."

Gómez Solís initialed the folder, nodded to the other man, and said: "Good piece of work. Thanks."

Hauer could have just as easily been sitting in Culley's office; he decided he had much to learn about his Mexican counterparts.

Gómez Solís smiled again; he *was* reading Hauer's thoughts (damn the man!). "A matter of time, Sergeant, that's what Culley Donovan says."

Hauer had to laugh this time; at himself. But that didn't mean he liked it. He waited for his host to finish spreading some pictures around the desk. The diploma had been returned to its drawer, and Gómez Solís looked closely at the pictures.

"These two work for this man, here." Pointing. "These are the dead men, right? Well, the one here,—pointing to a stockily built man of fifty-five or so—is the head man. He's sixty, and he's tough.

"At the present time, he is also in our State Penitentiary; but he's a free man legally and technically. I'll tell you about that later." And then, in an offhanded way: "He's also a marked man. But then, he's been *that* for over forty years . . .

"I know him, and knowing him as I do, I know he's angry, and he *will* act. But not when he's angry. He's a very careful planner.

"Now, my guess is that whoever it was that killed the other two, mistook Prosecutor Elder for this man."

Hauer opened his mouth, but Gómez Solís stopped him by raising his hand. "It's a guess, on my part. And only that: a guess.

"Don't fall in love with my theory, Sergeant. It's possible, yes; it may even be true, yes, but neither you nor I *know it for a fact*!"

Hauer was about to speak again, when Gómez Solís stopped him a second time: "Say you disregard my advice, where do you go from there? What have you *learned*? More importantly, what have you contributed to the case?"

Pause.

"I think you know the answer to that." Bland.

Hauer waited.

"Those are Mexican Nationals murdered in the United States. By whom? Other Mexican Nationals? If so, why? By Texas Mexicans? If so, why? By Anglo Texans? If so, why?"

Hauer shook his head. "Couldn't have been Anglo Texans."

Neutral. "Oh? Why not?"

"Well, one of the witnesses described them as Mexicans." He was about to say, "And what do you think a-that?" but he checked himself. Hauer considered his own situation for a moment: "That would've been dumber than dumb. It's taking it personal."

Gómez Solís smiled, rose, and walked Hauer to the door. Almost laughing aloud, he said to Hauer: "You want to know what I think a-that?"

This was entirely too much for Young Mr. Hauer; he was about to ask, rather sarcastically, too, if Captain Lisandro Gómez Solís, Captain of the *Cuerpo de Policía Estatal* and U. of I. BFA was a mind reader, when the Mexican, escorting him to the door, said, "I've got over twenty-five years on you; that's all."

He was about to hand over the envelope with the pictures to Hauer when he said, "The third man is legally free, as I said; it happens that he's in the Victoria Prison Hospital. Recuperating from an appendectomy; nothing vital. It came to him two days before he was to be released. He'll be out soon . . ." And then: "He was due out the day before the carnage, *la matanza*, that's why I said that Dutch Elder may have been killed by mistake. But don't put your money on that horse, okay?"

He handed Hauer the envelope and cautioned: "Be careful of those Mexican drivers."

Gómez Solís closed the car door, ran up the police station steps where a uniformed policeman saluted and held the door for him. He didn't look back.

"Something else for the folder." Hauer; under his breath. I wonder, he thought, I wonder how this is going to end?

He reached into his shirt pocket, ex-ed out Captain Gómez's name, and read the second name on the list Culley Donovan had given him: Lt. Harry Biggs, Jonesville airport security.

Hauer crossed the Amity Bridge to the northern back of the Rio Grande and found himself, as usual, in a snarl of downtown traffic. Turning right, the longer way to the airport but away from the main flow of traffic, he pointed his car to Jonesville's airport.

**Joe Molden's good, honest work
is shot down by Grand Theft–Auto's
sloppy record keeping.**

20

With Sam Dorson leading the way, they had decided that first morning that the cream-colored car was the first lock to be opened.

Until The Lab Man identified the bodies, made out the types of weapons used (not *which* guns fired since one needed the weapons to verify the test, as The Lab Man stressed once again), the Olds gave them something to hold on to.

That was the same Wednesday morning Rafe Buenrostro said he would read the statements again to see what he could find there, and said he'd keep in touch with The Lab Man. Rafe Buenrostro had found the slight indiscrepancy, the natural omission, about the car that had "almost runned over Kenny Joe", and Rafe had driven out there to see him, and Schultz if need be.

Culley had then assigned Joe Molden the chore of checking with the Valley's Olds dealerships for sales and transfers for the years '68, '69, '70, '71, and '72 for four-door, cream-colored Oldsmobiles. He was also to ask if any had been sold with luggage racks attached or if they had some added to them then or later on.

Molden nodded and went to work.

The same night of the triple murder, a Tuesday, Culley had received two phone calls at home. The first one was from Captain Lisandro Lee Gómez Solís, of the Barrones, Tamaulipas police, an old friend. He had not, Gómez explained, heard of the murders until half an hour before the call, at nine o'clock that evening, Mexican standard time. And, he wondered if he could be of service. He had, he said, what could be a possible lead for them.

One of Gómez Solís's men had called him earlier that day

to say that Andrés Cavazos de León aka *La Máquina*, and his good friend, César Becerra Garibay aka *La Tuerca*, had crossed the bridge at Río Rico.

As you know, Culley, he had said, the entrance to the bridge is perpendicular to Road 906. And, they were driving a red Chevy pickup truck, Tamaulipas plates.

Wasn't a red Chevy pickup one of the cars at the scene? Yes. Well, these two worked for Práxades Zaragoza, *El Barco*; Zaragoza was cooling his heels at the State Prison Hospital in Victoria. He had been due out the day before the murders, but an appendicitis attack kept him in the Hospital past the release date, etc.

Everybody in the world knew of the date of the release, of course, but no word had gotten out in re the appendectomy. See?

Yes, Culley Donovan agreed, that could be relevant. It was certainly *interesting*. A noncommital answer for an old friend, but he added that he'd be sending someone to see his old friend in Barrones the next morning.

After that conversation, Culley had called Dorson at home and said that the dead men had been tentatively identified by Gómez Solís. But, they both agreed, they would rather hear it from The Lab Man.

Dorson then suggested that Young Mr. Hauer be sent to Barrones to pick up copies of the photos and fingerprints, and the nice glossy of *El Barco* as a bonus.

And, Dorson went on to add, "He can pick up some education and no small amount of humility while he's there."

The second call to Culley that night had come from a Lt. Harry Biggs of the Jonesville Airport Security.

One of his men thought he might have spotted the Olds on his way to work that Tuesday morning; the man lived on Farm to Market 906.

Since Young Mr. Hauer would cross at Jonesville to see Lisandro Gómez Solís, he'd also be the one to send to see the man Biggs talked about.

Culley Donovan had assigned Sam Dorson to man the phone, start the folder, and to take messages from interested citizens, and from those phone maniacs who called in to report close relatives who were bombarding their homes with ray guns and poisoning the city's water supply. Other relatives reported cousins, uncles, etc. who were distributing dirty movies to children under the guise of sex education.

Dorson applied a system when manning the phone during these times: he would complain to the caller that there was a poor connection, or he would sound most interested and recommend to the caller to write everything down and mail it to them via express mail. At times he'd ask them to re-dial. This tied some of the lines, but it freed Dorson and the other lines. It usually worked, too.

Joe Molden walked in with a sheaf of papers in his hand, nodded to Sam and was about to start his series of calls to the Valley's Olds dealers.

He put down the phone before he dialed the first number, and said to himself: "Logically, the first call has to be to Grand Theft–Auto, not to the dealers."

The trouble with this was that he *knew* about G.T.–Auto. Unfortunately for Molden and for the rest of the citizens of Belken County, the Auto Division was headed by a hack who was close to Bollinger. One who had worked, quite openly too, for H.B.'s re-elections through the years.

It was easily the worst managed Division in the County Patrol. Most of the rank and file worked well, and he knew some of them, but, oh, that leadership, he thought.

In their favor, though, Grand Theft–Auto is pure hell on the border for the reason that the Rio Grande is a ridiculously easy river to cross. Although only one official ferry operates up in Los Ebanos, many other entrepeneurs run their own ferries in the shallows and deeps in the meandering river.

Still, the good cops at Grand Theft ran the Division the best they could; to its further detriment, however, Frank Jordan, the Division Chief, promoted cops in his own image.

It was one of these, a thirteen-year veteran sergeant named Joseph Posey, that Molden called when he started his first assignment the day following the murders.

This was the first piece of wrong information in the case, and it came from within as a result of a stupid, careless, and typically sloven mistake.

The Homicide Squad's log showed that a call had been made on 25 Oct '72 at 8:16 a.m. from Joe Molden to J. Posey, G.T.–Auto. The G.T.–Auto log read this way: "Joe Mullen, Homcide (sic) called on 25 Oct 62. 8:20 p.m."

Worse than the errors on time and the year, Posey hadn't bothered to sign or to initial the entry.

But that wasn't all.

"No luck," Posey had said. "No, no one's reported missing a '67, a '68, or '69, '70, '71, or '72 four-door cream-colored Olds. So far. Four-doors, right? And luggage rack, right? Is that what you said? Well, no. No luck."

Molden, much later, in the course of his search, remembered saying to himself, "Luck? What's luck got to do with it?"

Going on what Kenny Joe Bunton had said in his statement, the Olds was fairly new (Hauer's contribution: "or an older well-cared for car").

The number of Olds agencies in the Valley: four. He called the first one: the local one in Klail City. There were orders and sales registers to check; and transfers of titles, and owners' addresses, auto registration numbers, etc. Was all of this on file? Yes? Good, he'd be right over.

Two days later, he had a tally: Ninety-four cream-colored Oldsmobiles had been sold in the Valley from 1967 to the present. Molden thought on it and couldn't remember seeing *one* cream Olds in that time, Goes to show you, he said.

Of these, thirty-one were four-door models. He scratched sixty-three from the ninety-four.

Molden made his list: '67: 3; '68: 9; '69: 7; '70: 5; '71: 5; '72: 2.

Of these, sixteen owners had already parted with their once-prized beauties. They had either traded them, or sold them or wrecked and then sold them for junk parts.

Molden ran each of these down. The cars were in the new owners' driveways, in the garage, at work, at the shop, and so on. Four had been cannibalized and shipped to Mexico to be resold; nothing he could do with these, he said. Of the ones located, of course, none had been reported missing. And why should they? They were in the garage, in the shop, in the driveways, etc.

Of the remaining seventeen, three presented other difficulties: the owners had changed addresses, two of them had moved at least twice since the purchase; three other owners had died in their cars on the Valley highways.

This left eleven. And these, their owners had decided, needed some sprucing up, and as if on cue, they had gone to a bake-and-paint shop and had the tops painted green, brown, blue, and six had preferred pink tops. And so on, said Molden.

Thursday, 10:45 a.m., and Joe Molden was tired, but he-had-by-God gotten reports on all of them. It had been frustrating work, of course, but he was used to that. It was part of police work, he consoled himself, to be frustrated. It had been tiresome work, too, because the public is not as cooperative as it thinks it is; nor as cooperative as the police claim it to be; nor as cooperative as Jack Webb insistently and dearly wants to believe.

But there had been some cooperation on the part of some citizens: "They were assisting in the apprehension of a criminal." Molden didn't have to wonder where some of them had gotten *that* from. Too much TV; that's where, thought tired Joe Molden.

Tomorrow was Friday, *gracias a Dios*, he said to the face in the office mirror. And then: "God! I look awful." Ah, but tomorrow, tomorrow . . . they would meet and talk after the funeral, and something was bound to happen: It always had before. Mañana . . .

He also thought on the truth of why something always happened: it happened because they made it happen. He was thinking like a cop, he said. And, just like a cop, he then said: "Now where did I put that damn file?"

**The Lab Man leans on a mortician
and Mim Elder has a request.**

21

Elder's funeral was scheduled for Friday afternoon, October 27, three days after the murder; Henry Dietz had worked feverishly as had the other lab personnel, and on Thursday, Dietz, Irene Paredes, and The Lab Man's chief assistant, a fingerprint technician named Ted Pilkington, drove Dutch Elder's body to River Delta Mortuary; a clear disregard of the existing contract between the County and "those ghouls" as the Lab Man called them. But, as he also said, "This is for Mim Elder."

And it was; a personal favor. Dietz looked at a stack of expensive coffins, inspected them, and stood by the last one in the stack. He checked it for flaws and then he tested its solidity and workmanship. Henry Tolleson, owner and operator of River Delta Mortuary, stood by disapprovingly, but Dietz ignored him. Satisfied with the condition of one of the coffins, Dietz took Tolleson by the elbow and sat him down.

"Henry, it's going to be a small funeral; it's going to be a short service; and it's going to be absolutely *free*; free of interference from you, free of Harvey Bollinger, and it's also going to be free, *gratis*.

Tolleson glared at Dietz, but The Lab Man ignored this, too. "Now, Culley's going to say a few words at the chapel. My wife is going to play the organ, and Betty Chapman and Effie Dorson are going to sing *Strong Deliverer*.

"While the services are being conducted inside the chapel, Mim Elder's going to be out at graveside. Alone. And, she stays there as long as she wants to. You're to stay outside the chapel door. When she leaves, you come in and tell me about it, Henry. Now, was there any word you didn't understand?"

Henry Tolleson looked at his namesake and shook his head. There was fear and anger in his eyes, a dangerous combination at times, but not here; not from Tolleson. He coughed, and said, "Oh, yes, one question: If Mr. Bollinger . . ."

But The Lab Man raised his hand and stopped him on the spot. "He won't be there; he won't be at the chapel; and he won't be at graveside. Any other question?"

A look of incomprehension from Tolleson, and Henry Dietz let him sit there.

"Another thing."

Tolleson looked up.

"I hear of one photographer showing up, Henry, and you're going to have me round your neck every day of your life."

But Tolleson wasn't down yet. He pursed his lips, glared at Dietz, and was about to speak when The Lab Man was on him immediately: "You think not, Henry Tolleson? You have any idea what I can do to bodies out there at the Lab before your *boys* pick 'em up?"

Tolleson was going down, but The Lab Man wasn't through with him: "You couldn't pay 'em enough to work for you."

A long pause.

"You're in charge of everything, beginning right *now*. I'm bringing the body in through the front door. Dutch Elder isn't a piece of meat."

With that, Henry Dietz left the shaken Tolleson, walked to the county hearse and told Irene Paredes, "Scoot over, "I." You're driving this thing."

Irene Paredes looked across to Pilkington who pretended to be reading a stop sign. Irene started the engine, and The Lab Man said, "Take it to the front door, "I." They're waiting for us."

With a *yessir* from her lips, she wheeled the long machine to the front door of Henry Tolleson's River Delta Mortuary.

Henry Dietz did not say a word at the mortuary or after they drove away. When they arrived at the Lab, Henry Dietz went straight to his office, locked it, picked up the phone, and called Mim Elder.

On Friday morning, Miriam Elder had not found a way to keep Harvey Bollinger from attending Dutch's funeral. What could she do?

The funeral was a few hours away; she had to do *something*; one last something for her Dutchman. And then, a sudden inspiration: her best friend Barb Colunga! She'd call Barb. Yes!

Was there someway or something that her husband, Chris, could do to engage Harvey Bollinger's attention; something that would cause him to miss the funeral?

Was there an important stake-out somewhere? Some, ah, some big *show* that was strong enough to pull Bollinger away from the funeral that afternoon?

Had Chris mentioned anything along those lines?

Barb Colunga assured her best friend and told her not to worry.

"That would be the very last damn straw, Mim; having that buffoon at Dutch's funeral. You attend to what you have to do, and I'll come by for you at two o'clock sharp. I'll leave my car at your place, and we'll go in yours. You're not to worry. Hear?" Mim sighed and thanked her friend.

She smiled as she thought about "her Dutch." Two kids, and thirty years as man and wife. Not bad, she said, not bad for two kids who grew up together in an orphans' home up in Austin.

Mim Elder was neither particularly nor offensively religious, but at that moment, she thanked God. Suppose, she thought, suppose Dutch had gotten sick and suffered the way Corinne Donovan had suffered? No; Thank God, no.

And then she wondered if it were a sacrilege or something of the sort, because in the same breath she said, half-aloud and lovingly, too: "My God, but he loved to take me to bed." At this instant she stopped thinking about Bollinger; Barb, if anyone, would take care of that.

Barb Colunga was something that her best friend, Mim Elder, was not: the petite, green-eyed, red-haired—impish— Barb Colunga was a political wife. And, because she was both intelligent *and* smart, this also made her a dangerous foe. Some of the wives were bright and a few of them were pushy, but Barb Colunga, the daughter of a Mexican Methodist preacher, was also a person of character. And Mim believed when Barb said she'd fix it. If anybody could, Barb could.

Whatever it was Barb Colunga was going to cook up, Harvey Bollinger would not be in attendance at Rose Garden that afternoon. Thank God for friends.

It was done this way: Chris Colunga, the head of Grand Theft–Larceny, just happened to mention to his secretary, Marie-Eugenie Duarte, that he *might* miss Mr. Elder's funeral; yes, it *was* terrible, what with being best friends and all, but it was entirely *possible*.

You see, he had gotten a tip that a man responsible for some recent hijackings was in custody at Jonesville. The tipster had said that what started out a a simple highway violation, had ended up as a confession to something else.

And you know how those things are sometimes, Marie-Eugenie. And yet, there was probably nothing to it, but he had to check it out. Yes, a waste of time, more'n likely, but there it was. What choice had he but to check it out, right?

It was now eleven o'clock in the morning and Chris Colunga asked her to type a note for his lieutenants: Tim Ybarra and Stu Yates: "Going to Jonesville on business. If you can skip the funeral, call me at home. Leaving for J'ville around 1:00 p.m. If you can't make it, see you mañana. C.C."

She personally handwalked the notes and left them in the men's IN trays. Chris Colunga went into his office, began leafing through some recent cases, and then asked her to ring him at twelve-thirty. No later.

Marie-Eugenie memorized the note, but she *knew what it was all about*. At twelve-thirty, she watched as the head of G.T.–Larceny picked up his straw hat, walked out the door, and headed for the parking lot; she then waited exactly three minutes, and there he was, driving out of the lot turning left; he was going home.

She then called H.B., and he came downstairs to the office.

Bollinger then walked into Colunga's office, picked up the phone, and dialed the Jonesville jailhouse.

After a while, Bollinger stalked out, complaining that he couldn't get much information "out-a that dumb guard" at Jonesville. "Why, he had the nerve to tell me, *me*, that he had no idea what it was I was talking about. What hijacker?" he had asked. "Can you beat that?"

"It's close to one right now, Marie-Eugenie; I gotta go, and thanks again, hon."

Halfway to Jonesville he remembered the Elder funeral. He'd have to miss it.

"Can't be helped," he said; he turned the air conditioning to high; the weak norther had dissipated, and the temperature was now in the eighties on that 27th of October.

Bollinger went up to seventy miles an hour, turned off the police radio, and began preparing the questions he was going to put to the hijacker.

The owner of the light-blue convertible pays a visit. Friday morning.

22

At five minutes after eight, the inter-office phone rang; Dorson picked it up and handed it to Donovan. The Lab Man.

Dorson saw Culley's face light up, watched as Culley made a quick notation; he then heard Culley Donovan say, "Good for you, Henry."

The Lab Man must've said something else since this brought a chuckle from Culley. "A case of Noche Buena beer for all of us? Well, Henry, we're going to have to earn it . . . Compliments of *who*? Henry Tolleson? I don't believe you."

Cupping the mouthpiece and turning to the three men sitting around his office, he said, "Dietz. He says it's time for us to go to work."

"See you, Henry."

Everyone nodded except Molden who groaned. Dorson turned and winked at him.

And then, at exactly a quarter after eight, the three telephones came on and blinked. Culley Donovan, standing by the door, opened it, saw that the desk man was not at his post, and told Rafe Buenrostro and Dorson to pick up the first two lines; he'd handle the third, he said.

"Buenrostro. Homicide."

"Lieutenant! What luck, this is Jimmy Woodall; how are *you*?"

Ah, yes: Michael W. Woodall.

"Fine, sir; how are you?"

"Never better, Lieutenant; I wonder if you'd join Miss Lan— Estelle and me for dinner a week from tomorrow night? Is that convenient for you? A week's a bit sudden, I know, but you think you could make it?"

Delighted.

"Yes, I would. I look forward to it."

"Do you enjoy roast beef? Are you a beef eater?"

"Oh, yes; definitely."

"Good (genuinely pleased, too). So are we. It's a small dinner party; if you have a friend, she's invited, and gladly. Is six o'clock for cocktails too early for you?"

Rafe imagined that Jimmy Woodall, if he had to, could sell badminton sets in Antarctica.

"Too early did you say? No, not at all; thank you."

"No tie, Lieutenant."

"Pardon?"

"Ties, Lieutenant; don't wear one. Relax, eat, talk; have a good time."

I need a good time, said Rafe to himself.

"Six o'clock, then, and I . . ."

"Yes?" Expectantly.

"I look forward to seeing you and Mrs. Woodall again."

"Thank you; b'bye." Kindly.

Rafe Buenrostro took out his assignment book and wrote: M.W.W., 6:00 p.m., Sat. Nov. 4. He stopped and read some of the other initials on the same page. Ha! They stood for Allgood, Woodall, Pratt, and Krindler. Some page.

"I'm sorry, but Mr. Hauer is out for the moment. My *name*? Dorson, ma'am. No; *Dor son*. Yes, it does sound a lot like the band leader; yes ma'am. Yes, I'm ready: *Laura Sikes*. Thank you. Yes, I got that. Address?"

The conversation then took some five minutes, but it cleared up part of the mystery of the four-door, cream-colored Olds. The beginning of Joe Molden's frustration.

It had been agreed from the first day on that the car was most important. Everyone, Culley Donovan included, had looked at Young Mr. Hauer when he said it was *salient*. The car's chief importance, no question, rested on the fact that the four men had been in it; had been in it for a good period of time; and, had been in it together.

The length of the stay at the Kum-Bak had been negligible.

Brutal, yes; but negligible. But, the car, they said. Ah, the car. The car had been home for the killers for three-four hours, five perhaps. And, despite Kenny Joe Bunton's steadfast and unequivocal assertion that the men wore gloves, the unalterable fact (Culley here) was that The Lab Man and his group would go over every inch of that mystery car when they found it. And, they—the killers—had left something of themselves there.

What?

Well, that was for The Lab Man to discover.

When? Knowing Dietz, fast; and, better than fast, it would be done right the first time.

The *where* in the car would come next, and this would serve as the first open lock in the Chinese Box.

Dorson rang off, sat very still, and read his notes again. He then looked at Culley who was still on the phone and taking notes as well. Dorson threw a glance at Molden who was back at his own desk staring at some paper work. Sam reflected on what he had written down, and looked at Joe Molden again.

Culley thanked the caller, rang off, and said, "That was Biggs, from airport security. One of his men found a four-door cream-colored, Nineteen Sixty-nine Olds at the airport parking lot. It was probably there the day Peter went to see whatever-his-name-is who works for Biggs."

"Herb Mauck," said Molden as Hauer walked in.

All eyes turned to Donovan who went on: "Biggs has something else for us: the airport parking ticket stub with the time and date of entry. It seems that an attendant stuck it on the windshield; the electric eye was down that day, and they had attendants out issuing the entry tickets."

"Time and day!"

"It *sounds* good, but we'll have to see the car first." And then, offhandedly, "It's got a luggage rack." He half-smiled and said, "It *may* be a break."

A knock at the door. Hauer opened the door and saw a thin, deeply tanned teenager looking expectantly.

"Lieutenant Buenrostro?"

"Come in; the man in the blue shirt over there." The youngster looked at Hauer's shirt: it, too, was blue.

"Come along," said Hauer.

At the same time, Dorson went to see Culley with *his* good news: Laura Sikes, a bookkeeper for Colvin and Smart, had called in; she had wanted someone in charge of investigating automobile thefts. "She had come by personally on Monday—this Monday, Culley—talked to someone in Auto. That had been five days ago, and she hadn't heard from them since. So, she decided to call us. She asked for Peter, by name, and she said she knew your name from the paper."

Culley looked at the ceiling and said, "I wish to hell that Peggy MacDougall had never been born."

Dorson laughed aloud; it was his first good laugh since Elder's murder.

Both Dorson's and Donovan's description of the car fit: Laura Sikes' car was a Nineteen sixty-nine, four-door cream-colored Oldsmobile, luggage rack, Tex. Lic. No. ATS 444. And Biggs' report was identical.

Joe Molden listened with no small amount of interest and rising anger. Under his breath, but rather audibly, he said, "Those absolute Auto shits."

Hauer, who had led the youngster to Rafe Buenrostro's desk, jerked his head toward Molden's direction. The wording didn't surprise him; it was the heat in Molden's voice.

Culley tried to hold Molden down to a trot by saying, "It *looks* promising; but, we'll have to check her story out; and Biggs's too. The Lab Man'll bring some work for us around eleven or so, and I want us to be through here before then. There's a funeral to go to."

Molden nodded.

Donovan made a face: "Look, Joe; I know you've spent good time on . . ." He stopped in mid-sentence. "Rafe? What's up?"

"You-all want to come over here? I want you to meet Marty Lindstrom; his dad owns Lindstrom's Feed and Seed over on Hidalgo and Third. I called him up last night and asked him to come in this morning."

The youngster, the center of attention, shook hands all around.

Rafe said, "You old enough to drink coffee?"

That broke the ice some, and young Lindstrom said, "Nah; my track coach says it's bad for me."

Dorson laughed first, and said: "A lot he knows." He followed this with a sip from his cup.

Rafe Buenrostro said, "John Schultz, an eye witness, deposed that Kenny Joe Bunton had almost been run over by an oncoming car. From Bunton's statement, we learned that he had dashed out toward the farm road looking for help, he then stumbled into the irrigation ditch, but Bunton didn't mention the car at all. He had forgotten it. And, it wasn't that important to him, obviously, and certainly not as important as the shootings back at the Kum-Bak.

"For his part, Marty here didn't see Kenny Joe; he hadn't come close to him at all. But, from where Schultz was standing or running at the time, it may have looked close. A matter of perspective, then."

"I had asked Bunton if he remembered a car that passed him when he panicked and ran from the Kum-Bak."

"He did when I went back to see him. He described it perfectly: light-blue, two-door convertible, a young male driver, sunglasses, and a dog riding in the back seat."

Dorson: "That Bunton ought to be a cop."

"You'll remember that Kenny Joe said and then Schultz corroborated independently, that they had seen the Olds coming back the other way, meaning Jonesville. Well, I figured that the second driver, Marty, as it turns out, might have also seen the Olds. It's a high-embankment two-lane road, and that meant he'd have to make a U-turn right on 906 itself.

"Well, I started calling the gas stations in town to see if any one of them had a regular customer that fit Bunton's description of the car, and got Marty here. Last night, I spoke with his mother and then with him, and asked him if he had a dog. He said he had a black Labrador Bay retriever. That was the type of dog described by Bunton, and I figured I was in business."

"I'll be damned." Hauer; to no one.

Rafe Buenrostro turned to Marty and asked: "Want to tell us what you saw?"

"Sure. I'd skipped school a couple-a days, and I was coming back from an overnight trip to the beach; the norther had run me off, and the water'd got too cold out there. I had Bruno, my Labrador, with me, and I was clipping along the 906 straightaway, but nothing serious, when all of a sudden I catch up to a car. It was making a U turn right on 906, just like you said right now. It had stopped on my lane, on the way to Klail. A full stop. And then, it just made a U turn right then and there. It was crazy.

"That's some dumb driving, let me tell you. Well, I thought I was going to hit him or go off the road, one, and those two-laners do have pretty high embankments . . . you roll off one-a those, and you can forget it.

"Well, that car turned in a hurry, and I gave the driver . . . a hard stare. When I next looked in the rear-view, that car was flying. Close to a hundred, I betcha."

"Did you happen to catch the license when you came up to it? I mean, before it gunned off?" Rafe.

"Sort-a; I was pretty angry, see? It had stopped on my side of the road, and then the guy pulled that U turn on me. I didn't know what he was going to do next; driving around like that. And then . . ."

"Yeah?" Hauer.

"I shot him the finger."

Frown from Hauer.

"What's the matter?" Marty asked.

"Go on."

"Oh, sorry. Well, yeah, the license plates. I'm not sure about the letters, okay? I'm pretty sure it had two fours on it; maybe three. As I said, I can't give you the letters, but I'm pretty sure about the numbers.

"Yeah, two or three *fours* in a row. I didn't write 'em down 'r anything, but I did look."

Dorson and Donovan exchanged glances but said nothing. And then Lindstrom's eyes opened wide: "Jee-sus. Were those the guys that killed Mr. Elder?"

"Could you describe the car for us?" Culley.

"Sure. A sixty-nine Olds. It had those dark windshields on it, and it was a cream-color, like; and it had a luggage rack, yeah. Yeah, that's about it."

Rafe: "Marty, could we call on you for something else in case we've forgotten something here?"

"You bet. I'm working at my Dad's place after school, so I'm usually there . . . except for weekends." Smile.

"Thanks for coming by."

"Sure; I was worried when you called last night. I mean, it was kind-a late, and I'm glad you talked to Ma first. She worries a lot. You know how women are."

A man of the world Mr. Lindstrom. A man of the world who goes around shooting his finger at a bad set of people.

"Need a ride?"

"Nah, thanks; I've got my Dad's pickup out front. See-yall."

Culley Donovan kept his eyes on Molden who looked angry; angry enough to blow up at someone. At someone in Grand Theft-Auto, thought Culley. He looked at Joe Molden again: that's bad; he can't learn this job if he goes around trying to do somebody else's.

"Coffee up everyone. I think we're on to . . ."

He stopped.

Hauer, Sam Dorson, and Rafe Buenrostro looked at him when he stopped.

Culley Donovan decided to say something else. It was a reminder of what they were.

"We're a unit, and we work as a unit. We're not a mob here; we don't go all over the place. We do what we do, we all help, and we all contribute, and we all do the job. And . . . I'll remind you of something else; this isn't *our* case, it's Dutch Elder's. And, he's being buried this afternoon."

Rafe Buenrostro and Dorson sat in their chairs looking

straight at Culley Donovan. This wasn't for them; they knew. Hauer looked at the floor; Molden was looking out the window, but he was paying attention, nonetheless. Culley didn't embarrass him or even try to; he was merely pointing out the way things were; the way things worked *out*; this was their *business*; this was what they did for a living.

"Coffee for everybody, Sam."

"Coming up."

"Rafe, it's your meeting. Give us all you got."

They began the meeting at nine. It lasted until ten-thirty; at that time, The Lab Man called to say that Irene Paredes was bringing some material for them.

Back at the old stand.

Culley then told Henry Dietz that he had ordered a flat-bed semi from the motor pool.

Oh?

"We found the car, Henry."

"Good. Put Young Molden on."

A surprised Culley Donovan looked at the receiver, and said: "It's *Mister* Dietz, he wants to talk to you," pointing the receiver to Joe Molden.

"Thanks." Evenly.

The Lab Man, without explanation and with no word of greeting, said: "Stay out of Grand Theft-Auto; you're too young for ulcers," and with that he hung up, leaving an astonished Joe Molden with the phone receiver in his hand.

Molden looked at the receiver again and returned it to its cradle. He then turned to Hauer; they were headed for the men's room when Dorson stopped them.

"You didn't have a chance, Joe. The guys at Auto wasted your time by not reporting Laura Sikes's car, but she didn't make it any easier, either."

They looked at Sam Dorson, and then Hauer said, "My Aunt Laurie?"

"She's your *aunt*?" Molden. Hauer nodded. Dorson walked away and shook his head.

"Hold it, Sam. Why *didn't* I have a chance?"

"She had a fender bender eight months ago; she told me so

this morning. When she got the insurance money, she went to one of the bake-paint places, and then bought the luggage rack at Sears. The car was white to begin with, and she went from that to cream."

Molden didn't say anything.

Dorson: "You win a few, you lose a few."

Hauer: "And you drink a few."

Sam laughed at the old line and said: "When this is over, remind me to buy you a beer, Joe." Molden smiled and nodded at Sam Dorson.

Rafe Buenrostro looked up. "When the Lab Man sends in his report, he'll find the original paint."

Dorson pointed to Molden and to Hauer, who, in unison, yelled out: "Right!"

It was a unit again.

Friday afternoon.
The two bank shot.

23

Jehu Malacara glanced at his watch: 4:20 p.m. Terry Mac-Michaels, his friend from Treasury, had called to apologize for the delay: he and two men from IRS wouldn't be at Jehu's office until 4:30. Sorry.

A thank you meeting for good citizenship and cooperation, and so on. And so forth.

They must have a warehouse full of evidence by now, he decided.

He then buzzed for his secretary, Esther Bewley, to stop in for a moment. She came in through the side door.

"Esther, hold all calls during the meeting, will you? Except from Rafe, if he should call; I'm in for him."

"But nobody else, right?"

Nod. And then, "You terribly busy in there?"

A shake of the head.

"Take a seat." She did, and then he said, "You know what this second meeting with Terry Mac's about?"

"No." She looked at the troubled face, and said: "I know Mr. MacMichaels when I see him 'cause he's a friend of yours."

Nod from Jehu. "Well, it'll be out in the papers tomorrow evening, I suppose.

"Some Valley dope dealers bribed a number of tellers and junior and not-so-junior bank officers from the other two banks in town. They had thousands, maybe over half a million, Esther, in fives, tens, and twenties; street money that they wanted converted to hundred-dollar bills. Large transactions, okay? To do this, the dope guys—Irma Williger calls them that—set up two tellers at the drive-in windows to handle their cash: from two tellers to four to six, and from one supervisor to three and more . . . in each bank, Esther.

Then, they had an exclusive window. Plus, the tellers didn't fill out the forms recording transactions of over five-thousand dollars, and they were paid not to do so as well as to take in the money and set up special accounts for them. Special accounts, Esther; meaning the banks didn't know the money was there. In the bank.

"One of the dope guys then borrowed one-hundred thousand dollars from Texas State, no collateral and certainly no permission from anybody. It was repaid, but the tellers each got color TV sets for their help and one of the bank officers got a car which he then gave to his wife.

"They did other things, too, and I'm just hitting on a couple of examples, but you get the idea."

Nod.

He looked at her, and she said: "Thanks for telling me, Jehu." Trust and respect. And then: "You know me, Jehu."

"Since high school, Esther."

She giggled and became embarrassed by her inability to suppress the lifelong habit.

"And the meeting? Want me to do the same as always when Mr. MacMichaels shows up?"

"That's right; no announcement of any kind. He comes in with those people, and you walk 'em right in here."

"Will do."

"Thanks, Esther."

She stepped out, stuck her head in the door again, and said: "The phone's on; let me get it."

She put the transfer through and Terry MacMichaels's voice came over the receiver: "Being delayed a bit, here. Are you in a hurry, old chum?"

"Nah; I've been sitting here thinking about the people in the other banks. It's a damn shame, but . . ."

"Yeh; hold on a minute, will you?"

Jehu could hear two separate openings and closings of doors from wherever Terry Mac was calling him.

"Jehu, they went deeper and wider than our friends Tarver and Williger suspected it would. Twelve arrests are called for."

"Hnh."

"The IRS guys are busy writing a newspaper release huffing and puffing their work in this. It's designed to scare the citizenry."

"In the land of the free, Terry Mac."

"Know what you mean . . . and I know how you feel, too. They'll, ah, they'll be finished here in a little while, and when they do, we'll just pop on over. How's that sound?"

"I'll be waiting. Ah . . ."

"Yeah?"

"Aw, it's nothing; I'll see you when I see you."

I'm going to have to ask Terry Mac how Irma and Bessie learned of the doings at their banks, he reminded himself. He and Noddy and E.B. Cooke had continued to monitor their junior officers and the other employees for the past three months.

"I hate it," he said aloud. He had said it back then, and he was saying it now.

He then thought about Irma Williger and Bessie Tarver; it must have been nerve-wracking for them; and gutsy, too. He decided to act on something he'd thought about for the past month: he'd hire the two as soon as there was an opening, and there would be. The changeover for those low-paying jobs was fairly rapid.

They'd be happier over here, too, he decided. And no damned uniforms, either.

The phone. It was Esther.

Irene Paredes had called to say that Leah, her cousin from Jonesville, was driving in that afternoon; could Jehu call Rafe and see if he were available for doubling on Saturday?

Jehu Malacara picked up the phone and called his cousin at Homicide. The desk man picked up the phone at mid-ring, and said:

"Sergeant Contreras, Homicide Desk."

"Yes. May I speak with Lieutenant Buenrostro, please?"

"There's no one here, sir; I mean, the detectives are all at the funeral. For Mr. Elder, the prosecutor."

"I see; could I leave a message, then?"

"Yessir, I'm ready."

"Sergeant, tell him to call Jehu Malacara at the Klail First."

The desk sergeant listened carefully and thought: "I know *him*."

Contreras: "I sure will, ah, are you the Vice President at the Klail First?"

"Yes."

"Well, sir, you worked with my brother-in-law in the financing of a car wash business. His name's Oscar Garza."

Must be a slow day at Homicide, thought Jehu.

"Yes; I remember him; he wanted to operate a branch in Bascom, didn't he?"

"Yes*sir*, and he's doing pretty good at it."

"I'm glad to hear it." And he was, too.

"Sergeant, could you give Lt. Buenrostro an additional phone number, please? It's four-five-three, oh-three-seven-two."

"Seven Two?"

"Right."

"Got it. I'll see he gets it."

**Friday afternoon. The uncommon banker
thinks back on his life for a moment.**

24

Jehu rang off with a thanks. He leaned back and stared at the old wide-angle photograph marking the opening of the original Klail City High School in 1921. He wondered if some of the people in the photograph were related to those bank employees, busy at work counting out dope money for their new employers.

He also thought of the employees' families; this'll probably affect two-hundred people in this town, some way or another. And, it won't stop with the bank employees, either. Some so-called friends and close neighbors are unusually fond of relaying bad news fast, if it happens to others, he said to himself.

He swiveled about and saw the face of Gen. Rufus T. Klail looking down at him. Noddy hadn't wanted *that* picture in his office, he said. No, sir. E.B. Cooke had said that the signed Picasso on *his* wall was enough, thank you; and so, as a private joke between himself and his sense of humor, Jehu had chosen the old General.

A line from O'Connor's *Edge of Sadness* came to him: "As fine a man as ever robbed the helpless." The difference was that the Irishman Carmody must have had a sense of humor in him somewhere.

The General couldn't afford a sense of humor. After all, there had to be some things that even the rich couldn't afford.

Money. A curious thing, money, he thought. Now there's something without a sense of humor. And, ninety-five percent of the people who work for it sure as hell don't know how to use it. Not fully, anyway.

And this took him to banks and then back to the employees. Hmph. Jehu Malacara cocked his head this way and that, checking for remnants of a back pain that was now in its last stages of pain after three to four weeks of a constant nag. "And I'm back at the bank," he said half-aloud.

He thought: I could walk away from here and not look back. But walking away, just like that, would arouse suspicion; oh, yes. People who walk away from jobs and from a bank job, at that, and without explanation, well!

But, he'd walked away before. From this very bank, ten years before. What a cleansing *that* turned out to be. Without meaning to, he found out who his friends were; those who had some spine (as Rafe put it) and those who didn't. It reduced the hell out of that circle of friends. But those who stayed, stayed.

He'd been twenty-six at the time. A notion of returning to the warm embrace of his alma mater; graduate school. A half-baked idea, thinking back on it.

Scandal in Klail City. Jehu Malacara left the *Bank*; capital *B*, on that. And why did he leave? Well, why do you *think*? Right! He was a damn fool to do that, wasn't he?

And now he was back; been back since '65 after three years at Austin. Twenty-nine is a hell of an age to reach maturity, some people had said. But, they didn't say it to his face.

He had walked into Noddy's bank one fine day, asked Esther to tell her boss that Jehu Malacara was out front, wanting to talk to him. The old pirate had come running, had led him into the office with a "Hullo, you sanavabitche, what are you doing in my bank?" He had poured Jehu a drink and buzzed Esther with firm instructions that he was out. To everybody.

"I want to come back to the Bank, Noddy."

The old man had smiled and then burst out laughing. "Is tomorrow morning okay with you?"

No talk of an office, of the position, or of salary. And yet, they weren't friends. Friendly, yes; and respect, too. But: Jehu thought, and thought long and sadly, too: he'd betrayed Noddy Perkins. Not his trust; his daughter. Sammie Jo Perkins. *That* had stopped in '62, and *that* secret was ten years old.

Everybody should have one secret for himself, and that one

was his.

And so, he was back. From chief loan officer to Vice President and Cashier. And no, he wouldn't look back. He'd been back for seven years, and now at age thirty-six, most of the women he'd known in his twenties were married or divorced or whatever. And their splendid mothers and fathers had forgotten, or chosen to forget, what they had said about him when he left the Bank in 1962. (The social amnesiacs, Rafe had called them; and he'd been right). There was no bitterness on Jehu's part, either; they were harmless people who had nothing better to do. (The pious shits, Rafe had also called them; and Rafe had been right, again).

Jehu looked at his watch again. He buzzed Esther: "They're running a bit late, Esther. Look, if they're not here by closing time, don't wait for them; you go on home. Just tell Tom at the door to let 'em in."

"And Mr. Perkins, Jehu?"

"He'll be back the day after tomorrow."

The phone.

"I'll get it, Jehu."

It was Terry Mac again. "Still there?"

Wearily. "What's up, Ter?"

"Are you quite ready for this? They're having their pictures *took*. Some are in the next room and others are out in the hall someplace. Is that rich?"

"From the sounds of it, I don't want to be within a mile of either bank, not with all those guns."

"Twelve cars per bank, kid. We spare no taxpayer's expense. What do you think?

"I think it's embarrassing for everybody." Shake of the head.

Terry Mac agreed. And then Jehu said: "Aw, hell, Terry, it can't be any easier for you, either, can it? I mean, we know all those guys at the banks . . ."

"Yup . . . I think it just hit me, too." Pause.

And then: "Jehu . . . I'm calling off the meeting. They were just coming over to thank you for your fine work and . . ."

"Thanks." Bland.

"Tell you what, I'll call Pats right now; she'll know what to do to cure us, okay? I'll call you back in a sec . . . who you dating now, anyway?"

"Irene Paredes. You know her; she works at the Homicide end of the Lab."

"Sure do . . . Call her up, and I'll call Pats as soon as I'm done with these shits here. We'll drink a few. How's that?"

Feeling a bit better, Jehu said: "I'll bring some Riesling."

"Riesling? Now you're talking. See you sevenish, buddy."

Irene Paredes. Probably at the funeral. No, she's not; she's back by now. He dialed.

"Homicide Lab, Pilkington."

**Friday evening. Terry MacMichaels
relates the bringing in of the
hardened tellers.**

25

The arrest scenes at the banks were worse than Jehu Malacara had imagined. With twelve cars per bank, and eighty-four guns at the ready, it was as ridiculous as it was dangerous.

Aside from the County Sheriff's people and the District Attorney's men from Grand Theft-Larceny, there was also a sizeable host from the Klail City Police Department, various deputy sheriffs from Belken County, some local constables, agents from the Texas Department of Public Safety (troopers and Texas Rangers, equally divided), and then came the Feds: U.S. Customs, U.S. Border Patrol, Drug Enforcement Agency, various agents from the F.B.I. as well as other Treasury agents in various bureaus and administrations.

The special agents from the F.B.I. were headed by their Regional chief, Russ Vannoy, and it was the F.B.I. who arrested the narcotics smugglers counting their money at their own special windows. Vannoy's personal photographer came along armed with all manner of camera equipment plus two assistants.

But this was not an F.B.I. show, by any means.

Agents from the Animal-Plant Health Inspection Service (Dept. of Agriculture) showed up to search the dopers for grass, etc. MacMichaels rolled his eyes when he got to the etc.

Now, since two of the narcotics guys were Mexican nationals, the U.S. Department of State and its Mexican twin (Relaciones Exteriores) were represented by the American consul stationed in Barrones and by the Mexican consul posted to Jonesville.

The multiple agencies having border jurisdiction, and all fed by a seemingly bottomless Federal trough, were represented at the press conference by other civil servants; all herded and delivered to the Klail High School auditorium for a briefing, debriefing, and again: etc. MacMichaels took a sip of wine. The number increased since other representatives showed up, all invited, of course:

The United States-Mexican Consultative Mechanism—
    Border Working Subgroup,
The Southwest Border Regional Committee (SWBRC),
Other members of the Department of Justice not in on the
    arrest (Immigration and Naturalization Service),
The U.S. Treasury Department's Bank Enforcement and
    Operation,
and Special observers from Alcohol, Tobacco, and Fire-
    arms.

Terry MacMichaels described how the auditorium took on an air of festivity with friends waving to friends from the sister agencies on the planning, care, and the discovery of bank irregularities. Mesdames Williger and Tarver had not been invited, of course, but MacMichaels identified some of the sister agencies who live on and off the border:

International Boundary Commission,
General Services Administration (Bridge Construction),
Department of the Interior (National Park Service *and* the
    old Bureau of Reclamation),
Department of Commerce (Economic Development
    Administration),
Department of Housing and Urban Development,
Department of Labor,
and the Department of Transportation.

The Mexican colleagues had also been invited and were just as at home as everybody else in this environment. They'd been invited as observers and, as MacMichaels quoted one of the public information officers: "To show them how things are done over here."

"As if Mexican bureaucrats," added Terry Mac, "needed instructions on how things are done anywhere."

Captain Lisandro Gómez Solís of the Public Order Section did not attend. As he told Culley Donovan the following Sunday: "I sent my brother-in-law as a Special Observer. He works for the Secretaría de Asentamiento Humano y Obras Públicas and he was right at home; man doesn't have a thing to do with his time."

The brother-in-law, as instructed, did not remain for the final show; he drove on to Jonesville and brought back twenty cartons of king-sized filter-tipped Tareytons for Gómez Solís.

As most official Valley to-dos, this one ended with a barbecue, mariachi music, and with the usual renewed pledges of friendship, cooperation, collaboration, and continued goodwill among all of the governmental agencies on both sides of the Rio Grande.

The general press was not invited to the final event of the day, deadpanned MacMichaels.

**Saturday and Sunday.
The car comes home; a look at
the partners in crime on the
weekend.**

26

It was six o'clock in the morning, and a steady drizzle covered Klail City on the Saturday following the funeral, as Culley Donovan and Henry Dietz watched some workmen unloading a cream-colored '69 Oldsmobile from the flat-bed truck. They watched in silence as the winch operator lowered the car slowly, carefully, and directly in front of the first of three carports used by Dietz and his assistants.

One of Dietz's men, Ted Pilkington, a middle-aged finger-print technician, brought some coffee for both Donovan and Dietz. The three looked on as the workmen spread some long, dark-green plastic sheets and tacked them to the four walls of the carport. This done, Pilkington stretched the familiar yellow tape completely around the temporary shelter. He followed this by pasting the also familiar warning labels: EVIDENCE: DO NOT TOUCH: ORDER OF D.A., BELKEN COUNTY.

The drizzle was the soft kind, the seeping-into-the-ground kind; and Dietz complained that it was too chilly for an October drizzle. It wasn't, but most Valleyites complained since October also meant the end of the ninety-five degree weather which was more to their liking.

The drizzle wasn't expected to last more than a day or so, but the heat of the previous day had disappeared abruptly late Friday night when the second weak norther of the season descended on the Valley that last weekend of October, 1972.

The car landed as softly as a large cream-colored balloon, and Dietz lifted his chin in the workmen's direction; with that, the chains were removed, gathered, and secured tightly across the flat bed. The winch operator walked toward the group and asked: "Who signs for this?"

Dietz pointed to himself, and the winch operator indicated where he was to sign; the workmen were already inside the cab and looked impatiently as Dietz was busily signing six separate vouchers for the winch operator, for the flat bed truck, and for the overtime pay chits. The men in the cab were hungry, and one of them tapped the horn lightly.

The winch operator didn't bother to turn around; instead he looked at the men holding the coffee cups, and said: "I knew Dutch Elder." He hesitated a bit, but went on: "A kid brother of mine got into a scrape about two years ago."

He stopped again to look at them, and then he added: "Elder recommended probation for him; since then, my kid brother's been working for County Parks and Recreation because Elder went ahead and put in a good word for him. The kid's doing okay for himself there. You know what I'm saying?"

THe horn sounded again, more insistent this time; the winch operator threw another glance at the men holding the coffee cups before heading for the truck again.

Dietz turned to Ted Pilkington: "Put Irene Paredes on prints with you this morning." Pilkington looked at his clip board, made a notation, and walked inside the building.

The Lab Man wiped some of the drizzle off his glasses and said, "We'll have this car done to a tee for you by Monday morning. Everybody's working this weekend. Chili Morgan's more than half-done on the bodies and Ben Pardue'll complete his and Morgan's report by tomorrow night.

"It'll be on your desk by eight o'clock Monday morning."

Donovan nodded and The Lab Man then handed him three oversized brown manila envelopes.

"The photographs, Culley. We've a hundred and ten of 'em for you. You go ahead and keep these, we have another set upstairs."

"Okay." Donovan took the envelopes and walked toward his office, as The Lab Man stared long and hard at the cream-colored car.

That same Saturday at eleven a.m., Harvey Bollinger appeared on a local television program called "The Valley in Review," and he expressed optimism in bringing the murderers to justice. Quickly.

Within thirty minutes, Al Contreras, the desk man on duty at Homicide that Saturday morning, received twenty-three congratulatory telephone calls for his role in capturing the criminals.

A dozen callers also expressed their good will and their admiration for the hard working, dedicated officers of the Belken County Patrol. Al Contreras laughed about it later, in the locker room when his shift was over. After these calls, he said, the crank calls started coming in.

As Bollinger went on to predict "a speedy solution to this latest brutal insult to Belken County morality," Rafe Buenrostro was sitting in bed watching the end of the District Attorney's seemingly interminable monologue. The woman nestled against him, Sammie Jo Perkins, raised her head slightly, turned a sleepy eye toward the television set, and mumbled: "So that's what the old lady meant when she said the law was a ass."

"You awake?" He lowered his head, kissed her on the neck, and said, "I'll go make us some coffee."

She shook her head in disagreement.

"No?"

"No. I have a much better idea: Why don't you make us some love."

"In that case," he said, "you're going to have to wait until I take off my pajamas."

"You're not wearing any."

"Ah." He reached out, kissed her eyes lightly, cupped her face and then kissed her full on the lips, as she began kicking the covers off the bed.

"Rafe."

"What?"

"Let's do it on the floor again."

He looked at her, grinned, and slid off the bed where she was waiting for him.

At noon, out in their farm house ten miles from Klail City, Effie and Sam Dorson were also in bed and working on an old *Times'* Sunday Puzzle. "What's an anagram for *demand*, Sam?"

"How many letters?"

"Come on, Sam; *what's* an anagram for *demand*?"

"Damned if I know."

"Damned! That's it! I love you, Sam Dorson."

Sam looked at his pretty wife and said, "Well I'll be damned."

Effie Dorson then threw her pencil the length of the bedroom and said, "It's no fun doing a crossword puzzle with a person who is more interested in my body than in improving my brain."

"I know exactly what you mean." Mock serious. "But, just to show you what a kind person you married, I solemnly swear to work on the puzzle just as soon as I've ravished that All-American body of yours."

"Shall we leave the shades up and give the neighbors a thrill?"

"*What* neighbors?" Laughing.

"What *shades*? Come *here*, you clever little man."

Grinning. "It's been years."

She grabbed his neck, pulled him toward her as Sam Dorson began running his hands under her back, down her legs, across and up to the top of her brown nipples. He kissed them as her hand slid between his thighs and worked upward as she began to make room for him. He kissed her again, and then he placed his hands on her hips; as he began to move forward, he said: "Damned on demand."

"Ooooo; nice boy."

By three o'clock that Saturday afternoon, the drizzle was falling less steadily and less frequently, but the chill had settled in. The uninvited guest.

Myrna Molden and Bobbie Hauer had had enough of college football for one Saturday afternoon; fun was fun, but three hours of *that* was more than they could take.

Myrna walked to the refrigerator, pulled out two cans of Lone Star beer, pop-opened them, and took them to "the boys."

"Bobbie and I," she said, "are going to Monsieur Glen's and do some window shopping. What time will *this* be over?"

Joe Molden nodded in thanks, took a sip and looked at her. "Pretty soon; it's the last five minutes of the fourth quarter. Right, Pete?"

"Yep; and then the west coast game comes on after this one; CAl goes against SC or maybe it's UCLA versus Oregon; one-a the two."

Myrna Molden raised her eyes skyward, looking perhaps, for some sort of justice from on high. Finding none, she said, "We'll see you in a couple of hours, then. What time do you want to start the fire?"

"Just a minute, Myrn . . . . Aw, shit, look at that . . . What'd you say, Myrn?"

To a child. "The fire, Joe; for the steaks."

"Seven okay?"

"*Per*fect. Come on, Bobbie." (Pissed).

Hauer went to the bathroom, left the door open, and yelled out: "Where are they now?"

"It's still third and two on the four, but there's *a break in the action*." Chortle.

Hauer: "Yeah, you and Cosell."

Molden was about to say that this was not an NFL game, but he took a sip of beer instead. Friendship.

At seven that evening, Joe Molden and Peter Hauer were watching the charcoal fire with an occasional glance at the SC-Cal game; occasional since SC was already ahead 28 to Cal's zero with some six minutes to go in the first half.

Also at seven, Effie and Sam Dorson were rising from an early snack at Lombardo's Restaurant: Saturday night was

Italian night for the Dorsons. Afterwards, a movie or a good read, and there was always the bed.

Sammie Jo Perkins, in her eleventh year of an unsuccessful marriage to Sid Boynton, turned to Rafe and said in an affected but accurate la-dee-da: "The question eternal, Rafe: do you love me?"

"Yes." Serious.

"No embellishment?"

"I love you, Sammie Jo."

"I know; and I like to hear you say it, as the high school girls say. But, I happen to love you, too. And there's another *but*: All good things must come to an end." Playful.

"Sez who?"

"Right! Sez who? But only for a while. Sid wants to go to Houston, and I'm going with him. I have to keep an eye on him, Rafe. He never learns; seven months ago he picked up another boy at Montrose and was almost kicked to death."

Rafe looked at her again, but said nothing.

"Here, give me a kiss."

After a while. "Change of subject. I *know* you love me, and I know *that* 'cause I love you . . . God! I'm thirty-seven years old, *we're* thirty-seven years old, and I'm talking like a kid."

"Some kid."

"Hold me, okay? Just hold. Nothing funny, now. And kiss me, babe. Just one more."

Quietly. "I do love you so much, Rafe, and I promise I won't make an ass of myself when I leave mañana. Just hold me. Okay?"

Kiss.

By eight o'clock Saturday evening, Culley Donovan was tired; he'd been up since five a.m. waiting for the car to come in, and from there he had gone to his office to read the folder; he was going over his notes and reading them for the fourth time.

He then drove to see Mim Elder, brought her up to date on the case and returned to his office. He had skipped lunch and worked through early dinner; he then fiddled with some old files, put these away, and walked to the men's room.

As he urinated, he looked in the mirror. A tired face. Off went the tie, the shirt, and the T shirt. He began throwing water on his face, wet his hair, and then rubbed his face and head steadily for a couple of minutes. A quick rinse and back went the T shirt, the shirt, and the tie. An automatic ritual . . . one, two, three . . . three, two, one . . .

Automatic . . . Why? he thought, why had the killers headed toward Klail City after they butchered Dutch and the other two? They had driven to the Kum-Bak, walked in, and killed three men; they had walked out, re-entered the car, and the driver headed for Klail only to stop in the middle of the road, turn around, and then drive like hell—to make up for lost time?—to Jonesville.

To the airport? Maybe they flew in and flew out? Maybe young Lindstrom didn't see what he *thought* he saw; it happens. The others could've gotten out of the car into another one and then driven in *that* car and sent the driver to Jonesville. One man, not four . . . no, no, no, at that point we weren't looking for them, or for anybody; they had nothing to fear. At that point, we didn't know a thing.

All right, why had the driver turned right? Automatically? It's the natural turn. Okay. If the guy's a pro, he'd be on his toes, and . . . no, no, no. I'll give him credit for brains, but maybe he's a bit slow upstairs.

Why not?

Maybe—and then he stopped—"I'm a hell of a lot more tired than I realized," he humphed.

Ah, yes: speculation plus conjecture equals bullshit, so says that great and well-known phrasemaker of the western world, Culley Donovan. He laughed at himself, walked out of the bathroom into his office, and out to the main hall. He slapped Art Benavides, the relief desk man, and said, "So long, Art; see you mañana 'r Monday."

The desk sergeant's jaw dropped; surprised to the point of shock by the Captain's unfamiliar familiarity.

Culley had parked in Bollinger's spot; he smiled and then wound up laughing as he remembered Barb Colunga's little coup. He was in a happy mood as he headed home.

Tomorrow night, since they were now on a case, he and Rafe Buenrostro and Sam Dorson would meet with Lee Gómez Solís at the Lone Star Restaurant; this was Barrones' best, and it was owned by the Gómez Solís family. Good food, good brandy, and damned good friends; he thought of Corinne, his wife, as he pulled into the driveway of the empty house.

Four years a widower, and he wasn't used to it. What, for instance, did Rafe Buenrostro do on his weekends? Well, he loved to fish and hunt, but was that all he did? Donovan didn't know.

At first, he probably worked as I'm working now: to death. Hmph. What did Rafe Buenrostro do on his weekends?

Donovan opened the door to the back porch and forgot about his friend. He flipped on the television set in the kitchen, poured himself two jiggers of gin, crushed a dozen ice cubes, set the glass in the freezer, and went upstairs to shower.

He'd finished *The Pickwick Papers* the week before and was now deciding between *Our Mutual Friend* and *Dombey and Son*; he picked the latter, glanced at the TV set, flipped it off, picked up his gin drink and went to the living room couch.

He read less than fifteen pages, left the drink three-quarters full, and dropped off to sleep.

Sunday morning.

It was cool and drizzly again, and Sammie Jo Perkins had burned the toast for the third time. She gave it up as a bad job and jumped into bed to the waiting Rafe Buenrostro.

"I've got a great idea for a diet book, R.B. Wanna hear it?" Without waiting for an answer, she said:

"Chapter One. Take one healthy male to bed on Friday, suppress eating for the weekend, exercise regularly and vigorously, and *you'll be amazed* at the weight reduction.

"This offer will not be repeated, and this product is not sold at any store. Just send . . ."

Rafe Buenrostro laughed with her, sat up, rested his elbows on a pillow and asked: "And what about the rest of the book?"

"Ah. And you may well ask. Chapters Two through Ten— it's a big book—are all the same as Chapter One. Nine-point, plenty of space between the words and the letters and between the lines.

"Continuity is the secret, my boy," laughing and reaching down between his legs. "Oh, oh, the doctor better have a look at *that* little fella."

Rafe sniffed the air and said: "What's that?"

"Oh, the cook burned the toast again. What *shall* we do with her?"

Rafe rested his hand lightly atop Sammie Jo's navel, moved his hand down to the thickening red hair at the point of the Vee. "Well, we'll just have to get her out of the kitchen."

"Out of the kitchen and into the bed."

Rafe Buenrostro turned around, put his feet on the cool floor, and Sammie Jo asked, "And *where* do you think you're going, Lieutenant?"

"Brush my teeth."

"Oh *no* you don't; get back in here."

"Chapter One, is it?"

"You're damn tootin'."

The partners in crime meet and dine at the Lone Star Restaurant in Barrones, Tamaulipas.

27

Sunday night; eight o'clock. Rafe Buenrostro, Dorson and Donovan and Lisandro Gómez Solís have finished their charcoal-broiled venison plates. Servando Camarillo, a sprightly seventy-two year old waiter is standing some twenty feet away, arms folded; his two youngest sons stand slightly behind him and to his right.

According to Gómez Solís, Camarillo had worked for Lisandro Gómez Solís's father, don Aureliano, for the first thirty years of Camarillo's life; he began as a stable boy at age ten. For the past thirty-two years, he had made himself into a first-class waiter, a taster and connoisseur of fairly good and inexpensive Mexican wine, and had raised four daughters, all married to Texas Mexicans living on the northern bank of the river.

When his first wife died, Camarillo remarried a woman twenty-five years younger, and the nineteen year old twins standing behind him now were in their second year as waiters; they'd bussed for three, apprentice cooked for two, and then served their first year of waiting with their father at going-away parties, weddings, anniversaries, baptisms, reunions, and private dinners such as the one that Sunday night.

When Servando Camarillo waited at Gómez Solís's table— and it *was* his table, brought from home—Servando Camarillo waited on no one else. Age and rank, then, did accord certain privileges, and the management, in the form of Felipe Segundo Gómez Solís, didn't give a damn about service for others when his older brother showed up. It was not too frequent, alas, since Lisandro was an incurable workaholic, reflected Felipe Segundo. To be head of "La sección especial de la policía estatal del orden público," one had to be a workaholic.

Felipe Segundo walked up to Servando Camarillo and asked: "How's the *flan* tonight?"

"Así, así," and then in English: "so, so." A Spanish word play meaning tasteless, insipid. A useful word, *soso*.

The younger Gómez Solís nodded. "What do you suggest?"

"The peaches and pears were brought in this morning from Saltillo. *Lindísima fruta*, Felipín." Felipe Segundo put his arm around the old man and said, "Felipín: I'm thirty-two years old, and I'll always be that to you, won't I, old friend?" Camarillo gently pushed him away as Felipe Segundo nodded to Servando Camarillo's sons, and walked into the kitchen to look at those delicious *duraznos* and *peras* from Saltillo.

Also at eight o'clock that evening, Effie Dorson, Cora Dietz, Barb Colunga, and Mim Elder were sitting down to their Sunday night bridge session.

Mim Elder had prepared some snacks which all present swore looked scrumptious and of which all present swore to limit themselves to one each.

They didn't.

It was a fine night for bridge; the nasty weather was still around outside, and fine friends inside. And, every now and then, a hoot and a laugh as one or the other celebrated Barb Colunga's coup in getting Harv Bollinger out of town Friday afternoon.

This was Mim's first weekend as a widow, and she couldn't help wondering about what lay ahead for a fifty-one year old woman. A fifty-one year old grandmother. She looked around, decided that this was not the time to think about that and said: "Two diamonds. Partner."

"Now, now, no *partner*, no sighs, no signals," said Cora Dietz.

Barb laughed and it became infectious. This wasn't for Mim Elder's benefit, either; this was the way *they* played bridge.

The four men at the Lone Star were in for a longish night.

It was business, and it was visiting as well; a fine, old Valley custom, on both banks of the River. Newcomers chafed, but they either succumbed to the habit or they didn't succeed. Life *is* short and serious business can be, must be, conducted civilly. Civility also means taking one's time in eating or in listening or in the telling of a story; tonight's story (business) was deadly. But, all of them knew the rules. And, since they didn't meet as often as they would have liked, they did meet for these Sunday dinners when the Homicide Squad needed all the help it could get on matters where the northern and southern banks of the Rio Grande were concerned.

Lisandro Gómez Solís, too, did not, would not, hesitate to ask for help. A civil arrangement.

There had been several cases recently to serve as examples of cooperation, and the most recent of all had been during the Christmas season of 1971, the celebrated Peggy MacDougall case.

One week after she confessed—gloated, actually—how she had hacked up her husband, "My Norman," and with the evidence clearly against her, she dropped from sight and forfeited the full ten percent of her $100,000 bond.

She was gone before the day was over. Her lawyers, Jesse Maldonado and Curtis McIlhenny, had promised Judge O. Loren Ewald that their client would abide by the terms of her release, and now they had to face Judge Ewald on the day of the trial.

No one won with Ewald: the State, the defense; no one. After a public reaming-out in front of colleagues, a *harrumph*, and an incoherent lecture on morality, responsibility, and law and order, Ewald led the procession to his chambers. It wasn't a pretty picture there, either.

But, Peggy Mack had been found. She had holed up at La Quinta Medrano, in the heart of Barrones' business district; who would look for her there, right?

One of Gómez Solís's agents did; a forty-one year old policewoman had received the tip, reported it to her boss, and within an hour or two, the policewoman was dressed as a maid and keeping an eye on Peggy Mack.

The policewoman also gave Gómez Solís and Donovan's Homicide Squad a headstart: Peggy Mack had booked a flight on American from Jonesville to Mexico City, and she was due to leave the next day, a Wednesday.

After this, it was a matter for the Belken County Homicide Squad to wait around the airport for Peggy Mack to show up; a simple affair, then. But it wasn't.

For one thing, the flight was delayed out of Jonesville by some creeping Gulf fog which refused to go away. For another, there was a fight at the bar: The reporters and photographers from the Jonesville Herald and the Klail City Enterprise-News had become irritable and somewhat drunk after the six-hour delay. (Harvey Bollinger had informed—if not exactly invited, he said later—the reporters to witness the arrest by "his homicide squad.")

When a waitress refused the reporters further service, one of them followed her to the bar; he then pushed her, she spilled some drinks on a customer, and the bar customer then punched out the reporter. The other members of the Fourth Estate wobbled over to the rescue of their fallen comrade; this brought out the airport security guards who had a hard time getting into the bar in the first place: the door was jammed with passengers and onlookers who wanted to see what *that* was all about.

This allowed Peggy MacDougall to sneak into the now empty waiting room, down the ramp leading to the aircraft, and to board it with no trouble whatsoever.

Rafe Buenrostro and Sam Dorson, however, had spotted her and saw her walk past the guards and into the ramp. They talked it over with Donovan, and the three of them waited five minutes for Peggy Mack to find a seat or whatever.

Rafe then talked with Harry Biggs of airport security who ordered the waiting room and the gate closed. A general announcement requested all waiting passengers in the lobby to please transfer to gate six; the flight would be taking off shortly, they were told. This appeased them somewhat, but the put-upon passengers had nothing to do but to follow orders, and so they went on to gate six.

This done, Rafe, followed by Sam Dorson and Culley Donovan, entered the aircraft in search of Peggy Mac-Dougall. The aircraft commander had been in contact with Harry Biggs and continued to reassure the passengers that they'd be on the apron shortly and on into the strip in less than ten minutes; in the meantime, he said, why not enjoy a free drink on the house? This was followed by wild cheers from the crowd and by groans from the women working on the flight.

When questioned if she'd seen a six-foot blonde woman enter the plane five minutes before, a harried flying waitress motioned with her head and said, "Some big broad got in the john, just now."

With Donovan and Dorson standing in the galley, backs to the rear toilets, Rafe stood directly behind the toilets themselves. When the *Occupied* slot moved to *Vacant*, Rafe Buenrostro stepped backward and with his back to MacDougall's toilet, pretended to enter the one opposite. He turned around, nodded to the six-foot one-inch Peggy Mack, and she moved out to her a seat. At this moment, with her back toward Rafe and walking away, Donovan and Dorson moved in and each one grabbed an arm as Rafe Buenrostro took her by the hair, yanked it backward and said: "You're under arrest. Move it!" Hoarsely.

How goddammed dramatic, he thought. Still, this was business, and they led her out of the aircraft. As they did so and through the ramp and on out the gate, some bystanders saw three men escorting a woman passenger who was apparently in need of help. "Must have fainted," someone said. Poor thing.

A Belken County Police emergency unit was waiting outside and two good-sized male nurses took Peggy Mack inside and strapped her to one of the cots. She had passed out, and it was later determined (The Lab Man) that Peggy Mack had taken six valium tablets shortly before boarding the plane. This explained the ease of the arrest, why she had gone along peacefully, dreamily almost, as she waved and smiled at a grim-faced child sitting in a crowded waiting room.

The Peggy Mack capture was one of the most recent examples of the tacit, informal, north-south bank cooperation. It could be that the mayor of Jonesville and the alcalde of Barrones would not have approved, but then, they didn't need to know, either.

**Captain Lisandro Gómez Solís
builds a case for Culley Donovan.**

28

"Culley told me you've found the car."

Rafe Buenrostro and Dorson gave a nod, and Gómez Solís then said, "A fine birthday gift is what I call it."

Dorson was the first to speak up: "And whose birthday is that ?"

"Why, Culley's, of course. Yesterday: the 28th of October. St. Simon the Apostle, right?"

Culley Peter Donovan was as surprised as anyone. "I'll be darned," he said. "It sure was, you guys. My fifty-fifth."

"You didn't *remember*, Cull?" Dorson, surprised.

"Guess not; I was in the office yesterday until around five or six waiting for the car, and as it was, I didn't leave till eight or nine that night."

And then: "Thanks, Lee." With this, Gómez Solís pushed a smallish box toward him.

Rafe Buenrostro and Dorson first looked at the two old friends and then watched with curiosity as Culley Donovan began to unwrap the present slowly and carefully. Gómez Solís raised his eyebrows only slightly and Servando Camarillo's two sons walked up, guitars in hand, and they began to sing the "feliz cumpleaños" song; and then, the more traditional King David's song, "las mañanitas," reserved, usually, for early morning serenades.

The songs over, Servando Camarillo brought out a bottle of brandy, the snifters, and then he shooed his boys away. The old man closed the door to this semi-private room and made it completely private. He then sat at a table near the door, lit up a strong Delicado, poured himself a cup of coffee, and began to read a local newspaper.

When Culley Donovan had undone the ribbon and opened the small box, he discovered a key, a brass key. Old, but certainly serviceable, from the looks of it.

Gómez Solís smiled at him and explained: "Years ago, my father-in-law gave Estela and me a ninety-hectare piece of land on our wedding day. The key's for a hunting lodge, Culley; it's located a kilometer from the main gate. It isn't much, but it's clean, and the caretaker and his wife come by once a week to look it over, check for leaks, etcetera.

"Estela suggested we give you one of the keys for your birthday. It's private, isolated, and you now have the third key to the place."

Culley Donovan looked at the key and was obviously as touched by the thoughtfulness as by the generosity of his old friend. The most he could say was, "Thanks, Lee. It's a treasure; thanks."

But this was also a business meeting, and now, close to nine o'clock, Dorson pulled his chair back and said: "Be right back." He was on his way to call Effie Dorson who reminded him she was staying over with Mim that night; not to worry, it'd been pre-planned. And bye.

The Captain of the Orden Público section leaned back and picked up a leather case standing next to a floor-to-ceiling lamp pole. He then reached in his pocket, produced a key, and with it opened the leather bag.

"Notes," he said.

The three Belken County officers sat both relaxed and expectant in the easy atmosphere of Gómez Solís's special room.

"When Young Hauer saw the pictures of the dead men, I also showed him a glossy of Práxedes Zaragoza sitting between two women in some nightclub or other.

"I then told him that El Barco Zaragoza was angry; I might have misled your man there. Unintentionally, but unavoidable: my informants in the Victoria Prison had told me Zaragoza was angry-mad, and I inferred from that, that he, El Barco, had already heard about the incident at the Kum-Bak."

Rafe Buenrostro: "Was there time for him to have heard? I mean, Peter Hauer was here . . ." And then, "Yes. Sorry."

Nod from Gómez Solís. "And Zaragoza was angry, but not

because they had been killed; it was something else."

It's always something else, thought Rafe.

"It's a longer story than we have time for here, but it goes something like this:

"About twelve years ago, when the houses of prostitution were still in town—by the Old Mill section of Barrones—and marihuana was as plentiful then as it is now, Zaragoza and his two cronies had cornered a spot of the market in the Red Zone; it was a small spot, but it was tight, and it was controlled. When the houses were moved out to the Beach Road, they took their business there.

"Nothing big; but they were comfortable."

Smile.

"Now, these three have been—had been—together since they were all kids; young kids. Zaragoza must've been eighteen to their twelve or thirteen, and he started out doing the thinking and the fighting for them.

"By the start of World War II, they had made a name for themselves. Three small-time toughs making their mark in Barrones. Becerra and Cavazos were in their late twenties, and Zaragoza thirty-something.

"They'd roll all manner of G.I.s on leave or on a weekend pass; the usual for those times. They'd strong-arm some local merchants, too, when necessary, and bought off or paid some cops here and there, and they kept their control of the marihuana trade in the Red Zone.

"As I said, nothing spectacular. By Forty-six, changes take place around here, and our three men adapt: they invest here and there, on a small scale, and then they branched out at the end of that year: they began to hire out as *guns*. Independent guns who had their own protection, and that's important. They were brutal. Another way of saying effective, right?"

Wry. "Or, maybe I should say effective which is another way of saying brutal. They were both."

He flipped a page, and another, and stopped.

"Zaragoza kept doing the thinking, making the decisions, and by the Sixties, they could all look back to over thirty years of friendship." Pause.

He looked around and said, "And then, something happened to that friendship."

He opened the leather bag again, took out an official-looking document with ribbons, two gold seals and some unreadable and indecipherable signatures in rubric.

Looking at the documents, he drew another legal-sized sheet; he read that one and returned the two documents to a brownish envelope in the leader case.

Pointing to the envelope, he said, "Depositions."

"After more than forty years of friendship, Becerra and Cavazos cross their boss and mentor; probably the only friend those two ever had. It happened three years ago, and to let you know how well we run things around here, I just got wind of it a month ago."

The irony of the "how well we run things around here" was not lost on the other men, and they all smiled and looked at each other. Happens everywhere, the knowing smiles said.

"But, I think I can build a case for you."

Hearing Culley's phrase in Gómez Solís's rich baritone brought grins to Rafe Buenrostro and Sam Dorson.

"The double cross starts—started—with two-hundred and seventy-six pounds or 120 kilos of *cocaína pura*."

"Two hun . . ." Dorson.

"And seventy-six pounds, and the age-old border question: 'How do we get it across?' "

Sam Dorson let out a long, soft whistle, and this woke up Servando Camarillo who came up to their table; Culley Donovan smiled at him, and Rafe Buenrostro explained that their friend meant no offense, had not called him.

"But is there that much cocaine in the world?" Sam Dorson.

Rafe nodded as well. "How could one group have so much? I mean, that . . . comes to fifty, sixty, seventy million dollars."

Servando Camarillo coughed slightly and asked if they needed something. Looking at the table brought negative responses except from Dorson who said, "Hay café, por favor?"

Servando Camarillo brought Dorson his fresh cup of coffee. That done, he returned to his chair and poured himself a second cup.

Gómez Solís: "Becerra and Cavazos broke their friendship with Zaragoza for 276 pounds of cocaine. A long friendship, but can you imagine the size of that load?" He looked at the floor for a moment.

"You have to keep in mind how we operate; I answer only to the *Juez de instrucción*, the Judge of Instruction, for want of a better translation. I report the major disruptions of public order, as you know: capital crimes, grand larceny, armed robbery at knife or gun point, etcetera. And *he* is the whole authority; he decides whether I have a case or not. I am an arm, an enforcer of the laws. Nothing more."

Long pause.

"I need his permission to investigate, charge, arrest, etcetera. Only *I* can ask, and only *he* can give or deny permission.

"A lot of power for two men, but there's a check and a balance. With this preamble out of the way, I'm going to present a hell of a coincidence. Laura Sikes, the same Laura Sikes of the Oldsmobile . . ." He stopped.

"What's the matter?" Gómez Solís.

"She's Hauer's aunt." Dorson, grinning.

Gómez Solís's laughter startled old man Camarillo, and the Captain had to wave him off; with his back to the wall, Gómez Solís slapped at the wall with his open hand, and a sliding door opened. One of Camarillo's sons walked in.

Without a word, he handed the Captain a bill for the dinner. Gómez Solís signed it, handed the younger man two ten-dollar bills and a twenty for his father.

He said, "You know how long it takes the state governmental bureaucracy to reimburse vouchers?"

A running joke.

"Gracias, don Lisandro." The young man walked to the front of the room, helped his father to his feet, and held the door for him and for the Captain's party.

Walking out he said: "All of our border officers, customs men, bridge personnel, inspectors, and informants report to my office daily. They cross to the northern bank of the river, visit some of the Valley towns, and return with bits and pieces of information, raw data, some hard facts, etcetera.

"Danilo Elizondo compiles the lists for me by category, but it's not important how it is done, and you already know the way I operate. I'll stop here on that.

"Now, Laura Sikes (smile) has been smuggling small amounts of marihuana for some ten to twelve years; about the time, then, that El Barco, Mr. Boat, and those two very dead henchmen came into the business."

There was some very intent listening going on as all four stood by the door of their dining room.

"She doesn't know it, of course. Has no idea, in fact. It's planted. My men and women tell me that Mrs. Sikes and several other friends play *canasta uruguaya* every Sunday afternoon."

Culley: "Canasta?"

Dorson: "In the Seventies?"

Gómez Solís smiled and nodded. "Yes; I know what you mean."

He then handed each man a bottle of brandy as a gift and went on: "Anyway, Mrs. Sikes and her friends meet once a week, and have for twenty years or more, to play canasta. Their games begin right after mass or some church service, they have a light snack, and then their six-hours of canasta at somebody's house. We're talking of anywhere from twenty to twenty-four players; or, six to eight cars a week."

Outside. The drizzle had stopped, and the Gulf breezes started to warm up Belken County once again. The four men stood on the sidewalk facing the Lone Star, and the Captain said, "You'll be able to *see* what I've been leading up to and Mrs. Sikes's part in all of this. We'll have to go across the street."

Kitty-corner from where they were standing, stood an open no-food bar: drinks and a marimba player were the entertainment there.

"There's a new marimba player in town; up from Chiapas, most likely. He plays it soft, and he knows every tune Agustín

Lara wrote and sung in every whorehouse he worked in, in Veracruz and Mexico City . . . before Agustín turned respectable and started writing that claptrap music for the tie-wearers."

Tie-wearer being Gómez Solís's term for *arriviste*.

The four men removed their coat jackets and crossed to the open bar. A waiter, who looked older than Camarillo, brought them a bottle of Courvoisier. "Brought all the way from across the street (gesture) and made this very morning." The waiter smiled. A border joke as old as he was.

Gómez Solís was smiling but not at the waggish old man's humor. He was savoring the rash of information his inform-ants had gathered, he said. He then laughed in public, but not too loudly, because *eso no se hace*; it isn't done, you know.

Someone coughed.

"The women stop playing around six or so, and after pow-dering up, I suppose, they drive to Jonesville, cross the river, and have a big Sunday dinner at my brother's restaurant. Very nice, very relaxed."

He pointed to the place where they had just left; and then he said: "They park there, in the reserved-for-customers parking. And then they leave for home, as they usually do, about ten o'clock or so. Tonight, for instance, they were out of the restaurant at 10:05"—Smile. "Young Camarillo brought the bill and the time."

"Anyway, the bill is paid, the tips counted out, and a 'We'll see you next Sunday, Philip the Second'."

Sam Dorson was smiling from ear to ear, and then burst out laughing; must be the brandy, thought Dorson.

"A lookout at the parking lot watches their cars for a fifty-cent tip, and you know how that goes. But, the lookout *was* in the employ of Zaragoza's little operation. Someone else from Zaragoza's gang would slap a two to three kilo brick under the left fender, one per car, nothing big. The brick remained firmly in place with the best epoxy your country is able to produce.

"Small potatoes: eight cars, eight bricks; six cars, six bricks. Mrs. Sikes and her friends are above suspicion—as they should be—and their cars are not stopped on either side of the river. We certainly never stopped them, we *knew* what was going on, and we kept tabs on the small stuff, which usually led us to bigger stuff, and so, we let them operate. Your side never stopped them either; but *there*; it was friendship and familiarity as longtime residents of Klail City, Belken County.

"The only times the women stopped, they did so voluntarily to pay the bridge toll or the Texas state tax on liquor. But that was it. They stopped on their own.

"That same night, one or two mules would cross the Amity Bridge—green carders, all of them—and drive to Klail City collecting their *mota* from under the fenders. As your Goethe says in Spanish, Sam: "Sin prisa, pero sin pausa.""

Dorson nodded slightly. All eyes on Gómez Solís.

"Unknowingly, then, the canasta players have been smuggling the stuff for years: fifty to fifty-three weekends a year for some ten to twelve years; and, it does come to something, doesn't it? But, it was an investment for us; we let *that* go by, kept an eye on the mules' larger operation, and went after the bigger game.

"We don't tell our friends in Vice across the river everything."

Nods.

"As you may have inferred by now, my people have the addresses of our unsuspecting smugglers, and when the Sikes car was stolen, it was reported in my office immediately.

"Who would steal it? A competitor? No. Why take the car? Take the brick and that's it. But no."

Pause.

"Brandy, anyone?"

Dorson and Donovan held their glasses up. Rafe shook his head.

"The car was stolen, and you were looking for it. And, it was all connected. A coincidence. It was absolutely crazy, but it happens. And, we've all been through that at one time or another, right?"

Grins, smiles, and nods all around.

184

"The man who stole the car last Sunday night is a Texano Mexicano; his name is José Francisco de Paula Estudillo."

"Packy Estudillo?" Rafe and Dorson, together.

"Le meme."

Dorson: "He couldn't have known."

"Agreed. A mule had already made the pick-up at the Sikes' car port. Estudillo is a car thief, nothing more."

He looked at the three of them; they knew it was going to take time; it always did. But credit where credit is due: the case was being built little by little, carefully, and, to be sure, none of the three was falling asleep.

"So, señor Estudillo cops the car and drives it to his home; Zacarías Malacara, one of Rafe's Mexican national relatives, right?, reported that Packy arose early Monday morning, drove to Bascom, and parked the car in the Klein Mart and Mall parking lot, and then left it there."

Rafe Buenrostro turned his glass upside down and waited.

"Zaragoza has been up in Victoria Prison for three years; Becerra and Cavazos have kept the business going with no one to do their thinking for them, and then they were *taken over by a new partner*. I don't know who he is, but I *do* know he exists."

Sigh from Gómez Solís. "Now, you realize that with the double cross, and El Barco's fury when he learns of the double cross, and all of this tied to those two hundred and seventy pounds of cocaine I talked about . . .

"And, I've been saying that Mrs. Sikes and her friends *had smuggled* marihuana for ten or twelve years. I also kept saying *was* or *did* or *whatever*, because last Sunday, accidentally, we discovered that the packages were smaller: in short, the last marihuana smuggling had taken place four weeks before; and, cocaine had been smuggled over for the last four shipments. Well! Smaller packages, but heavier; same procedure, but no longer small scale.

"Marihuana is grown in bulk, so what's in a brick? Right? But cocaine is something else. They made four trips with the cocaine, but since we didn't know, we let the cars go by as usual. Last Sunday, a week ago, we arrested two mules in

185

Jonesville; they were *new* to the operation . . ."

In Jonesville? It became very quiet. Mexican cops arresting somebody, *anybody*, in Texas?

"Arrested is a nice way of saying it, of course. Let's say our people drove the mules back to this country which they love so much.

"That same night, we rounded up the epoxy men, sweated them, found what was left of the cocaine, confiscated it, weighed it, did the arithmetic and came up with a total figure of two-hundred and seventy-six pounds. We have thirty pounds. Period. And, unless the rats have gotten to it, the stuff's in the Judge's safe and under guard."

The upshot of this part of Gómez Solís's story was that Becerra and Cavazos were frantic. They'd been crossing marihuana for years, and they'd got themselves a new partner when they switched to cocaine. And now, they'd been blown. To add to this, the realization that El Barco Zaragoza was being released from Victoria Prison in two-three weeks hit them full in the face.

"Their small, profitable operation had been rocking along, and then they crossed their man. And, they're on the run: they *know* we've got part of the cocaine, and now they've also got El Barco to worry about."

Rafe Buenrostro cut in, quietly but firmly: "You realize we have to report the illegal arrest, don't you?"

A shrug of the shoulders. "I agree, but this was our chance, and we took it. But you're right, you have to report it; I'll take my lumps." Pleasantly.

"Well, Zacarías Malacara was waiting for my other man to show up when he tells them of the Estudillo caper. The mules had picked up the cocaine, and *then* Estudillo stole the car. On his own, then, Zacarías Malacara decides to stay across the river, sends our other agents to report to me in the morning."

An offer of more brandy; refused gracefully.

"That Monday morning, Zacarías follows Estudillo to Bascom, to the Klein parking lot. He stays around for three hours keeping an eye on the car and on the car thief who is keeping an eye on the car as well.

"At exactly 12:05 noon, some shrimp, Zacarías's own words, picks up the car. A man in a suit is with him."

"A short guy? A shrimp?" Dorson.

"A red-faced guy. An albino; red as a shrimp, you know. *Un camarón.* The man is wearing dark-green glasses and a brown beret that'll cover the white hair I suppose. The albino drives around the block to a Gulf station, has the car checked out, and then returns it to where he picked it up.

"Zacarías follows right behind, and sees the man and his companion get out, cross the street and enter a room in the first floor at the motel. Brinkman's."

"In Bascom." Dorson said unnecessarily.

"Zacarías called in, and one of my assistants told him to come home. The report was taken and typed, a notary swore in Zacarías and took a deposition." With that, he pointed to the leather case.

It was quite a story; and now, they were up to Monday, the day before Dutch Elder was murdered.

Gómez Solís went on. "When Estudillo took the stolen car to the albino and friend, Becerra and Cavazos were in immediate danger, but they didn't know it, of course. *We* didn't know it. Besides that, the two were worried about El Barco—as they should've been—and he was due out any day now. In either case, their lives were on the line.

"They'd cut El Barco loose, and they had themselves this new partner whose identity remains a secret." Disappointment. And then: "And we've sweated a good number of people, but nothing . . ."

A shake of the head by Gómez Solís. "A dead wall. But, Zacarías can put the albino, the other man, and the car, in the motel." Brightening up. "And, he can put them there that Monday morning when Estudillo delivered the car."

Now *that's* style, thought Dorson to himself.

"As for Estudillo, he is now an accomplice; he stole a car that was later used in the commission of a capital crime. Now . . . I think you'll have your hands full proving that he knew he stole a car to be used for a capital crime . . ."

Maybe, thought Rafe Buenrostro, but at least we have the car thief; next step: who paid him? A choice there: the albino, the other man. At the least.

"That . . . that Tuesday when Dutch was killed, one of my men at the Río Rico bridge spotted them in a red Chevy pickup, made the two, and then marked the time they crossed. Becerra and Cavazos were dead seventeen minutes later; Weaver's place is on 906, and that's some ten miles from the bridge."

"The question right now," Culley broke in, "Is not so much who killed them as who set them up?"

"Yes," agreed Gómez Solís. "Two options: Zaragoza, for the double cross—though I don't think so, and the second: the new partner who, one, was afraid of Zaragoza, with good reason, and two, intended to take over a small but profitable low-risk operation . . ."

"Which wasn't a small operation any longer since the traffic was now cocaine." Sam Dorson.

"With marihuana on a larger scale." Culley.

"Quite a case," said Rafe Buenrostro, that sterling phrase-maker.

With that, Lisandro Gómez Solís, key in hand, opened the leather case, transferred a paper or two from one of the long brown envelopes and said: "Here's your second birthday present, old friend." He passed the documents on to Culley, thus signalling the end of the dinner party. They shook hands all around and left Gómez Solís at the table.

As the three men jaywalked across Aldama Avenue toward Donovan's car, they heard footsteps running toward them. Rafe Buenrostro looked up and saw Gómez Solís. He was waving at them.

"He's waving goodbye," said Sam Dorson.

"No. That's a motion for us to stop, to go see him."

"Well, let's go see what he forgot." Culley.

Gómez Solís met them halfway, in front of his brother's restaurant: "One of Servando Camarillo's sons just gave me something for you. Mrs. Sikes and her friends missed their second delivery tonight."

Smiles.

Rafe Buenrostro took the opportunity to ask: "Do you know when Práxedes Zaragoza will be released from Victoria?" Does he know? Dumb question, R.B.

"Oh, in a week or ten days. The doctors aren't sure; he *is* sixty-one years old, you know."

"I hope we get this out of the way before his release from the hospital." Rafe Buenrostro looked directly at Gómez Solís.

Sighing. "I know what you are thinking, Rafe, and you're right. He'll go on a tear and Public Order around here is going to be a joke."

All four agreed on this as Dorson took the car keys from Donovan and went on ahead to fetch the car. "You all stay here."

Gómez Solís was pointing out where Laura Sikes's car and the cars belonging to her friends usually parked. Nice, and dark enough it was; but there were no parking lot attendants that night.

"Goodnight, Lee."

"You use the key, Culley, or I'll tell my wife."

A wave of the hand.

**Art and killing, and
the art of killing.**

29

The Lab Man's reports were not marvels of style, but then, they didn't need to be. On the other hand, they were precise, on time, descriptive, and stamped with the Dietz trademark: accurate.

Rafe Buenrostro was at his desk on his second reading of the Lab Man's report on the Kum-Bak Murders; the newspapers had so baptized them. The television people, a more imaginative crew, had labelled them "The Crime of the Seventies," although the Seventies were but two years old. "Thus," said Dorson, "matching the decade's age to theirs."

The taxpayer has been sufficiently trained to admit strangers into his living room as long as there is a distance between them: sanitary napkins salesmen, constipation pill saleswomen, insurance agents, whatever. The taxpayer is also sufficiently trained to look at perfectly horrible scenes as he and his family eat their dinner as they gape at the evening news.

In the Kum-Bak murders, however, the taxpayer missed the good stuff that Tuesday afternoon. And he did so because a television producer had vomited his three-hour lunch over a cameraman and over most of the equipment being set up in the area.

He had wanted, he said, "A first-hand look at this mess." He had called it that without first having seen the mess. And what he did see had made him sick to his stomach; it also cost him the services of the cameraman for that day. So, the lone Belken County television station carried pictures of the Kum-Bak Inn, of the grounds, and of Molden's and Hauer's looks of consternation; and, the taxpayers saw the two men on the

Five o'clock News, on The Ten o'clock Report, and, to round off the day, on The News at Midnight.

The taxpayer must have wondered what the blond man with the wavy hair (Molden) and the one with black hair (Hauer) were doing walking back and forth with their hands on their hips, and apparently (if they were cops), doing very little about the traffic chaos on Farm Road 906 where a lone policeman and two civic-minded citizens (Buenrostro and Dorson) were attempting to clear up the traffic tangle.

The newspaper reporters identified Molden and Hauer as Lieutenant Buenrostro and Captain Donovan, respectively, of the District Attorney's office. The television announcer read the copy handed to him and identified the two as Lieutenant Dorson and an unidentified Federal Agent attached to the District Attorney's office.

Buenrostro burst out laughing when told of the name mixup, and thought: "It figures." He went back to reading the Lab folder. He finished the second reading and there'd be a third and fourth, if necessary. He meant to memorize the material. It was deliberate work; some went as far as to call it slow, but he was comfortable with his own procedure.

Once the case was closed, he would begin to forget the main points almost at once, and he was comfortable with this procedure as well.

As he read the preliminary report, he recalled Irene Paredes's reaction to the bloody mess. She had seen a small part of it, but that had been enough. As it was, she had seen more than the aggressive television producer.

Rafe underlined some of Dietz's notes and thought on Irene again, and on her reaction to the bloody mess on the floor, wall, and counter of Theo Weaver's country beer-joint.

The Lab Man's report had told him many things when he finished the second reading, but Irene Paredes's look of horror, anguish, and revulsion had told him much more; it was neither precise nor accurate, no, but it told a screaming truth to anyone who had looked into her eyes that day: "Stay away! Don't go in there!"

There is something antiseptic about distance. For one, a person can gaze at a painting—no matter how horrible and gruesome—provided it is far enough away in distance and in history. The scene may even be enjoyed with a certain detachment: the way one looks at the American Civil War battle scenes in those round buildings in Atlanta and Gettysburg.

Conversely, proximity is an on-hands matter, and thus the notion of Antiseptic Distance tends to be erased. A third element, familiarity, also shapes one's acceptance or rejection of that which is neither distant nor at hand.

If the distance is past history, that, too, is a further remove. If the distance is present history, the horrible war in Vietnam, for example, it's closer, true, but what one sees are moving pictures or freeze frames of pictures.

Pictures do not bring the horror as close as *the real thing*. Oh, some Vietnamese cop blows a man's head off with a .45, and it's frightful, unpleasant, and ugly. But it's a movie, a picture. It's real, and yet, it is film. And, it happened so far away, too. Add the racial origin of the people involved, and that too, is at another remove.

A village burned out by phosphorous bombs is even more horrible, of course, and one sees kids and the old folk on fire, running in the middle of some village street, with no idea why *this* is happening to *them*. But that, too, is a movie; it's real enough to the people, and they were burned and they did jump into the river to extinguish the phosphorous on their bodies and when they left the river, the phosphorous reignited on them again. But, it was so far away. We were touched, of course, but we were also detached.

A painting, because it is static, is at a still further remove, and so, no matter how vivid our imagination, a bloody battlefield scene remains at an acceptable Antiseptic Distance; and, one admires the horses' leaps and bounds, the smoke from the harmless cannon, and one walks away, satisfied to have recognized foolish Raglan's order for the suicidal charge, and then one moves on to the next magnificent antiseptic masterpiece; Waterloo, say. And so on.

Our minds again fill in what the artist, purposefully, left

out for us to fill in. But our eyes don't see it; our eyes may not agree with those of the people standing next to us, either. A thousand pictures out of one original, if seen by a thousand people.

But none of it is real. It isn't, for a closer example, a broken-down beer-joint on some Farm to Market Road with a hundred people milling about, smelling death, and enjoying the excitement, but not seeing it, as one also does not see death in a painting.

The television producer saw death, and became ill on the spot. And then, his plastic wife was horrified when her husband threw up on her freshly made broccoli and cheese casserole. And how could *he* explain to *her* that what she held in her lovely hands reminded *him* of the shit at the Kum-Bak? A picture in his mind which time would erase, but not completely.

What Irene Paredes had seen was real. And real, because there is nothing antiseptic about a fingernail attached to an index finger floating in a schooner of red beer. Or, about one brown-and-white, wing-tipped spectator shoe with blood oozing out of the still encased foot which has been severed from its ankle, which is now resting under someone's chin. Or about hair, bone, and teeth imbedded to the door of the men's toilet, and blasted there by a well-oiled shotgun in the hands of an expert firing at some stranger at short distance.

And this is what Irene Paredes saw in less than one minute, but why go on?

Ah, because she couldn't forget what she saw; bloody stumps covered with men's clothing for no reason she could think of; spent cartridges spewn on the floor and bobbing up and down like tiny brass boats between an upturned wooden table and a part of a man's body arched around it.

She had fled.

Sensibly enough, thought Buenrostro. There's nothing like proximity, he thought, to bring the truth to the folks back home; to the fat, the smug, and the well-fed. To the stay-at homes who bitch and hiss and moan about "This dreadful drug problem we now have in the Valley" (If they only knew!) and who demand, "Why doesn't the police—(The Police!)—do something about it?"

Well, he thought, we were; but it sure as hell wasn't much, he had to admit.

Irene Paredes had fled. But, he wondered, would she forget? And if—he stopped thinking; a tap on the shoulder.

"Can I have dibs on the Lab Report, Rafe?"

Hauer.

Nod.

Oh, yes; she'd forget. But not entirely.

And, he knew *that* from hands-on experience.

**Monday Morning, as promised,
the preliminary Lab Report.**

30

30 Oct. 1972

TO: C. P. Donovan. Belken County, Homicide.

FROM: H. Dietz. Belken County, Criminal Laboratory

SUBJECT: *A preliminary report* on the multiple homicide committed on 24 October 1972.

No physical evidence accompanies this *preliminary* report; no other copies are available to other County entities as per office of D.A. policy. Person (s) signing this report is (are) responsible for its confidentiality.

Original of report is in office of H. Dietz, Laboratory Director.

/s/ Henry Dietz

I.   VICTIMS

1.   Elder, Gustave Ambrose.   b. 3 Mar 1917
                                      d. 24 Oct. 1972

Property: 1. Nineteen dollars. Sixty-five cents.
           2. One Schaefer fountain-pen, brown. Initials: *GAE*.
           3. One Zippo lighter.
           4. One pack, Camel cigarettes.
           5. One two-blade pocket knife. E-Z Cut Brand.
           6. Tex. Operator's lic. No. 11761811.
           7. Amer Ex Card. (Confirmed by spouse).

8. Photographs. (Identified by spouse).
9. Insurance Card. Allstate. Expir. Date: 1 Dec 72.
10. One billfold, black.
11. Miscellaneous papers (identified by spouse).

Body Tag: GAE–1.

Personal Data: See, personnel file at Office of District Attorney. Belken County.

2. Becerra-Garibay, César.   b. 13 Mar 1918
                                          d. 24 Oct. 1972

Property: 1. Five-thousand, three-hundred twenty-two dollars. ($5,322. U.S. Cy.) Torn.
2. One cashier's check issued to deceased Becerra by Banco de Comercio, Barrones, Tamps., Mexico. Date: 20 Oct 1972. Amount: $7,000. (Moneda Nacional, Mex. Cy.) Torn.
3. One cashier's check issued to deceased Becerra by Banco Monciváis, Barrones, Tamps., Mexico. Date: 20 Oct 1972. Amount $7,000. (Moneda Nacional, Mex. Cy.) Torn.
4. Two lottery tickets. Lotería Nacional de México, Nos. 33-8888-01-16; 33-8888-01-17. Torn. Drawing date for above: 3 Nov 1972.

Body Tag: CBG–1

Personal Data: No criminal record on Belken County file.
Disposition: Information requested on 26 Oct 1972 from Texas Department of Public Safety.

3. Cavazos-de León, Andrés.   b. 18 Apr 1919
                                          d. 24 Oct 1972

Property: 1. Two-hundred dollars ($200. U.S. Cy.) Torn.
2. Seven-hundred forty-six pesos ($746. Moneda Nacional. Mex. Cy.) Torn.
3. Address book, brown, spiral. Torn in three pieces.
4. One billfold, dark-green. Torn in four pieces.
5. *Permiso de operario.* Tamaulipas. No. 676-22-959 (Driver's Lic.) Torn.
6. *Permiso comercial.* Tamaulipas No. 431-22-700. (Commercial operator's Lic.) Torn.

Body Tag: ACdL.–1

Personal Data: No criminal record on Belken County File.
Disposition: Information Requested on 26 Oct 1972 from Texas Department of Public Safety. "
Seventeen (17) Traffic Violations Outstanding. Parking meter violations. Dates to be given chronologically on Final Report. (Initialed by H.D.).

NOTES: Victims' effects tagged, identified. Being held until adjudication of case as per order of District Attorney.

/s/ C.N. Looney, Jr.
Custodian, Property Dept.

II.   FINGERPRINTS:

1.	Becerra-Garibay, César.	On premises.*
2.	Bunton, Kenneth Josiah.	On premises.*
3.	Cavazos-de León, Andrés.	On premises.*
4.	Elder, Gustave Ambrose.	On file Belken County District Attorney
5.	Schultz, John Gunther.	On premises.*
6.	Seventy-nine miscellaneous fin-	

gerprints on premises lifted. Unidentified. Request for identification of above sent to F.B.I. Regional Office, 26 Oct 1972. (*initialed by H.D.*).

* On premises includes building and motor vehicles present at scene.

/s/ T. N. Pilkington
/s/ Irene Paredes

III. (Underline one) THIS IS A Final—*Preliminary* Report.

Findings: Elder, Gustave Ambrose. Body Tag: GAE–1.

Victim died of two shotgun wounds to head. First shot removed upper-third of left-side of face and head. Second shot severed head from upper torso.

Result: Death instantaneous.

Disposition of weapon: Weapon unavailable for disposition.

Findings: Becerra-Garibay, César. Body Tag: CBG–1. Subtags: (2,3,4,5,6).
Six .230-grain bullet ammunition (g.b.a.) wounds to head. Six orifices.
Twenty .230-g.b.a. wounds to upper torso. Eighteen orifices. Two bullets lodged on leftside, rib cage. Removed.
Sixteen .230-g.b.a. wounds to lower torso. Sixteen orifices.
Nine .230-g.b.a. wounds to right arm. Seven orifices.
Two bullets lodged on wrist and elbow area. Removed.

Nine .230-g.b.a. wounds to left arm. Nine orifices.

Five .230-g.b.a. wounds to left leg. Five orifices.

Five .230-g.b.a. wounds to left ankle. Five orifices.

Results: Death instantaneous.

Left arm severed. Right hand severed. Left arm severed at elbow. Left ankle severed. Genitalia severed.

Disposition of weapon: Weapon unavailable for disposition.

Findings: Cavazos-de León, Andrés. Body Tag: ACdL-1. Sub tags: (2,3,4,5).
Seven .230-g.b.a. wounds to head. Seven orifices.

Nineteen .230-g.b.a. wounds to upper torso. Sixteen orifices. Three bullets lodged in upper thoracic region. Removed.

Eighteen .230-g.b.a. wounds to lower torso. Sixteen orifices. Two bullets lodged in groin area. Removed.

Eight .230-g.b.a. wounds to left arm. Five orifices. Three lodged in wrist, elbow, shoulder area. Removed.

Nine .230-g.b.a. wounds to right arm. Eight orifices. One bullet lodged in elbow. Not removed.

Results: Death instantaneous.

Right arm severed. Left arm severed. Left hand severed. Genitalia severed.

Disposition of weapon: Weapon unavailable for disposition.

NOTES: .230-grain bullet ammunition has a muzzle velocity of 918 feet per second. The pressure per square inch in the Thompson sub machine gun chamber is 12,470 pounds.

This laboratory tested an identical weapon using identical ammunition at 400 yards (1200 ft.). The .230-g.b.a. went through four (4) pine boards (3/4 inch thick) spaced one-inch apart. A second test with .230-g.b.a. at 400 yards (1200 ft.). also went through four (4) pine boards (3/4 inch thick) and spaced one-inch apart. Results conclusive. At Point Blank, a .230-g.b.a. will penetrate six to seven pine boards placed one-inch apart. Becerra and Cavazos were shot at Point Blank; severed parts of body attest to muzzle velocity and pounds of pressure in chamber of Thompson machine gun using .230-g.b.a. (For your information: .200-g.b.a. has a higher muzzle velocity: 945 feet per second. Faster because lighter). (Initialed by H.D.) Ammunition for Thompson sub-machine guns is the same used in the caliber .45 U.S. Automatic Service Pistol, 1911 Model. Type L drum has a 50-cartridge capacity; number of wounds received by Becerra: 68; Cavazos: 61. Type C drum magazine has a 100-cartridge capacity. Changing of drums to reload not a difficult oepration, but operator must first remove the winding key by lifting the flat spring thereon and then sliding the key off. Drum magazine must then be introduced from left side, and care should be taken in loading, etc. Statements by Bunton and Schultz, your file, attest the time spent by unknown parties at Kum-Bak was less than thirty seconds. Undersigned conclude Type C drum magazine was used by unknown parties in both homicides. Without weapons on hand, undersigned unable to ascertain which model used. Weapon may, then, be any of the following: 1921, 1923, 1926, 1927, 1927A, 1928, 1928A, 1929.

/s/ Henry Dietz, M.D.
Director
Criminal Laboratory
Belken County

/s/ B. Carney Pardue, M.D.
Associate Director

Henry Dietz had paper-clipped a personal note for Culley

Donovan:

Culley: Ask Young Mr. Hauer why the letters *L.* and *C.* were used by the manufacturers to describe the drum magazine capacity. Drive him crazy for a while.

Henry

**Young Mr. Hauer reads, with no
small amount of interest, the
file on one Packy Estudillo,
car thief.**

31

Peter Hauer had gone over Estudillo's fat file for three-and-a-half hours; a cram course in the art of stealing automobiles.

Estudillo, fifty-two years old this fall of 1972, had stolen his first car in 1932, at age twelve. His accomplice, John "Butter" Wilkins, had supplied the muscle power to crank the engine of a maroon-colored Model A Ford.

Packy, too young to have learned about fences or about transporting the car to Barrones, Tamaulipas, for profit, took the Model A for a joy ride. Unfortunately for him, it was only the third time in his young life he had driven a car, and he ran the Model A into a ditch some two miles from where he and his friend had broken into it.

At least twelve witnesses identified them, and so Packy Estudillo and his partner in crime were arrested within half an hour by a Klail City policeman.

His friend, Butter Wilkins, was eighteen years old, not sixteen as he had told the police at the time of arrest. Found guilty, he was given a three-year probated sentence.

Packy, at thirteen, was packed off to the Willett School for Boys. The judge must have decided that Packy needed seasoning. Packy survived and thrived.

Released on his fifteenth birthday, he got his first and last job (gainful employment, read Hauer) as a mechanic's apprentice at Bud Odem's Ford in Klail City. Packy Estudillo couldn't get away from cars.

At eighteen, and with Butter Wilkins again a willing companion, Packy, a better driver but still no businessman, grabbed a four-door La Salle and drove it to San Antonio; a city he had heard of but of which he knew absolutely nothing.

Luckily for them, the road from the Valley to the Alamo City, some two-hundred and eighty miles distant, is a fairly straight, unbroken stretch of road.

They were going to the zoo, he said later.

Packy and Butter parked the car at a corner of Broadway and Hildebrand (San Antonio Police Records) and then walked to the zoo a few blocks away.

Bored, they said, with watching the caged animals, Packy and his friend decided to return to the La Salle for a spot of driving. They became lost in the park and abandoned any idea of recovering their fine machine. They did, however, find a green Ford roadster parked in front of a large Baptist church near the zoo. With his friend as lookout, it didn't take Packy four minutes for a hot wire job, and they drove off. They drove northward before they realized they were on their way to Austin, the wrong way.

They turned southward and drove for some four hours; night closed in on them, and they were still some two hundred miles north of Klail City. They parked the car alongside others standing by a Tourist Court, locked it, and went to sleep in a nearby school playground.

In the morning, they counted their capital and decided to leave the roadster right where it was, and they hitchhiked down to the Valley.

At Ruffing, the northernmost town in eastern Belken County, they stole yet another Ford, abandoned it at the outskirts of Klail and walked into Pérez's Pool Hall for a very late breakfast that same evening.

An Army recruiter had spent most of the day at the pool hall and both Packy and Butter engaged him in a game of eight-ball. One thing led to another, and before the evening was over, the Non-com had paid for the games and the beer, and Packy signed up for a five-year hitch in the First Cav that year of nineteen thirty-eight.

With Packy out of the way, Butter, the source of the stories in the file, told the Klail City police that Packy had forced him to steal the very first car, and "there was nothing I could do, was there?"

The police were sympathetic and drove him to Pérez's Pool Hall and waited until Butter Wilkins volunteered, signed the enlistment papers, and stood by as he was put on a bus to Fort Ben in William Barrett.

Butter Wilkins went AWOL after three months, was brought back to his mother's house in Klail, given a suspended six-month term in the Fort Ben stockade and summarily transferred to Fort Bliss in El Paso.

Packy liked the Army, but not the horses provided by the First Cav; he behaved himself reasonably well, however, and sought a transfer to a Quartermaster unit where he drove weapons carriers, jeeps, six-bys, and was doing that and a little black-marketeering in Paris when the War ended in Europe that Spring of 1945.

Peter Hauer read on and discovered that the two friends were both discharged in mid-Summer of '45. After this, Butter married, moved to Edgerton, Texas, in the western part of Belken County. In the meantime, Packy Estudillo returned to Klail City to start a new life.

Fighting veterans of World War II, the pair of them.

Five years later, by mid-Summer of '50, Packy Estudillo was suspected, charged, and arrested, repeatedly, but ultimately not convicted, of stealing anywhere from thirty to forty cars in that period.

Ten years later, Hauer discovered, Grand Theft-Auto was now on its third file folder on Packy and placed, correctly or not, just about every other stolen car, truck, or pickup on Packy's charge sheet. No convictions, again. He was convenient, they needed an arrest, and so it went.

Trouble was, of course, *everybody* knew he was a car thief, but the year and a half at Willet School, to date, had been the only jail sentence.

Till now, said Young Mr. Hauer. Fifty-two year old Packy Estudillo was going to fall; the Olds had been used in the commission of a capital crime.

Dead certain and dead to rights, nodded Young Mr. Hauer.

He read the final entry, initialed the folder and was about to return the file to Grand Theft-Auto when he asked Sam Dorson if it were safe to do so.

Dorson frowned, was about to say he thought the question asinine, but instead he asked: "Made a list of friends, accomplices, and acquaintances; the man's kith and kin?"

"Yes." Hurt.

"Past addresses? Phone numbers? Recent doings?"

"Of course." Resentment.

"Is his present address or whereabouts given?"

"No."

"I didn't hear you, Peter."

"I said *no.*"

"Then hold on to the file; put the stuff in your desk, and *we'll* fill in that little item ourselves. You and I'll find Packy Estudillo."

"You and I?" Pleased. "We're going after him?"

Dorson smiled broadly. "Damn right, but before we go get that Willy Sutton of cars, let's make a list of his favorite bars, and preferably, those with dice games in the backrooms."

Hauer looked at his notes; there was no mention of any gambling. "He shoot craps?"

Dorson; smiling wickedly. "No; he bets with the house."

"He *is* a shit, isn't he?" laughed Peter Hauer, and he began making a list of the favorite beer joints and dice rooms of one Packy Estudillo.

Sam stayed at his desk thinking what method would be the best to grab the elusive Packy; he then looked at Peter Hauer scribbling away, and said to himself: "He'll do; but first, we'll see how he handles that old smoothie."

**In which the best laid plans
are *agleyed* by an itchy finger.**

32

The car had been washed and vacuumed professionally before it was parked and abandoned at the Jonesville airport lot. A thorough check via phone and by personal visits from Molden, Hauer, Dorson and Buenrostro to thirty-one filling stations and seven car washes in Jonesville revealed no cream-colored Olds with one, two, three, or four men who had come in for a car wash.

A blank.

The Lab Man had phoned Culley Donovan and promised that something would turn up, and that he or one of his people would find it.

Yeah sure.

But when? And, in the meantime?

In the meantime, more telephone calls and more personal visits to gun dealers. And pawnshops. And fences. And this took time, but time is the one element that policemen everywhere count on. Where the public becomes as bored as a child with its Christmas toy, the police's appetite for curiosity increases. To add to this, The Lab Man, too, relished the hard-to-harder problems that faced him and his assistants.

The Olds, scrubbed clean, as it had been found at the airport, had been brought in the flatbed to The Lab Man's garage the day before. The area, roped off by Pilkington that Saturday morning, was gone over repeatedly by the men and women who had foregone vacations, time off, and weekends to work on the Dutch Elder murder.

And then, as The Lab Man promised, the evidence revealed itself (as it usually does when it is there). It wasn't in plain sight, of course, but it *was* there. And, it was found, as usual, as a result of hard work and a little luck.

The Lab Man dialed the Homicide Desk three days after

the delivery of the Olds. Dorson was alone, working on the folder, and reading the reports submitted by Buenrostro, Hauer, and Molden after all four had met to talk about "what it was they had up to now," as Culley had requested.

A buzz.

Dorson looked at the phone; inter-office call. The Lab Man? It was.

"You sitting down?"

"What've you got, Henry?"

"A break, Sam. A stupid, ordinary break, but a break, for all that. And for us: one good, clean, clear fingerprint."

Tentative. "Anybody we know?"

"Yes, as a matter of fact. An old chum. Packy Estudillo."

Mmmmmm. We could put Packy watching the car in Bascom, and now we can put him in the car . . .

"But Packy's no gunman, Henry. I doubt if he even knows how to fire a gun."

Dietz (and Dorson could imagine the smile), "Yes, yes, and a third yes, but Irene Paredes found the print, lifted it, and then took it in those long, talented hands of her's and (triumphant) *identified*, it and some partials." (Relishing every damn syllable, thought Dorson).

"Well?"

"What I said, Sam, my boy; the print belongs to one Jose Francisco de Paula Estudillo. Oh yes, our boy is in the shit, somehow."

Dorson listened and waited for the other shoe to clump down. But, there was none.

This was the straight goods.

"Sam? You still there?"

"What?" And then, "Sorry, Henry; yeah."

"Now, Irene'll be down there in a few minutes; she should be there by now."

"Henry, thanks. As an old friend."

"Part of the job, my boy; part of the job. Bye, now."

Irene's knock came on cue. Dorson opened the door to a smiling Irene Paredes.

"Hi, Sam; my boss call you, yet?"

Wearily. "Yes."

She looked at Dorson who then spread both hands in the air and said "Kamerad."

Smile.

"I'm glad it was you who made the I.D. check."

She nodded and handed him the folder. She waited for the question she knew was coming.

Ahem. Dorson. "Where did you find this beauty, anyhow?"

She was ready. "On the inside panel of the glove box; he left some partials on two half-empty lipstick holders, three poor partials on a picture postcard addressed to Mrs. Sikes by a friend who was on a train ride to Topolobampo, and a very good partial on a rouge-pencil cartridge."

"The little darling, though, was on the inside panel. It's his, all right."

"Ah; so Packy couldn't resist a little-look see, could he?"

"Who is he, Sam?"

"A car thief, but this being the Valley, he now specializes in pickup trucks. He crosses 'em himself or he hires out a ferry. Brazen.

"But, he's no gunman, "I." Everybody can tell you that, himself included."

"But he was in the car, Sam."

A smile and a nod. "And you put him there, all right. Good piece of work, Irene."

"Thank the person who invented white powder."

"Oh?"

"Yeah; some of it spilled accidentally as I was nosing about; it fell on the inside panel. Rafe'll love that, won't he?"

"Ah, yes; and he needs a good laugh now and then."

Irene looked at him and hesitated whether or not to ask a personal question. She went ahead: "Ah, I understand you're a Roman Catholic now."

Sam nodded and said, "And I scored as a godfather, right off the bat."

"He's a lucky child."

Surprised but pleased. "That's very kind, Irene; thank you. It's a, a, a nice thing to hear."

A wink and a 'bye' and she was off to her own work.

**Packy Estudillo makes a decision and
a telephone call.**

33

Jose Francisco de Paula Estudillo was counting the cigarette butts in an oversized ceramic ashtray standing on a
nightstand. There were eighteen, and he selected three of the
longest, straightened them out very carefully, and laid them
on another nightstand to the right of his bed. No matches. He
got up, walked over to his tiny closet, patted a couple of his
coat jackets and he found a matchbook: Brinkman's Motel, it
read.

Oh, shit. It was that *dumb* job that put me where I am right
now.

He turned around, walked to the nightstand, picked up the
longest one of the cigarette butts and lit it. Back to bed.

Staring at the ceiling, he noticed that some of the paper was
beginning to come off; but, he thought, it's been like that for
four years.

He then said: "What I need is a lawyer."

And then, almost in the same breath and behind that
thought, a new one: "No; what I *need* is one a-them psychia-
trists. *That's* what I need."

"I must be crazy," he went on. "But it's my fault."

He was about to mash the cigarette and suddenly remembered where that one had come from and thought better of it.

Oh, it was easy to get the name of that goofy-lookin' red-
faced guy from the motel clerk, but whoever heard of a guy
named Vena Cava? And then? Oh, I was real smart, all right.
I asked for and got the room number. Dumb shit.

He moaned. "I'm in the shit . . ."

Another moan. "*Enmierdado; en la caca-cuacha-mierda.*

Hope eternal. "No, maybe not. A good attorney could get
me off; they've done it before. A-course it cost me some, but
still, what's a few dollars compared to time in the County

Jail? Or Huntsville. Huntsville? Jee-sus." He stopped.

He stopped talking to himself and discovered he needed to talk; he had to, or he'd explode. No, he thought, that's not right: nobody *explodes*.

"Now, a lawyer . . ." Whining. "But I don't have any money just now. And that's the *truth*."

Packy Estudillo was an excellent, a first-rate car thief. His credentials at Grand Theft-Auto attested his talents in this regard. He was, however, an inveterate gambler, and when he won, he won big; and, when he lost, he lost the same way. Right now, he was stone broke. "*Bruja*," he said, using the popular border slang for the English *broke*.

Gambling. And some sex, but he could go, and had gone for six months without a visit to any of the Valley's whorehouses, north or south bank.

New thought. "That's it! I could hide out at a whorehouse. A massage parlor, as they now call 'em here."

Another thought: "I could lay low there for a whole. Or cross over to Barrones, or go to little Control. No, not Control, it's too damn small, I'd stick out like a prick in traction . . . Barrones. Ya."

Quietly: "I got friends at some of the houses in Barrones . . ." He stopped. "Am I *crazy*?" With Becerra and Cavazos dead, I'd be killed on the spot."

He wouldn't. But, he had no way of finding that out. Given his character, Packy always listened to the last person who talked to him. In this case, himself.

"All right," he said. "The massage parlors on this side. I could lay low *there* for a while."

"No; what if some damn cop comes in for some personal business?" And the cops are already looking for me, right now. There, out in the streets. Right this very minute. Jesus."

They weren't.

And then he almost burned the tip of his thumb; "Damn butt," and he dropped it in the ash tray.

He picked the second one, and his hand shook when he saw the Brinkman matchbook.

The sky was falling on this little chicken, and his limited

brain power was draining away that morning. "And now," he said, "on top of *everything* else, I'm hungry." He yelled at the ceiling: "What am I going to do?"

He started to laugh and stopped only when he fell exhausted to the bed. "I'm going nuts! That's it. Cart me to Flora—yeah, that's where I belong . . ."

After this, he cried some more. He also curled up in the bed and closed his eyes: visions of the State Prison, and the County Jail, and out of nowhere: A Whataburger stand. "No!" he screamed out.

Had he fallen asleep? No, there's the lit cigarette butt. I've lost my notion of time, he thought. "That's it! I'm really crazy . . ." and he sobbed some more. He looked intently at his index finger and thumb and saw the smoking piece of paper and tobacco. Shit! He put it out. He then brought both feet to the floor, put his face between his hands, and rested his elbows on his knees.

"I'm imagining things. No one's looking for me; I'm not important. I'm not, really." But even he, Packy Estudillo, couldn't convince himself that he was not about to be apprehended by ten cars full of cops, each one with a bull horn and barking out: "All right, Estudillo, come out with your hands on your head, or we'll torch the place."

Would the cops really set the place on fire? "Cut it out, goddammit! I'm crazy, that's all. Crazy."

And with that he fell backward on the bed, his feet on the floor, and he fell asleep.

He awoke two hours later and immediately looked at his wrist: no watch. "What the hell?" And then he remembered; yes, the dresser. Yeah. He walked there, saw his face on the old mirror, and he saw the face of a very sick fifty-two year old car thief. He began to sob.

"I need help."

The time was ten a.m., and Packy Estudillo decided to make a telephone call; but first, a drink of something, and a cigarette.

He went to the tiny kitchen, opened the refrigerator and looked at a dried-up lemon, at a plastic spoon, at something green in a salami wrapper, at a Dixie cup which had spilled over and the chocolate contents of which had splashed on the white porcelain; and then, his eyes landed on a jug of Atmo-Spring Water.

Water? Yeah, what the hell.

He uncapped the jug very deliberately, took a drink, and noted absently that the cold water hurt his teeth. He recapped it carefully, deep in thought, and said: "Fuck it."

He went to the nightstand.

"I'm calling Dorson; I call those crazies at Auto, and I'll never see the sun again." He took out a Valley directory from under the nightstand, looked up Belken County and asked for Homicide. He placed the receiver between his neck and ear, lit the last cigarette butt as he heard a voice say:

"Sergeant Horn, County Homicide desk . . . . Hello?"

"I want to speak to Lieutenant Dorson." Relieved.

"I'll have to check. Hold on."

Check? What does he mean? Dorson'd better be working, goddammit. He's a cop, ain't he?

Dorson's voice came over the line. "This is Sam Dorson."

"Oh. Hi!"

"Lieutenant. It's me, Packy . . . . Estudillo."

Dorson looked at the receiver, he said to Hauer: "Estudillo."

Hauer picked up the phone on Rafe's desk.

"Lieutenant, this is very important."

Toward a true definition of a
desperate criminal.

34

Sam Dorson looked steadily at Peter Hauer without either looking at or seeing him at all. Dorson's mind was on Packy Estudillo.

Dorson had noted something in the car thief's voice. Hysteria? Produced by what? Some irreconcilable fear. But of what?

Packy had stolen *that* car; but, at this stage, he'd have no idea of Irene Paredes's find, or of Gómez Solís's yeoman work. And, what a mine of information that fine venison dinner had turned out to be, Sam thought.

He laughed, and Hauer looked up at him. Dorson laughed again, savoring the thought: Laura Sikes, you trusted bookkeeper, you; you're a smuggler, and you'll get the twenty-year jolt you got coming to you for smuggling pot! And for over a decade, Your Honor. Jug the old reprobate; contributing to the delinquency of canasta players!

This tidbit, though, would have to stay with Culley and Rafe. A damned shame. Still, it's more fun to know a secret than it is to tell it, right?

And then he said aloud, "What a job!"

Hauer shook his head. He thought: "Rafe Buenrostro's kind-a spooky, but he's not *crazy*."

But Dorson was gone again. Back into the world of one Packy Estudillo. Poor little runty bastard was climbing the walls and sniffing the glue off the ceiling by now . . .

"Come on, Petah," he said rather suddenly, "we're going after one of the top one-hundred most wanted men in Belken County."

On the way to the car motor pool, Dorson thought: "Poor Packy; fell in with a bad crowd when he was thirteen years old: himself. And now, at the pinnacle of his career, he calls us for help. . . . And he *needs* help."

Hauer put the folder away, ran across the motor pool, and caught up with Dorson.

"Where's your .38?," Dorson asked.

"What?"

"This." Reaching behind his back, Dorson drew out the gun in the middle of the parking lot; he pointed it skyward.

"You said that Packy . . ."

"I said nothing of the kind. I said we're picking him up. Go get it and bring some uniform who's on duty."

"For Packy Estudillo? I've *read* his file, Sam."

"Great! And, while you're at it: have the uniform call the ambulance. Now!"

"You're . . ." but Hauer stopped. *Crazy* was hardly the term for Dorson. Hauer stopped one of the uniformed patrolmen and asked him if he were available. He was. "Wait here," said Hauer. He went into the office, called the County ambulance himself and gave them the address.

A paramedic then asked:

"Should we bring oxygen?"

"Oxygen?"

"Yeah, it's procedure."

"Well, if it's procedure, why ask?" Asshole.

And then Hauer said: "Dorson was right; it's procedure to go armed when making an arrest." Peter Hauer was unusually hard on himself, and never more when he said: "Dorson may be crazy, but I'm just plain dumb."

"Where's the uniform?"

Looking back: "There he is. You know him?"

Dorson threw a glance at Hauer.

"Let's go; the skinny son-of-a-bitch is probably raving mad by now."

Packy Estudillo wasn't mad, but he did need some sleep, some liquid, and a little food. They learned later on that he was dehydrated enough for an overnight I.V. to bring him around. When Dorson and Hauer arrived at Estudillo's address, and Dorson had driven like a madman, the driver and two other paramedics were already there, arms crossed and leaning against the ambulance.

A woman paramedic motioned with her head to the ambulance and said, "He's in the rollaway cot in there. Which one of you is Dorsey?"

Hauer grinned at the *Dorsey*, and the woman mistakenly said to him, "He's been asking for you."

"The hell he has," said Dorson. "He's been asking for me; go on, open the goddam door." She pouted, but Dorson chose to ignore this. Turning to Hauer, he said: "Drive the car back, stay at the phone. I'm taking the patrolman with me. We're going to Klail-Cooke. Scoot."

Dorson turned to one of the parameds. "Is there drinking water or glucose back there?"

A shake of the head.

"Take us to Klail-Cooke, then. *Now*." He followed the patrolman and secured the double-door on the ambulance.

Sam Dorson was convinced that Packy Estudillo, desperate enough to call him, and rattled by hysteria and shock, must have known something; must have seen something; was, perhaps, trying to repress what information he had. Poor little son-of-a-bitch. . . .

Sam was angry at himself. He had missed something somewhere. He was out of step.

Packy. Hmph. Probably knew where the murderers were or had been, and, Packy was foolish enough to take chances like that; oh, he knew Packy Estudillo. He thought of Hauer's "I've read his file," and Dorson, aloud, said: "Shit."

The patrolman, a two-week rookie didn't make a sound; didn't move.

A given, said Dorson to himself: The killers are not across the River. Gómez Solís got that part between Jonesville-Barrones and Ralámpago-Río Rico sewn up; farther up the Rio, he couldn't say . . . but Dorson was sure about those twenty to twenty-five miles. Yes.

Aloud: "They're not in Klail."

The local police had checked the motels, the one downtown hotel, and the rooming houses; a shakedown of the massage parlors merely confirmed that massage parlors, like cops, worked twenty-four hours a day.

The patrolman looked at Dorson suspiciously and looked down again. Dorson didn't even know the rookie was there. Aloud: "Since they're not in Klail, that leaves Jonesville to the east and Flora, Bascom, and Edgerton to the west of Klail City."

The northernmost town in the Valley was Ruffing. But, there was a roving Customs Patrol unit there; so that was probably out.

"No, they're in the Valley some place. And on the northern bank of the River."

When he looked down, he saw Packy Estudillo looking up at him. "You're in a bad way, Packy."

Nod.

"But you're safe here."

Smile. Estudillo turned his head, sighed, closed his eyes, and went to sleep.

The patrolman who had accompanied Dorson still had no idea what he was doing there. Hauer hadn't told him.

Oh, yeah, he learned about ass-chewing detectives at the academy . . . and for God's sake stay away from those Homicide guys; they're the worst. And here he was, two weeks out of the academy and who was he with? Some maniac called Dorsey who talked to crooks, and called 'em by their first name. Shit.

What he *did* know was that that little runt down there, sleeping like a baby, needed a bath. In gasoline, preferably. And *then* with soap and water. Phew!

He looked at the detective again, straightened up and tried to look efficient.

Dorson had forgotten about Packy Estudillo and was now thinking of the conversation with Gómez Solís. He reached for his note pad, took it out, read from it, and put it back again.

Did he miss something? He needed to talk to Rafe; he got on his feet, crouched in the careening ambulance, and looked out the back windows. He then took out his service revolver, checked it, and reholstered it. The Patrolman watched him, but didn't say a word.

They rode in silence the rest of the way.

At the same time, Hauer was walking back to the Court House on his way to Homicide. He saw two men as tall as he was, headed in his direction. Hauer decided to take a chance.

"Excuse me, are you Jehu Malacara?"

Jehu replied that he was, extended his hand, and after Hauer said who he was, Jehu introduced Terry MacMichaels.

"Been looking for Rafe, have you?"

"No, as a matter of fact; is he around, though?"

Hauer said he didn't know, but they could try Homicide. MacMichaels then said, "Gotta go, Jehu. What time you and 'I' showing up?"

Jehu nodded and said, "Seven-thirty. On the nose. Give a kiss to Pats for me."

MacMichaels laughing. "The hell I will; give it to her yourself." He waved goodbye.

Jehu and Hauer walked toward the basement of the Court House, and Hauer asked: "You and Rafe are cousins, right?"

"Oh, yeah."

"Yeah, that's what I thought." And Hauer then ran out of things to say to the banker who, obviously, had other matters on his mind.

Jehu Malacara's silence was nothing personal against Hauer. He'd been talking to Treasury agents half the morning and all that afternoon, and he was drained of further conversation. It was an effort to make chit chat; it'd been a long day.

Treasury knew the rules and the regulations in banking; and so did Jehu Malacara; the difference was that he lived the Rules and Regulations; abided by them, and saw to it that they were carried out. Daily. This day's work had been tiring but necessary; happily enough, it had been devoid of the State Fair atmosphere following the bank arrests the past Friday, the picture taking and posing, and the embarrassment caused to those people in the other banks.

He was tired, that was all. At the hearing, Judge Erasmo Rivera asked his recommendation as to bail for the tellers and the other bank officers; Jehu said they were local people, they all had families, and they wouldn't go anywhere. They'd been shamed enough for a lifetime, he added. And there was the trial to consider, and eventually, to suffer through.

Judge Rivera, older than Jehu, but a long-time friend, agreed. The arraignment and charge were carried and then the judge called in the attorneys for the tellers and the junior bank officers and told them of his decision. To be released on their own recognizance. The Government did not oppose Judge Rivera's order.

Chances were very good that most would admit to a confession of judgment—plea bargaining, the press called it—or some other agreement. Jehu Malacara certainly hoped so; he was thinking not only of the tellers and junior bank officers (some of whom he knew) but also, and most of all, of their families. He tried to imagine what their kids would go through at school. He gave a brief shudder.

Bessie Tarver and Irma Williger's "narcotics guys" were in their cells upstairs; part of the Court House's fifth floor was a secured partition reserved for Federal prisoners.

Judge Rivera had said to their attorneys that their clients could afford bonds of $700,000 each. He raised his hand: "The Fifth Circuit will be happy to hear your motions, counselors; I'm not. I'm not in the position to do so."

He went on. "You do have one choice this afternoon." He smiled, too.

"You can go through that door," pointing to it, " and face from fifteen to twenty reporters from the newspapers and the television, or you can take the other door which leads to the freight elevator, and that'll put you out of the building through the prisoners' ramp."

The lawyers rushed to the second door.

Jehu Malacara, who'd been present with Terry MacMichaels during the arraignment and the good cause hearing, stayed with the judge until a deputy marshall herded the reporters and the television people out of the hallway; a fire measure, he explained.

It was at the end of the meeting that Jehu Malacara had run

into Peter Hauer. They walked into the Homicide Squad's front room; it was empty. Hauer shouldn't have, but he opened Donovan's office. It, too, was empty.

"Struck out," said Hauer lightheartedly.

Jehu Malacara was thinking of the "narcotics guys" at the moment and not at all at what Hauer said. Jehu blurted out: "I couldn't agree more," to a surprised Hauer.

With that he left the detective in the otherwise empty offices. He turned right and ran into Sergeant Al Contreras: "Ah, Mr. Malacara. We talked on the phone, remember?"

Jehu looked at the man closely and nodded. An idea. Could he use the phone? Sure. A local? Automatically.

"Fairly local; I'm calling your lab."

"Here, I'll dial it for you."

Irene Paredes herself answered the phone.

"It's Jehu."

"Well, hi, sailor."

"Pretty busy?"

"Right now I am, but we're still going out tonight, aren't we?"

Jehu sighed and said, "Let's stay over there till eleven or so . . . we can leave then, okay?"

"What do you have in mind?"

"You."

"Good! I'll pack a few things and we'll go to your place straight from Terry Mac's . . . or: we can cut out the middle-man and not go to Terry Mac's at all." She laughed as she said this and loudly enough for The Lab Man to look up at her.

Irene waved to Henry Dietz and went on: "We don't have to be there till seven, right? Why don't you come by here, at the lab. Let's say five o'clock, that's just twenty minutes from now."

"I'm calling from Homicide." Laugh.

"You bankers are all alike." Dietz looked up again. And then Irene Paredes said, "Come on up; I want you to see where *I* work . . . and I want to see you anyway. Come on."

**With Packy Estudillo in the hospital,
the world gains a gourmet.**

35

Culley Donovan had no idea if the gunmen were looking for Packy or not; he also didn't know if they were in town or not. It didn't matter. Safety was safety, and "Precaution supersedes everything else."

God, he thought, I have simply got to stop thinking like an Academy manual. Jee-sus.

A double room would do it. He was resolutely against having some uniformed policeman out there, sitting on his duff, getting familiar with the routine and the help, and then letting his guard down. No; that wouldn't do, and he didn't believe in another Academy gem, either: "The armed guard at the door is your first line of defense." Shit; there I go again . . . I must be getting tired, he thought.

There'd be policemen and patrolmen, all right, and he'd place the local help from the Klail City P.D. on each of the four entrances to Klail-Cooke; he'd have two County Patrolmen by the elevators, and two dressed as orderlies and moving about the halls of the third floor, Packy's floor.

When Bollinger first heard of the 24-hour rotation, the first thing he said was, "That's quite an expense, Culley."

Culley agreed with him wholeheartedly; this disconcerted Bollinger. Well, how long you planning to keep them there, then? *Only* as long as they are necessary, but not one minute more. Promise.

That had satisfied H.B. and more so when Culley said he apologized for taking so much of his time.

"Not at all, Cull."

Cull. Hmph.

Harvey Bollinger rang right back. "Just keep me informed, okay?"

It was the *okay* that usually weakened what position Bollinger ever tried to hold. He was forever seeking corroboration as a modus vivendi.

The day following the first afternoon and night with an I V feeder in him, Packy Estudillo had wolfed down nine meals: his three, and the rotating guards' other six.

He loved the food, he said. "Nothing like it," he told Dorson, "in the world."

"I know," said Dorson.

The County Patrolmen who worked the shifts while sharing the room with him would pass their trays to him, take his empty ones and place them on the wheeled metal table. And gladly.

Paula Simpkins, a Senior County Patrolwoman, knew something about food and enough not to eat *there*, as she called the Klail-Cooke Hospital. The day before, she said, they were served pea soup, an unclear green aspic concoction, plus another gelatin of some sort resting rather uneasily on a chard of lettuce, as well as a lumpish pie-slice of meatloaf. The dessert, said Paula Simpkins, consisted of a powdery oatmeal cookie.

Today's salad, she went on, was the piëce de resistance: half a canned peach with cottage cheese, and I'd like to see that cottage burned to the ground, she sniffed. And, she asked, guess what was in the peach's pit cavity?

A green maraschino cherry, that's what. She also said that if she didn't know, and she did, where her mother-in-law was at that moment, she was ready to swear that the woman had hired on as a nutritionist there, at the K-C. Packy loved it, Simpkins said, dispirited and unwilling to make a fight of it.

When another officer was about to describe what *he* passed up, Simpkins raised her hand and said she didn't want to hear about it and walked out.

In search of her mother-in-law, Dorson thought when he heard Simpkins's story.

On the morning of the third day, Packy Estudillo was holding court; he had decided, he said, to reform. In some ways, he amended. To begin with, he beamed at them, he was giving up smoking. "The doctors here say it's bad for your health."

Ah.

"That's commendable." Dorson.

Packy grinned and although he didn't quite understand what Lieutenant Dorson had meant, he, Packy Estudillo, knew it was a sincere compliment. Dorson was his friend; Dorson had saved his life.

The others in attendance were Joe Molden, Donovan, and Rafe Buenrostro.

Donovan kicked it off and said, "Tell us what you know." An original beginning, he thought.

He had received a registered letter, the first one in his life, he marveled; there was a note in it, unsigned, and a one-hundred dollar bill clipped to the note. A nice card; good, hard paper, too. The note said they needed . . ."

Donovan: "*They* needed?"

"Lemme think . . . You're right: *was* needed. A four-door car was needed—*se necesitaba.*"

"Passive voice, imperfect tense," thought Rafe Buenrostro. Very good, Packy.

The letter was in Spanish.

They needed a four-door, late model car, in the very best of shape. And, if this arrangement worked out, he'd have other jobs at the same rate, or higher. Higher was underlined. He remembered *that.*

Buenrostro was about to interrupt and then stopped himself.

On the back of the note, Packy went on, was the address where he was to deliver the car: Klein's Parking Lot, by Klein's Mart and Mall. The Bascom Klein, Packy explained, not the Edgerton Klein.

"When did you sign for the registered letter?" Donovan.

"Ah, a Saturday."

"How can you be so sure?"

Cause I stole the car on the following day: Sunday. I stole it at night, right here in Klail. I drove it to Bascom bright and early Monday morning, left it at the Klein Mart and Mall in Bascom."

Donovan. "And then what did you do?"

Meaning: And what was it that caused your mental collapse?

Giggle. "I had searched the car, but it was clean. Nothing; I even pulled off the backseat, and *it* was clean underneath; oh, a few women's pins, bobbie's, and a Kleenex or two, but nothing else. Clean."

"Did you open the glove box?" Buenrostro; a test of continued probity, that was all.

"How did you know that? Is that a guess?"

They looked at him but said nothing. Molden's eyes were going from one speaker to the other. Fascinated at watching the team work a willing witness, but noting the tests and probes for reliability, all the same.

"Oh, okay; I did, but there wasn't anything there, either, 'cept some funny-looking pencils with no erasers on 'em."

Dorson thought: "The man is fifty-two years old, and he doesn't know an eyebrow pencil from a No. 2 Mirado. Amazing."

Packy's answer had the ring of truth to it, too. But more than that, he couldn't fake the surprise of holding a pencil that was at least half metal and to no purpose that he could see.

"And I left them there, okay?"

"And then?"

He nodded and said, "I waited around."

"Where?" Donovan.

"There, in Bascom, at Klein's parking lot; well, no, not *there*, where they could see me, but half a block from there, from where I could still see the car pretty good. And I saw him," he added.

Silence.

The same thought came to the three detectives: Zacarías Malacara, Gómez Solís's man who'd been tailing Packy since he stole the Sikes's car.

"I saw a albino."

"What?" All three together, and they looked at each other.

"A albino. You know, *cara colorada como un camarón*. A shrimp. And dark glasses, 'cause the sun hurts their eyes. Well, this one had on a flat hat. No, not a hat, but it was flat. Not even hat-like; no, not a hat, but it *was* flat. Like a cap, but with no bill. It's flat, okay? And another guy with the shrimp, the albino."

Ah. Gómez Solís mentioned a shrimp.

The detectives looked at each other and nodded.

"Well, the shrimp, he has a buddy with him; they get in the car, and I said, 'Oh, shit, 'n me with no wheels.' I remember saying that, but guess what happened?"

"What?" Molden, excited.

And all four looked at him.

"Go on." Rafe Buenrostro, gently.

"They . . . the shrimp, 'cause he got in the driver's seat, drove around the block. That's all, around the block; they stop at a gas station for a while, and then they drive off. A bit fast . . . not too fast. But good driving. I can tell about good driving. Right?

"Well, they parked it back where *I* left it. Yeah. And then, they, ah, got out, and walked across the street to a motel. Right there."

"That's Brinkman's stinkhole." Dorson.

"Yes, it is, how'd you know that?"

"And what did you do?" Donovan.

"Well, I—giggle—I crossed the street, counted the doors on the first floor, 'cause that's where they went to. Room 107." Giggle. Packy Estudillo's hands began to shake a bit.

"Both went in together? The same room?" Molden.

"Together, yeah. Who're you?" To Molden.

"And then what did you do?" Donovan.

Smiling and very proud of himself: "I went to the clerk there, and told him I was looking for a cousin of mine; an albino."

He looked at the detectives for approval.

"Go on." Rafe, quietly, but firmly.

"Well, he said, the clerk did, you come to the right place.

225

A talkative little fart, the clerk. I come to the right place 'cause my cousin was in Room 107 with his three buddies; been there for two days, and were planning to stay a week or so. Maybe longer."

Sunday. Monday. Tuesday, the day of the murder. And this was Wednesday. A week later. The identical idea came to at least three of the detectives. And if the four men had decided to leave early?

And if they hadn't?

"Go on." Rafe Buenrostro; no emotion.

"Well, that's it, the clerk said Mr. Cava was there, and then I said that that wasn't my cousin's name. Well, he's a albino, ain't he? And I said *yes*, but that's not my cousin's name.

"Well, I was just trying to get the hell away from there, but the clerk he said, 'Look, read it yourself. There's his name: Vena Cava'."

With that, Rafe Buenrostro and Sam Dorson burst out laughing; Donovan tried to suppress a smile, but failed.

Vena Cava, indeed.

Packy Estudillo squinted his eyes at Molden who stared back at the little wreck of a man.

"Well, anyways, I said that wasn't my cousin's name, 'n I got out a-there, and . . ."

Packy's eyes became glazed and he fell back as he began to shake. He swallowed hard, and said: "I need a drink. Anything. Anybody got a cigarette? A drink? Ah, ah, ah, who's got a smoke?"

Culley Donovan reached for his pocket and came up empty. Naturally. He made a face.

"Just a minute." Rafe Buenrostro. "Look at me; over here. Look at me."

But Packy had shut his eyes. He wouldn't look at anyone; he had remembered something. Rafe Buenrostro thought he knew, and that's why he wanted the car thief's attention. Packy turned and opened his eyes; he focused on Dorson and said: "*You're* my friend, Lieutenant, you saved my life, remember?"

"It's okay, Packy. Listen to Lieutenant Buenrostro, he's got

226

something to say to you."

Buenrostro: "Was there someone watching the motel?"

Packy: "No. No. He . . ."

Buenrostro: "He was watching . . ."

Packy: "Yes; I, ah, I, I thought I saw him at K-K-Klein's lot, and then I thought I saw him on the sidewalk, later. By the motel. And then . . ."

Buenrostro: "He was a cop." Rafe Buenrostro omitted saying that the man Packy saw was Gómez Solís's man, Zacarías Malacara. He had followed Packy from Laura Sikes's house to Packy's late Sunday night and then on to Bascom, the next day.

"A c-c-cop, you say. You sure?"

"Go on." Donovan gently.

Breathing back to normal.

"Well, this cop got into his car and drove off. I didn't see him again. I thought he was after *me*; and I didn't know he was one of you . . .

"God, I was scared; I had no way back to Klail so I stole a car." Giggle. "I stole a Japanese car. Reliable."

Settling down now.

"So I went to my room, 'n I stayed there. I guess I was there a month. It was awful."

Molden was about to say something, but he saw Dorson's hand waving him away.

Rafe: "Did the cop talk to you?"

Packy: "No. Yes . . . please . . ."

"Go on." Donovan.

"That's it; those guys were there . . . they're the ones who killed the Dutchman, not then, but . . . I mean Mr. Elder."

Dorson suddenly: "You hungry?"

"Yeah! Boy, there's something about the food in this place I really like."

Packy's eyes were beginning to glaze again. Donovan rapped on the door and a sergeant named Gabriel Cantú walked in as the others walked out.

From Estudillo's hospital room, Donovan led his small army to the coffee shop on the first floor. A waitress all in white: shoes, cap, apron, dress, and hose came over and heard Dorson's order for two coffees; but, she thought, there's four guys.

"Two?" She repeated. "You sure?"

They didn't hear her, she turned around and bumped Molden with her hip. "Sorry," he muttered; she said it was o——kay, and then wiggled off.

"Rafe, you'll take Joe and Pete to Brinkman's. Sam and I'll be at the office; when you call, whether those guys are there or not, I'm calling Lee Gómez and ask him to come over. An unofficial visit."

Buenrostro left the table after the word *visit*; they'd have to drive to the Court House to pick up Hauer and then drive the nine miles to Bascom. He looked back, half-way to the door.

Molden made a face, got up, and ran to catch up with Rafe Buenrostro who was reaching in his pocket for the car keys.

"Where the other guys go? The one with wavy hair?" She meant Molden.

"What two guys? Those coffees are for us. Come on, put 'em down." Dorson.

"You, ah, want cream and sugar to go with that?" What a *strange* person, she thought, looking at Dorson.

Donovan tasted his and winced; Dorson finished his cup in one gulp, looked at Donovan and shook his head. "This guy learned to make coffee at the Jonesville airport," he gasped.

As it was, the waitress charged for four coffees. There was no time to argue, and Dorson paid.

The four guests at Brinkman's Motel.

36

From nine o'clock that Wednesday morning until four that afternoon, Felix Leal had been trying, unsuccessfully, to reach Dr. Juan José Olivares on the telephone. And although Bascom, Texas is less than twenty miles from Soliseño, Tamaulipas, it's an international call.

The local telephone company, a very independent outfit called the Belken-Dellis Telephone Company (We Cover the Valley) was on strike; and, had been on strike for ten days.

Management was doing the best it could 'under the circumstances' to provide service, not recognizing, of course, that it itself had caused 'the circumstances.' At the same time, the *Klail City Enterprise-News* and the *Jonesville Herald* were enjoying the increases in revenues and they printed the two-page ads from the B & D Telephone Co. decrying the strike, and the one-page ads listing the grievances by the linemen and operators. The newspaper editorials attacked the unions for insensitivity for cutting off the Valley from the rest of The Free World. Washington, of course, was on tinterhooks.

Calls to Soliseño, then, were chancy.

Felix Leal had not heard of the strike, did not know of the stalled negotiations, and, come to that, had only one subject on his mind at the time: money. A payment in full that was due him and his three partners sitting around the room: Alejandro Garza, Zenobio Treviño, and the driver of the abandoned Oldsmobile, Enrique Salinas, a lifelong friend.

So far, Dr. Olivares had paid them two-hundred and fifty dollars each as a down payment plus one-hundred dollars to hire a reliable car-thief. Dr. Olivares had recommended a man named José Francisco de Paula Estudillo who was supposed to have been a professional in his line of work as they were in theirs.

Leal had no complaints on the selection of Estudillo: it had been a good car, and *they* had taken good care of it, too. They had had it waxed and washed, and the only inconvenience to the owner, he thought, had been the four days the car turned up missing.

They had used it that Tuesday for less than five hours; Estudillo had left the car in a shopping mall in Bascom where it stood with two-hundred others parked there in the October sun. On Tuesday, Leal had gone with Enrique Salinas again to pick it up; two suited-up businessmen getting into their car. They picked up their associates at Brinkman's Hotel and from there, they drove directly to the *cantinita* nine miles east of Klail City; a total distance, then, of some nineteen to twenty miles to Weaver's Kum-Bak. A funny name, thought Leal. Salinas had said that they weren't English words. Czech, maybe. Czech! What did Salinas know?

Dr. Olivares had assured them that Práxedes Zaragoza, El Barco, would be with his two partners, Becerra and Cavazos at that little place. El Barco had been due out on the previous Sunday, and the three were to meet and talk on the American side; it was safer. A sort of reunion and business party, then. They'd be riding in a red Chevy pick-up truck.

When Leal and the other three pulled into the Kum-Bak's parking lot, they saw two pick-ups: one was the red Chevy with Texas plates, the other was a beat-up pick-up with oversized tires.

Leal and his crew were to go in the place, run everybody else out, and then, and only then, were they to execute El Barco and the other two.

Descriptions were given over the telephone, understood, and then Leal discussed the simple operation with the other three.

Felix Leal picked up the phone again; the tone came on as before, he dialed '9' again, reached the outside line, dialed the 803 Mexico Area Code, dialed the number to Olivares's home, corresponding clicks to the number dialed, pause, and then a ringing on the other side of the River, three rings, and then the phone line died on him. Again, "Chingada madre!" The other three didn't bother to look up. Leal had been trying for hours to make that call, and it was always the same: the tone, the dialing of the number 9, the area code, the phone number, the clicks, the ringing, and then the dead line. He swore again.

The driver, Enrique Salinas, was asleep on the floor; he had gone to bed as early as ten o'clock on the previous night; and there he was: thirteen hours later, fast asleep.

"It isn't natural," Leal had once said to him, but Salinas had shrugged his shoulders and replied: "It is for me." And that was the end of the subject; they'd known each other, had worked with each other, for close to thirty years. There had been some minor interruptions in their association due to several brief but harsh stays in the tough jails of northern Mexico.

Both had wives and children and money enough for relative comforts; the conjugal visits were a help. They were also life savers, too, since the homosexual community behind bars was dangerous to life as well as to limb. Prison humor, he said to himself.

The other two companions, they were hardly friends, Alejandro Garza and Zenobio Treviño were also norteño types; northern Mexicans. And, from the last names of all four men, it would have been safe to assume that they were natives to any three of the northern Mexican states: Tamaulipas, Nuevo León, or Coahuila.

Neither Leal nor Salinas knew the other two; they didn't know them well or otherwise. They had been highly recommended, however, and after Leal had seen them in action eight days ago, he agreed with the recommendation: good, efficient, and not given to talk.

Garza, who spoke no English whatsoever, spent his time reading American adventure stories available in Spanish. After having finished one, he'd go back and underline entire pages; he moved his lips to read. But, he was a fast reader, nevertheless. Zenobio Treviño spent his time doing pushups, and when not doing that, he spent the day and night cleaning, oiling, disassembling and assembling the sub-machine guns. After this, it was back to the exercises. He spoke no English, either, but he had memorized the names in English of each of the parts.

Felix Leal, for his part, was a shotgun man; he had sawed it off personally in his garage workshop in Barrones, and he kept the twin-barrel gun in as good condition as Zenobio did both Thompsons.

Tools of the trade.

When Leal was not shooting people for a living, he worked as a bartender at the Camelia Bar in Barrones. It was a workingman's place with full kitchen service to supply the workers with *botana*, the free and salt-laden appetizers.

The extra salt was intended to make one drink a second beer which then made the drinker hungrier, and the *botana* came. One ate, got thirsty again, and one ordered another beer, and so it went.

Undaunted by his past failures to reach Dr. Olivares for a resolution of some sort, Felix Leal once again had dialed '9' and he heard the familiar clicks and the ringing. The line rang six times before it went dead.

Leal had not met Dr. Olivares, and he was sure that the others hadn't either. The money came as he had said it would, so that much was certain. He'd worked for people he knew and that didn't mean he trusted them either. But, as long as he pays, that's it.

"Puta madre." The variation in the language again didn't cause any of the others to look up. He pursed his lips, locked his hands behind his neck, and stared at the ceiling.

Now, he thought, it could be a bad connection; *that* I would understand. But, what if Olivares picks up the phone, and then hangs up; he can then say he answered the phone but that there was nobody at the other end when he did so. That the line would go dead on him, and that was that.

Leal thought, 'He would never double cross me. Us. I'd kill him. But, if I did that, then I wouldn't get my money, and I couldn't pay these two off. But, what if——he stopped. He didn't want to think of *that*; no.

He kicked off his shoes and immediately went back to his *what ifs*. What if these two think I'm stalling them? What if they think that Olivares and I are . . .

No. That's crazy.

But what if Olivares—Está tratando de hacerme un cuatro—is trying to do a number on me? Yes. Engañarme como a un chino— diddle me like a Chinaman does his wife, from behind?

He wouldn't do that. I'd *kill* him, but then if I killed him— back to that again. He scratched his left ear, worked his fingernails into his balding head, and looked at 'those two.' The contract had been done by phone; how the good Doctor got his telephone number only the Doctor knew. But, the money was in dollars, and it got there on time. And, the car thief had been a good one. Hmph. He looked at the other two again.

Garza was reading one of his paperbacks, and now Treviño had tied a handkerchief around his eyes and was assembling both sub-machine guns at the same time.

Felix Leal made up his mind not to worry about Dr. Juan José Olivares; his chief worry, really, was the immediate money: the motel cost them $20 a night, they had rented it by the week, and the clerk agreed that if they guaranteed him those seven days, he'd only charge them $17.50 a night, and the eighth day, today, would then be a free one, if they wanted it.

Food was another concern, but this expense was up to each one, and 'those two' could do what they wanted about that.

Bascom, a town of seven-thousand, and thus slightly smaller than Klail City, had any number of small cafes. The only condition was that the four could not eat together nor in the same place at the same time. This, too, worked well and to everyone's satisfaction.

But, *when* was the money to be delivered to them?

Dr. Olivares had given strict orders not to call on him at home on weekends. Fair enough. This was a weekday, and how else could they reach him, but by telephone? They couldn't very well go across to Tamaulipas so soon—no, not with that son-of-a-bitch Gómez Solís having every damned cop, farmer, cow, pig, and chicken working for him. No; it was at least a three-week wait, and *then* they'd all go home.

And, it wasn't a matter of leaving 'those two' on their own. Ha! They were 'big city boys' from Monterrey, but they didn't know either the northern or southern banks of the Rio Grande. Babes in the woods was what *they* were. And Leal's mind went on along on these lines.

"Chin—gao." Softly. He craned his neck over the side of the bed and saw Salinas starting on his fourteenth hour of sleep. "No; no es natural."

From thoughts on Dr. Olivares, he switched to the *cantina* and saw the red Chevy pick-up, the two wide-eyed farmers that flew the hell out of there, and he saw Becerra and Cavazos. He knew of them, but then, *everybody* knew of them; what surprised him was Práxedes Zaragoza, El Barco; the Boat. He had heard he was the stocky type. Hmph. But, Zaragoza had been inside for some two or three years, and that was enough to cause anyone to lose a few pounds.

And he was dressed kind-a funny, too. Baggy pants and that silly green and yellow baseball cap. Probably lost his mind in prison; syphilis'll do that to you, he'd heard. Teach *him* to go around fucking those whoreboys at Victoria; those guys are liable to give you almost anything. Like the plague, or worse. Yeah.

What did he yell at me? "Oye?" Listen? No, no listening from you Señor Boat; see if your *mother* can hear this, and Leal again saw the first barrel tear one side of the man's head off; the second barrel made the decapitation complete.

The trick, of course, was not to have any blood spatter on you, 'cause the blood's there, ready to leap out of your skin, boom! like that. The trick was in the distance—not too far or that shot'd spread, and not too close or you'd get a bath—the distance, then, and the holding of the gun: it had to be level, not butt down, barrel up. Straight, level, even; that's how El Barco had left the world, arms outstretched, like a cop directing traffic.

But the damned noise! Not from his shotgun, no! It was those infernal machine guns. El Barco's men, well, they were in pieces and the noise bouncing all over the place, and those holes that cut right through the wall. That wood be any drier, and the whole place would've caught on fire. God, they're noisy. El Barco's men were in pieces; and the larger parts of them seemed to bounce around and bump against each other as Garza and Treviño were walking out, their backs to what was left of the dead men.

Outside, they had walked calmly enough; the two partners opened the back doors, and he got in front. None of them said a word on the way to Jonesville.

But! That damn Salinas must have been asleep at the wheel 'cause we drove toward Klail City a good piece before he stopped and turned right there in the middle of the highway. And then I had to slow him down to fifty or sixty or he'd-a driven into the middle of Jonesville doing a hundred miles a damn hour.

I guess he's getting old; hell, we're *all* getting old, except for 'esos dos'—'those two over there.'

The phone!

Leal counted the number of rings and picked up the telephone on the seventh ring. He shook the sleeping Enrique Salinas and motioned to the other two who were staring at the telephone. "La lana," he said. The wherewithal.

A voice said, "Habla el señor Reséndez?"

"Es usted el señor Hernández?"

They were in business.

Dr. Olivares would deliver the money in person. Room 107. Yes. Fine. There was a phone strike, had Leal tried to reach him? Yes? Ah. Well, he was calling from Jonesville, and he'd be in Bascom at seven; seven-thirty at the latest.

**The helpful clerk at
Brinkman's Motel.**

37

Rafe Buenrostro stood at the counter and pressed the service buzzer. It was a small lobby; its main decoration consisted of a miniature plastic palm tree in a half-barrel; unknown guests through the years used the barrel as an ash tray, and no one had bothered to empty it since then.

Hauer stared at the barrel and turned his head away from the smell. Molden stared at the plastic miniature as they waited for the clerk to show up.

Hauer leaned over and looked at some old-looking candy boxes inside the glass counter. "I think they sell used candy here." Molden grunted at this and sat on an overstuffed chair; he jumped up almost immediately.

Hauer turned around. "What happened?"

"Damn spring or something pinched me. Did it tear my trouser leg in the back, Pete?"

"Nah." Without looking.

The clerk came running in from some backroom somewhere, saw Rafe Buenrostro at the counter, smiled, and asked: "You three gentlemen together? Y-all want a room?"

Rafe laid his gold badge and I.D. on the counter; the clerk nodded and asked: "Yessir?"

"We need your help."

Hauer and Molden looked at each other: *Help?*

"Yes*sir*, Captain."

Rafe Buenrostro smiled at him and said, "Are the four men at 107 in or are they out for the day?"

"Mr. Cava's party?" The clerk then looked at the clock. "They're in. They usually don't go out till seven; seven-thirty, the latest."

"What can you tell me about telephone calls there?"

"Well, what with the strike 'n all, you know, they got one

today, and one last week."

"Where from?"

"Met-sico; both of 'em. From Soliseño; you know where that is?"

"Sure, that's . . ." Molden stopped.

"Good. When'd they get the first call?"

"Let's see . . . ah, it's on the daily charge sheet. You see, I only . . ."

"Excuse me, is it handy?"

"Sure thing; it's right around here, be with you in a sec. Okay?"

The door opened, and the clerk turned his back to the counter. An underweight brunette walked in; she looked them over and said: "Okay, who wants the blow job?"

Molden and Hauer turned around to say something, when Rafe Buenrostro coughed; she looked at him.

"We're the police." He smiled.

"Oh." She hesitated, and then said: "C-c-can I go?"

Rafe nodded and Molden and Hauer stared at him. Is he crazy? That's solicitation, for Christ's sakes!

She closed the door, swung her beaded purse and headed for Klein's Mart and Mall across the way.

Now *that's* a good lay, she said to herself.

Rafe Buenrostro looked at the clerk who then said: "The ledger, yes. Just a sec."

Rafe turned to Molden and Hauer and said, "Pete, cross over and get into that paint store; you can see the room from there. Joe, you—" he stopped. "Off you go, Pete."

"Right."

"Joe, there's a bench across the driveway over there. Leave your jacket here, and take off your tie; got a quarter for the *Enterprise*?"

A shake of the head.

"Here; get the paper, roll up your sleeves——" to the clerk: "Be right with you." When Rafe turned around, Molden was already on his way, paper in hand. The coat and tie were on the dangerous easy chair.

"Here you are, Captain. Last week; from Soliseño,

Tamalee-Pass, from a Mr. Nieves Hern-and-ees to a Mari-Ano Res-endez."

"No others then?"

"Well, yes; the one today, but that's it."

Nieves Hernández and Mari—Buenrostro stopped at mid-thought. Crooks with a sense of humor, and history; using the names of the legendary smugglers—*contrabandistas*—and borderers, too, from the choice of *those* two names.

"Any other calls, incoming or outgoing?"

"One-oh-seven? No sir."

"You're here every day?"

"Yep."

"*Every* day?"

" 'fraid so, sir." Hurt.

"No other calls, then. And both from Soliseño?"

Nod.

"All incoming calls written down?"

"Yessir, and outgoing, too."

"Outgoing?"

"Oh, yessir. The United States government requires it."

Since when, wondered Rafe Buenrostro. Some Federal shits have got this poor guy working for 'em. Hmph. Bastards want to bug, bug! but get yourself a court order, first.

He smiled at the clerk. The clerk relaxed and asked if there were anything else.

"Sure is; could I borrow your phone?"

"Local? . . . I mean, sure, go ahead."

Rafe said, "I'm calling Klail City; that's a toll free, isn't it?" Friendly.

"Oh, sure. You, ah, you want me to leave you to speak in private, Captain?"

Rafe Buenrostro shook his head and then said good-naturedly: "I'm a lieutenant."

"Ah."

Rafe dialed and waited until someone put Donovan on the line. "They're here, Culley. They go out around seven; seven-thirty." Looking at the clerk who was nodding in agreement.

Dorson on the other line: "And they're *there*?"

"Oh, yeh."

Culley: "We can have the men in Bascom and ready to go in . . . in forty-five minutes. Top. That'll get us there a good two hours plus before they're scheduled to leave. Where do they go? To eat or something?"

The clerk mouthed: *to eat.*

And then: "Rafe, where are the children?"

"Got'em outside, watching the place."

"Go——od. Sam and I'll get on the phone here and call the Bascom P.D., and whatever else we need to do. Looks like we're in business, son. See ya."

"Yeah."

Rafe asked the clerk for the phone number for the paint store across the street; he called there and told Peter Hauer to remain indoors. Rafe then looked across the motel parking lot and glanced at Joe Molden who was reading the Bascom paper.

The police were ready and assembled as Culley Donovan had said they would be: forty-five minutes, give or take a few. The unmarked police cars stood some two blocks away and there was no possible way of detecting them: no guns drawn, no sirens blaring. The cars blended in with the others at Klein's Mart and Mall.

Donovan: "There doesn't have to be any shooting if the three of us handle this."

"Let's do it." Dorson.

"Sam and I'll get the door." Rafe Buenrostro.

"Good." Culley then rattled on the window pane and asked a patrolman to come in.

"I'll take your shotgun, Guzmán."

"It's loaded and ready to fire, Captain."

Donovan glanced at him; he wondered if the kid would fire it, given the chance. "You never know," thought Culley Donovan.

The clerk was enjoying himself. Dorson sneaked a look at him and thought: "Probably thinks he's watching some damned TV cop show . . ."

Things were ready to go, but Rafe Buenrostro showed no

signs of moving. Instead, he stared at Klein's Mart and Mall; the parking lot. He seemed to have made up his mind about something.

"One thing, Culley . . . that mysterious partner Gómez Solís mentioned made a couple of calls here, but no idea when he's coming over to see these people or if he is."

Both Dorson and Donovan looked at him.

"It's my guess that the mysterious partner he told us about hired these four here to get rid of Becerra and Cavazos at Weaver's Kum-Bak . . ."

"And with them out of the way, he's in the clear; that it?" Culley Donovan looked intently at his young partner who was looking straight back at him.

Buenrostro then said, "The mysterious partner is the only man that Gómez Solís hasn't been able to nail for us." And then offhandedly: "By the way, have you heard from Gómez lately?"

"No; his office said he was mediating something between the governor and the mayor of Barrones."

Donovan then turned to the clerk and said, "Unplug all the telephone lines. Now."

"Yessir."

"Is there a backroom somewhere around here?"

"Yessir."

"We don't want you to get hurt."

"Oh, no sir. I mean, yessir."

Culley Donovan nodded and said, "You've been a big help." Smiling. "Go on, now."

"It's got no windows, sir; 'n I sleep behind this counter." Pointing.

Nod from Donovan; he looked at his wrist watch. "Let's slow down just a bit. *They're* here, and we've got two hours before they go out to eat or whatever."

"What's on your mind, Cull?" Dorson.

"Something Rafe said just now."

Dorson. "You mean about Gómez Solís not being able to name—nail—that guy for us?"

"Yeah." Donovan, quietly and almost to himself. And then,

"Why did you say that, Rafe?"

"Well, Gómez Solís himself said he'd known about the plants on the women's cars for years, but he laughed it off as small potatoes."

"So?" Dorson.

"Well, he also gave us Packy's name, and he knew exactly when Becerra and Cavazos were going to be at the Kum-Bak. He told us so himself."

Dorson, the devil's advocate. "He's got a world of informants, partner."

"We all know he's got informants, and he credits them for much of his information. But, he's in a position for a lot of information himself. A hell of a lot. It's like an orchestrated score almost. Like some of those cheap lyrics where one can guess what the next word or line is going to be."

"You got more, don't you, Rafe?" Dorson.

"And you've been thinking about this for some time I imagine?" Donovan, slowly, evenly, but interested above all else.

The clerk went to a corner, sat down, and listened. Who were they talking about? Some friend from Met-sico? He pointed his right ear at them.

Cough. Rafe: "Well, if Práxedes Zaragoza dies . . . ," he stopped. And then, "If he dies of an appendectomy at Victoria Prison, the mysterious partner is home free because both Becerra and Cavazos are also out of the way, dead . . ."

"And the 276 pounds of *cocaína pura* will then belong to one man." Dorson.

"It's *what ifs*, Sam . . . yeah; but, look, let's send Gabe Cantú to Barrones right now. He's got friends. *Informantes*. He'll find out if the mayor and governor are there and if Gómez Solís is meeting with them. It's not every day that the governor comes to the border."

"You're a suspicious so-and-so." Culley, laughing. "But I'll go along for now."

Donovan rattled the pane again, and Guzmán came in: "Put those things away somewhere," pointing to the walkie-talkies.

"Yessir."

"Bring Sergeant Cantú over here."

"Yessir."

Culley Donovan looked at Rafe and said, "Anything else?"

Rafe Buenrostro nodded. The Zaragoza-Becerra-Cavazos friendship, he thought. Partners and friends in crime . . . blown away by 276 pounds of cocaine . . . No. There wasn't that much cocaine in the world for those three to betray each other. Not those three. Those were *old* guys; they knew each other, their wives, kids, families . . . and then a new partner comes and that friendship is blown away, just like that?

Bullshit.

Rafe: "Lisandro Gómez Solís knew Laura Sikes's car had been stolen before we did. Remember how much he enjoyed the irony of the coincidence? Huaer's aunt and all that? It appealed to his sense of humor, and that's how we were meant to take it."

"And we did." Dorson.

"How hard was it for him to manufacture the coincidence?" Rafe continued looking at Klein's parking lot. "And then there's Zacarías Malacara scaring Packy Estudillo . . . it might not have been Zacarías at all. . . . He could have used Zacarías's name and mine too . . . it blinded me for a while."

Donovan. "You don't think Packy told us the truth, then?"

"Oh, I think he did. He left some things out because he had no idea how much he knew. But Packy came to us, and he did so because he cracked up.

"A lot of *what ifs*, Rafe." Dorson, again.

A knock at the door and Sgt. Gabe Cantú came in. Culley Donovan took him aside and then led him out the door. He turned to Rafe:

"What set it off, Rafe?"

"The phone calls here, I guess. The calls came from Soliseño; it's there on the clerk's record. . . . Who owns the village of Soliseño? The ranch? The *municipio*, practically? They do, the Solíses . . ."

"But we have no solid proof, do we?" Dorson.

Rafe looked at Donovan first and then at Sam Dorson. "No, no proof . . . and first things first . . . room one-oh-seven."

Culley Donovan looked out the grimy screen door in the little office and saw Joe Molden in shirt sleeves having a good read or pretending to. Donovan stepped out to the sidewalk, took out his handkerchief and blew his nose; a patrolman came up to him.

Everyone was to stay inside the cars, and that included any local constable or cop roaming by. They were to wait for a second signal from Captain Donovan.

Just then, an almost new, long, four-door Ford station wagon with Mexican plates was making its way up a Bascom side street, some four blocks from Brinkman's Motel. On the front and back of the station wagon's plates were two identical emblems denoting the man's profession as a medical doctor. He wasn't one, but if passers-by made that assumption, they were welcomed to their mistake.

The driver of the car was a man in his fifties; seated next to him was a youngish, smartly-dressed Mexicana who turned and smiled to three little boys playing in the back of the wagon.

The man took in the numerous Belken County patrol cars and local police cars as well as the activity looming up on both sides of the street two blocks away from Brinkman's.

He then looked down at a black medical bag which held some ten-thousand dollars in it. He patted it and drove past Brinkman's looking straight ahead. To a passer-by he was a wealthy Mexican shopper in for a spot of buying at Klein's Mart and Mall.

It now appeared as if he wouldn't have to pay the money to Félix Leal and his men for services rendered. He had had every intention of doing so, but what with all the police milling about . . . no, he thought, that wouldn't do. At all. He smiled again: he was ten thousand to the good, and with those four out of the way. . . .

The man placed his right hand on the woman's thigh, squeezed it, and said: "It's such a lovely day, isn't it?"

She smiled back. He then suggested that they do some shopping at that new place, over in Klail City, just nine miles away; the Park Fair Mall, he explained. It was a surprise he'd been saving up for her, he said. He'd buy the boys some additions to their five-engine Lionel train collection. Yes, that's what he'd do. As for her, well, she should look around; pick out something nice. Something?

"I mean that in the plural, María de la Luz: *some things*." He smiled.

"After that," he went on, "we'll see how our new Texas home is coming along. I think we'll like living out on the island part of the time, don't you?"

She smiled again. She was very happy; and, she thought, very fortunate to have married this older man, this considerate man.

As the man completed the right turn leading to the Klail City highway, Rafe Buenrostro and Sam Dorson with their service revolvers drawn, waited for a signal from Donovan. When it came, they kicked in the paper-thin door to Room 107 at the Brinkman Motel. They knocked the door off at the hinges cleanly and completely, and right behind them, Culley Donovan jumped expertly between them, shotgun in hand. Dramatic as hell, Rafe thought, as he looked around the room.

Two of the men in the room raised their hands quickly, automatically; the third man, blindfolded, held some machine gun parts in his hand. The fourth man, a red-faced, woolly-headed man, woke up, rubbed his eyes, and asked what the noise was all about.

**The partners in crime
send the Elder case to the
D.A.'s Office.**

38

Young Mr. Hauer took charge of the Homicide Squad's files, as he said, "to bring order to a world of chaos." The next year, 1973, would see computer tapes replacing the handwritten files. "And that," said Hauer, "will really screw 'em up again. Irretrievably." A computerized pun, he said, to no one's benefit.

That same morning, a week after the arrest at the Brinkman, Culley Donovan learned officially what he had heard from Sgt. Gabe Cantú: Captain Lisandro Gómez Solís had put in for a medical retirement and was off on vacation somewhere in the state of Guanajuato. Donovan shook his head slightly and said to himself that Guanajuato was too far south for Lee Gómez; did not, then, believe the official version.

At the same time, the Lone Star Restaurant in Barrones was sold off as well, and Felipe Segundo Gómez Solís was said to be managing the family's interests in the coastal port of Tampico, Tamaulipas. Two-hundred and seventy-six pounds of cocaine, reflected Donovan, go a long way.

Hauer then knocked on Culley's door to say he'd gone to the Lab as Donovan had instructed; Hauer returned to his desk, but he was restless. He had worked on a "big case," and had been "part of the team." He wanted, needed, to *do* something. He was antsy all day, and that night, he read bedtime stories to four-year-old Peter Hauer III until the little tyke dropped off exhausted. This done, he walked into The Master Bedroom, as the building contractor had proudly called it, and told Bobbie Hauer to take off "Those godly-damned hair rollers." Surprised, but pleased at the same time, Bobbie Hauer jumped out of bed, ran to check on Petey

Three and returned to their bedroom.

She began climbing out of some new shortie pajamas (they *worked*, she told herself) and smiled at Peter Hauer who was sitting in bed, waiting for her.

For his part, Joe Molden visited his uncle, Sheriff Parkinson, for an hour or so. Walking back to Homicide, Joe Molden considered his role in the case. He'd gotten his picture in the *Enterprise*; true, not with Rafe or Sam, but a picture was a picture, and in the state papers, too.

As for the picture in the local paper, Dorson told him that "A picture in the paper is worth a thousand words in Shanghai." Molden had no idea what Dorson was talking about, but then Dorson was always saying silly things like that, he said.

"He'll never be Division Chief," Molden said. Coveting that post for his own self, of course.

Molden picked up the phone and called home.

"Myrn?"

And who else would answer the phone? thought Myrna Molden.

"You got beer for tomorrow's game?"

"Yes." Resigned.

"What's for supper tonight?"

"Meat loaf." And she hung up.

Women! thought Joe Molden.

On the previous day, a Thursday and quite early as usual, Culley Donovan checked in, left word where he was going, and checked out again. He drove to farmer John Schultz's house.

Nothing important but something that Culley wanted to clear up. For himself.

Culley wanted to know why Schultz had been so sure when he insisted that the killers were Mexican. And Mexican nationals, to boot.

When he arrived at the farm house, Schultz was standing

on the east porch, working a churn.

"Ripe dates," he explained.

Donovan hoped he hadn't made a face.

"Date butter, Captain; the wife's own recipe. Two hours in the ice box, and she's ready to go." Culley looked around and took in the forty to fifty stubby palm trees surrounding the farmhouse.

The man must have the world's market cornered right here, he thought. He was afraid Schultz might offer him a sample. From a sample to a pound, from a pound to the hospital, paraphrased Culley Donovan.

To avoid that possibility of the offer, Culley decided to make it a very, very short visit. He got to the point.

"Mr. Schultz, why were you so sure those men with the guns were Mexicans?"

Schultz looked surprised. Why, he'd heard those people were already in jail.

"Oh, they are, but . . ."

Laconically: "The shoes."

"The *shoes*." Not a question, but near it.

Right. Real *mexicano* leather, they was. And, thick leather soles, weather stripping, and those high, snappy heels and a high-bright shine on the rounded toes. Mexican. Damn good shoes, too. All three pair. Them people know how to make 'em."

"Leather," Schultz repeated.

Donovan, mystified. "You saw all that?"

"You bet. I kept my eyes on the floor when I walked out-a there."

"So you didn't see the stocking masks or the gloves?"

"I guess mebbe I did, and I must-a thought they *looked* funny, but I was only there—me and Kenny Joe was—a very *short* time, and I kept my eyes mostly down when I walked out of there."

"I see." Encouragingly.

Schultz then looked up, smiled some, and said: "Well, yeah. I looked up some, but all I saw was them three machine guns, and one a-them motioning for me to get the hell out-a there. *Git*, it said, and I did; so, all I really saw was the shoes."

Culley Donovan considered telling Schultz that the machine-gun pointing at him had been Félix Leal's shotgun. He was about to decide he wouldn't tell Schultz, but the cop in him was too much; he had to say it.

"What you saw that morning, what the gunman motioned with, to you, was a shotgun." Definite but not unfriendly.

Schultz looked at him, kept to the churning, but said nothing.

Culley nodded, thanked him, and thought about the churning date mush and the potential offer. He made for the car.

He had his hand on the door handle when Schultz called to him: "Captain."

"Here it comes," sighed Culley.

"It-a, it looked like a great-big-huge-cannon to me, Captain," and he broke out in a gap-toothed smile. Schultz then waved to Culley Donovan with one hand, keeping the churn going with the other; never missed a lick, he told his wife later that day.

Later that same afternoon, Culley Donovan and Sam Dorson called Bucky Chapman from the D.A.'s office down to their basement offices. Rafe Buenrostro, at his desk, had finished initialing the folder showing the case was complete when he was called outside by Art Benavides, the Desk Man.

Bucky Chapman walked in, sat down, smiled at Donovan and Dorson and looked toward Rafe's empty desk. "Where's the third *vir* of this triumvirate?"

Dorson grinned and winked at him. "On a long distance call. From Houston."

"From Houston, eh?" And then, in his best prosecutor's voice, Chapman asked. "And how do you know that for a fact, Lieutenant Dorson?"

Culley Donovan laughed as he answered for Dorson: "He's a cop, Counselor." Wink.